THE
SEED

A TRUE MYTH

Grace Todd

"It's rare, but sometimes one reads a book that is so absorbing that one can't put it down, so filled with truth that one can never 'un-see' it, and so profound that one will never forget it. *The Seed* is that kind of book. The 'experience' of reading *The Seed* will haunt me the rest of my life. I don't even have the words to describe that 'experience.' Experience it for yourself and then give this book to everyone you know."

Steve Brown, Author; Key Life radio broadcaster

"There are not adequate words to convey the beauty of this extraordinary journey. Erik has taken the journey, and tells the Story in a way that will awaken your imagination for it and reignite your desire for union and communion with Love—for life without end in the Love Fractal. *The Seed* will grow on you and in you as you read."

Chuck DeGroat, PhD, Associate Professor of Pastoral Care and Counseling and Senior Fellow, Newbigin House of Studies; author of *Wholeheartedness, Toughest People to Love,* and *Leaving Egypt*

"Here, in this beautifully written fantasy, Erik Guzman has done what many writers try to do without success. He's made that old story of God's love for sinners come alive in a new, illuminating way, the way of Love. *The Seed* will both remind you of the old story and teach you new truth about the repeating 'pattern of Love in the world' and how we are loved, not for what we do but because we are His. Buy this book. Share it with your family."

Elyse M. Fitzpatrick, Author of *Home: How Heaven and the New Earth Satisfy Our Deepest Longing*

"Erik Guzman is one of the most exciting, insightful, articulate, economic, and powerful writers on the planet. I hate reading fiction, but I LOVED this book"

Jim Henderson, Executive Producer of Jim Henderson Presents: William Paul Young, Author of *The Shack*

"In his 'true myth,' Erik Guzman brilliantly tells all of our stories. Allow yourself the disorienting and reorienting experience of going backward to find the seed and discover all the unlikely places Love has been growing in between the empty, pain-filled, and cynical places in our hearts. No other story has invited me in quite the same way to let Love find me, no matter how terrifying and startling, and then to let Love grow within and remake me."

Sharon Hersh, Professional counselor; adjunct professor; speaker; author of *The Last Addiction: Why Self-Help Is Not Enough*

"*The Seed* captures your attention and sizzles with fun and brave theological vitality. You don't know why yet, but it doesn't get any better than life in the Love Fractal. This story will lead you to explore the contours of what it means to hear God say, 'I love you because you are mine.'"

Justin S. Holcomb, Episcopal priest; seminary professor; author of *On the Grace of God* and *God Made All of Me*

"Imagine hearing a brand-new version of your favorite classic song. You recognize the familiar melody immediately, but the instrumentation is original, the phrasing fresh. You have always loved this song, and now, thanks to the artist, you love it even more. Now open this book. If you're like me, you will find yourself smiling over and over again."

Nate Larkin, Founder of the Samson Society; author of *Samson and the Pirate Monks: Calling Men to Authentic Brotherhood*

"Why are we in so much pain? Why do we hurt each other? How is it that we've become so disconnected from the divine, ourselves, nature, and each other? In vivid parabolic storytelling, Erik Guzman channels George MacDonald and J. R. R. Tolkien in *The Seed: A True Myth*. Mysterious dragons, dark forests, living trees, and love fractals greet us as Erik lures us on a path where allegory meets biography. Highly recommended!"

Mike Morrell, Founder of the Speakeasy network; writer

"The Inklings taught us that we need good stories and Guzman has given us one here. At each turn of this book we meet truth breathed through myth—the biblical story perceived through a vivid imagination. The geek in me loved every minute."

Ryan M. Reeves, MDiv, MA, PhD, Dean & Assistant Professor of Historical Theology, Gordon Conwell

"I am undone. I just finished *The Seed: A True Myth* and I can't stop weeping. What a hope-building, eternity-embracing, eye-lifting, heart-exploding book. I am so grateful for Erik's work. Truly. I can't remember the last time a Christian book moved me in this way. You will not be disappointed."

Jessica Thompson, Speaker; author of *Everyday Grace: Infusing All of Your Relationships with the Love of Jesus*

"Along with Brennan Manning, Henri Nouwen, and C. S. Lewis, Erik Guzman has managed to write in such a way that the unconditional love of God is experienced through man's words. I have been profoundly affected by this True Myth."

Zach Van Dyke, Teaching Minister at Summit Church, Orlando, FL

"A colorful, right-brained feast that satisfies the soul and stimulates the imagination."

Frank Viola, Author; speaker; blogger at frankviola.org

"In a religious tradition frequently marked by walls, divisions, and differences, *The Seed* provides a grand story of spiritual journey— one that is interwoven with all times, places, and beings, and where every action is completed with redemption. A beautiful and compelling book."

David Wimbish, Vocalist in the Collection

"You've never read anything like Erik Guzman's *The Seed*—an ambitious, beautifully written yarn that skirts the line between allegory, fantasy, and myth in extremely inventive fashion. He has somehow managed to capture a great deal of the wonder and weirdness, urgency and beauty, of the biblical material that inspired it—a major breath of fresh air, in other words. No matter how well you think you know the 'old, old story,' no matter how high or labyrinthine your inner walls have grown, this is truly a tale that will 'take you by the tail' and not let go! You've been warned."

David Zahl, Editor of The Mockingbird Blog; author of *A Mess of Help: From the Crucified Soul of Rock n Roll*

"Erik Guzman's retelling of the Bible's story of creation and redemption bears fascinating elements of Carl Jung, C. S. Lewis, and the Brothers Grimm. If you don't blink you can even spot Ayn Rand and Jack Kerouac. It's a wild ride from start to finish, and you'll never be bored. Here's to the Love Fractal!"

Paul Zahl, Episcopal minister; theologian

The Seed

A TRUE MYTH

Erik Guzman

New
Growth
Press

www.newgrowthpress.com

New Growth Press, Greensboro, NC 27404

Cover Design: Trish Mahoney, The Mahoney Studio, themahoney.com

ISBN: 978-1-942572-79-4 (Print)
ISBN: 978-1-942572-80-0 (eBook)

Library of Congress Cataloging-in-Publication Data

Names: Guzman, Erik, 1972- author.
Title: The seed : a true myth / Erik Guzman.
Description: Greensboro, NC : New Growth Press, [2016]
Identifiers: LCCN 2015041435| ISBN 9781942572794 (softcover) | ISBN 9781942572800 (ebook)
Subjects: LCSH: Interpersonal relations--Fiction. | Labyrinths--Fiction. | GSAFD: Allegories. | Christian fiction. | Fantasy fiction.
Classification: LCC PS3607.U985 S44 2016 | DDC 813/.6--dc23
LC record available at http://lccn.loc.gov/2015041435

Printed in China

23 22 21 20 19 18 17 16   1 2 3 4 5

This book is dedicated with Love to my wife Paisley and my three children: Hannah, Madeline, and Ezra.
Here's to life in the Love Fractal!

Contents

Author's Note about Fractals

I was a teenager the first time I saw a fractal. Well, that's not entirely true because fractals are everywhere. I just didn't have a name for them yet. I was walking through the mall and one glance at the screen displaying the fractal had me mesmerized. The video went on and on delving ever deeper into colorful, seemingly chaotic shapes. However, as the magnification of the images continued, clear patterns emerged and kept repeating. It was like staring into infinity. The particular fractal I saw that day was a computer-generated visualization of the Mandelbrot set. (Search for Mandelbrot fractal videos online and you'll see what I mean.)

Years later I was blown away when I found out that all of nature is formed by these self-similar repeating patterns called fractals—the universe, galaxies, planets, mountains, clouds, waves, plants, and even the human body.

Given my fascination with fractals, I couldn't help but let them make their way into this book. Still, I realize that not everyone geeks out on the stuff that I do, so here's a simple example of a fractal that helps to understand what exactly they are and how they work.

Picture a tree. The branches are smaller versions of the trunk, each bearing ever smaller branches with leaves and seeds that each contains another tree. A tree is a pattern made of repeating versions of itself, and that's the very definition of a fractal.

So, tuck that bit of knowledge away, and as you read I hope it will be helpful when you encounter the word *fractal*. More than that, I hope you'll realize that this entire story is a fractal with you and me and all the world as a part of it.

"In the end the only events in my life worth telling are those when the imperishable world erupted into this transitory one . . . everything else has lost importance by comparison."

– Carl Gustav Jung

1

Shadows

Any true father would lay down his life to protect his children, but death took the hunter's family without giving him the chance.

He raced through the woods, his spear tight in his fist. Towering trees looked down on him as he dodged branches and leapt over jagged red rocks in pursuit of his prey. The hounds barked ahead. They picked up the scent after breakfast and pulled the hunter from a morning haze of self-pity out into the hot summer afternoon. The barking moved toward the edge of the forest. His feet ached in his boots. Sweat soaked his threadbare clothes and ran from his graying hair into his beard.

He had to stop for water.

The hunter finally paused, panting and groping for his waterskin as the noise from the dogs echoed through the trees in the distance. He drank deeply and then gasped for air.

He checked his pack and noticed his daughter's little music block almost fell out. He stuffed the instrument deep into the bag and tied the opening shut. His hands went to his knees as he tried to catch his breath. He closed his eyes and a memory of his wife and children overtook him.

His younger daughter and his little boy laughed as they played by the river, taking turns swinging from the rope he'd tied to one of the branches above. They leapt from the riverbank and flew through the air, their squeals disappearing in splashes of clear water. His older daughter sat in the tree and watched from above, her feet swinging with the rhythm as she plinked away on the music block he gave her—her karimba. He marveled at how quickly she was maturing into a young woman.

On the shore, his wife sat with him in the sun, her back to his chest and her head resting on his shoulder. He kissed her head. Her amber hair tickled his nose.

"I wish we could live in this moment forever," she said.

"What about tomorrow?" he asked, stroking her hair. "We have a tower to build."

She nestled closer. "I will love you tomorrow too."

He smiled. "You're a good woman. What would I do without you?"

"I'm sure you'd figure something out."

"Humph."

Suddenly, the children's laughter faded and a familiar darkness flooded his memory.

The shadow.

It took everything from him. When the hunter found his family, it was already too late. The shadow hunched over the bed, its back scraping the ceiling. His wife and children were huddled together, pale and lifeless . . . cold. The image haunted him and made his blood boil.

The hounds barked in the distance.

Forcing his eyes open, he cursed the shadow for invading his thoughts, but in reality he preferred seething rage to the pain of remembering the good days long gone. Whatever it took, he would avenge them. He would find the shadow and kill it, or die trying. His anger required total devotion.

"God, give me strength," he prayed. "Give me justice."

He put his pack on his back and began running after the dogs again. His heart thumped in his chest and his legs burned, but he would never relent.

Consuming hatred drove him on.

His pace faltered when he heard the hounds' deep barks give way to baying.

Could they have it treed?

Adrenaline sent the hunter into a sprint. After years of tracking the shadow, he hoped it was finally his chance for revenge. The woods became thinner and light splashed across the mossy carpet. There were fewer obstacles, but he still wasn't close enough to see the baying hounds. "Get it! Get it!" he shouted as he raised his spear above his head.

It's mine now.

A yelp of pain came from one of the dogs. Then another.

Thoughts of victory were premature.

He couldn't run any faster. Fierce growling and barking, then a sharp cry were followed by a horrible silence. He staggered and stopped. Through eyes stinging with sweat, he could see a wide-open space ahead in the distance beyond the trees, but he couldn't see the hounds.

Where are you, damned monster? He grabbed his spear with both hands and crouched, breathing so hard he feared it would give away his presence.

He inched forward, deliberately inhaling and exhaling, willing his heart to slow. Whatever happened next, he would fight the shadow until his last breath.

He ascended a short, rocky incline and stepped into a meadow beyond the edge of the woods. Squinting in the sunlight, he scanned the horizon.

Nothing.

No sound except the buzzing of insects in the tall grass.

The hunter turned around and bent down. The hounds' tracks just stopped. His dogs vanished from the earth. He looked closer at the grass surrounding him and saw red droplets sprayed in arcs on the blades, like crimson dew. He touched the blood and rubbed it between his fingers, wondering why the shadow pierced his dogs' hides, why it didn't just pull the life out of them into its nothingness the way it stole his wife and children.

While the hunter crouched, perplexed, he didn't notice the shadow approaching until it was too late. Darkness engulfed him before he could look up.

The ground sped by beneath the dragon. Trees, fields, rocks, and flowers blurred together in a rushing river of greens, browns, grays, and touches of yellow and red. It had all burned before, but life kept insisting. A stream flowed into the palette mixing in an array of blues and whites. Water filled the landscape below, adding a roar to the whistling wind passing over the dragon's wings.

His name was Wyrm. With no arms or legs, he slithered on the ground, but he preferred the sky. His body was long and slender. From his smoking snout to his shredded tail, his scales were polished ebony. Black teeth as sharp as needles filled his mouth. His eyes were bottomless pits.

All of a sudden, the churning waters dropped away and mist engulfed the soaring serpent. Droplets beaded and whisked down the length of his body as he closed his eyes and flew blind through the clouds. He shot past the falls into the warm air beyond, caught an updraft, and opened his black eyes. An expansive, grassy plain stretched out beneath him. The great height extinguished the sensation of speed. He passed over the labyrinthine town of Ai—its inhabitants about their morning routines—and off into the distance toward a vast forest that grew far from any people or civilization.

Wyrm ruled over everything below him and everything beyond the horizon. The whole world was his kingdom, but he stayed hidden from view. Flying high and unseen, he became more than a mere dragon. His prophets spoke his words, but never spoke his name. He let his legend grow over the generations until he was worshiped as almighty God.

He governed through his blood worms. They filled anyone who would accept their influence and power. His workers tended his kilns and built his towns. His kings led the people according to his will, and the worms in his spies made sure he knew everything that happened in his kingdom. Most accepted Wyrm's rule, no matter the difficulty of his demands, in exchange for protection from the shadow.

Wyrm flew over the forest following the scent of the hunter's fire. The smell of animal flesh cooking grew thick and then dissipated, leaving a trail of greasy smoke to follow to its source. He drew his wings in close to his sleek body and spun into a dive, then unfolded his wings with a snap, pulled out of his rapid descent, and leveled off, still high above the woods. He let out a high-pitched screech that only the hounds could hear, then looked back. Trees obscured his view, but he could see the dogs chasing him, darting in and out of patches of light with the hunter behind. Wyrm had been watching the miserable man for many seasons and everything was in place to put his plan into motion. He screeched again and flew toward the edge of the forest, slow enough for the hounds to keep up, leading them on into the afternoon.

Looking back again, Wyrm noticed the hunter had stopped. He circled above, unseen. He was eager to oblige when he heard the hunter's plea for help.

Wyrm bolted toward the tree line and led the hunter's hounds out into the open. He dove, sunk his teeth into one of them, and

shook it violently before swallowing it whole. The remaining
hounds barked and bayed as he circled back around and snatched
them from the ground one by one. He belched flames as he
ascended higher.

The hounds didn't provide the nourishment he needed, but
their disappearance would draw the hunter out of the forest, leaving him vulnerable and confused. He beat the air with his wings
and spun around. He gained altitude until his next target emerged
from the trees. He stopped flapping and glided in to take the hunter.

Wyrm swooped down without a sound. He pulled out of his
dive just above the baffled hunter, snuffing the light of the sun and
engulfing the man in the shadow of his wings. The dragon cracked
his tail like a whip and sent the hunter flying into the woods.

Wyrm landed on his belly and slithered toward the forest. As
soon as he entered, he felt the shadow's maddening presence. He
turned toward its pull. It stood like a crooked tree erased from the
woods, an emptiness that warped the world around it. The shadow's branches reached out over the hunter's limp body.

"Why are you here?" Wyrm hissed. "He asked for me."

The twisted shape didn't move.

"Haven't you made him suffer enough?" Flames lit the dragon's mouth as he spoke. He lifted half his body off the ground and
extended his wings. "He gave himself to me."

Suddenly, the shadow shrank and disappeared.

"Coward," the dragon growled.

He slithered toward the unconscious man and encircled him.
"I will give you the strength you need," he said. "We will have justice." Wyrm looked down at his shredded tail on the ground and
then sunk his fangs into it. Black blood poured from the bite. The
oily substance pooled around the hunter's head and dripped from
the dragon's mouth. Large drops landed on the hunter's face. The
blood bubbled and black worms emerged from it like maggots from

rotting meat. They crawled into the man's mouth, nose, ears, and eyes as Wyrm hissed, "Welcome to your new home, my children."

The wound on the dragon's tail clotted with the same black worms that had just entered the hunter. He slinked through the trees and out of the forest, then took to the air.

2

A Common Enemy

Screeching echoed in the moonlit forest. The trees' jagged shadows reached into a rocky field beyond. A young couple, grubby and dressed in animal skins, dove behind a boulder.

"Why?" the woman asked above the piercing noise. "Why does it follow us?"

The man covered his woman's ears and pulled her to him. She was trembling.

It sounds . . . almost sad, he thought.

She pressed his hands tighter to her ears. "Why?" she whimpered.

He shook his head to silence her, but she shook hers back.

During the day, the shadow pursued the couple without making a sound, driving them ever deeper into the wild. But at night, its tortured song in the woods drove the man and woman into each other's arms, if only for a brief moment.

The mournful shrieking stopped. Silence persuaded him to peek from behind their hiding place.

"Be careful," the woman whispered. "It could come out."

He shushed her while scanning the edge of the forest, then quickly ducked down.

"What?"

"I thought I saw something move."

She stared into his eyes. "We need to get out of here while we can." She turned, but he grabbed her wrist and jerked her back.

"Sit!"

"Let go!" she snapped, tugging herself loose.

He relented and held up his hand for her to be quiet. "Just wait."

He carefully peeked around the rock again and before he even understood what happened, he glimpsed it—the shadow! It stood as tall as a tree and blacker than midnight, far off at the edge of the woods. While motionless, it hid in plain sight, its outline blended with the darkness of the forest. Then, in an instant, the shadow moved, revealing its presence as it silently glided through the trees. As it passed, everything near it, even the light from the full moon, bent toward the shadow's center.

The man spun back and stifled a groan, covering his eyes with trembling hands and rocking uncontrollably.

"I saw it," he said through clenched teeth.

She grabbed his arm. "Did it see you?"

"How should I know," he whispered. "You know it doesn't have any eyes."

"Which way is it going?"

"Couldn't tell." He continued rocking, but slower. "I hate looking at it. It's so . . . empty." He opened his eyes to see her watching him. He regained some composure and stopped moving back and forth. "Just seeing it . . . it's like I'm dying. Like it's going to suck me into it. It's a horrible nothing."

"What do we do?"

"What we always do."

"But it will see us."

He looked at the field in front of them. "We've outrun it before."

She nodded, but fear shrouded her face. He knew what she thought. They could run every night until their legs gave out, but they would never get far enough away. It would never stop coming. If they didn't keep moving, it would consume them.

"Ready?" he asked.

"Do we have a choice?"

"No."

The woman closed her eyes and took a deep breath. She looked at him and got to her feet, crouching behind the boulder.

If she could keep going, so could he. He got up, crouched next to her, and without a sound the couple ran for their lives.

The hunter opened his eyes. His head throbbed. He felt for his pack, but it was gone.

The karimba, he thought.

He tried to get up, but just lifting his head off the ground left him dizzy and nauseated. A sharp pain in his side told him ribs were bruised, maybe broken. He lay still, dazed, looking at the gray sky through the trees. It was early morning. Not a sound except for the ringing in his ears, high-pitched and disorienting.

What happened? Why didn't the shadow take me?

He considered another attempt to get to his feet, but the earth wouldn't stop spinning and his back was stuck to it. He gave up.

He didn't move again until thirst drove him to it. This time he didn't try to lift his head, he just reached for his waterskin and poured the last of his water into his mouth. He coughed and managed to roll over.

Breathing hurt. He spotted his pack through blurry eyes. It lay a few feet away, still tied shut. A surge of strength helped him onto his hands and knees. Having gotten that far, he thought he might be all right. It was just a matter of time. He crawled to a boulder and pulled himself up to stand. Wincing, his legs buckled beneath him and he slipped on the loose rock under his feet. He fell back to the ground and yelped at the piercing sting in his side. Ribs were definitely broken and the pain made it near impossible to pull enough air into his lungs.

God help me, he prayed silently. *Don't let me die like this.*

"What was that?" the man looked up from the small rabbit he was skinning.

The woman stopped, her hand frozen on a berry she was about to pick. "It came from the trees."

The night before, the shadow's shrieking never returned, but the couple kept running until they were tired enough to hope that it was too far away to attack. They took turns watching while the other tried to sleep. The shadow didn't reappear.

In the morning they moved on, traveling along a stream that flowed beyond the edge of the forest. They stayed out of the trees for fear of the shadow catching them without warning. It had always found them before and they were sure it would eventually find them again. Out in the open, at least they could see it coming.

The man stood, clutching his stone blade. He hadn't retrieved his trap yet, and if they had to run he didn't want to leave it.

A labored groan came from just inside the woods. Something was hurt—or *someone.*

The woman whispered, "Can you see anything? Is it an animal?"

He swatted at the air in her direction.

"Is it one of them?" the woman whispered, barely audible.

He turned and scowled at her, then returned his gaze to the trees. Whatever it was, it sounded big. He wondered if it was a trick of the shadow, luring them into the woods with fresh meat. *Could it be one of the pale ones?*

In the early days of their wandering, they came across a walled town filled with the others. Before that, they thought they were the only ones like them. The others walked upright too, but their skin was drained of color. The pale ones rode on large four-legged creatures the likes of which they had never encountered. The man and woman kept their distance and moved on. They never met one of the others face-to-face.

"No. It's not safe," the man decided out loud. He bundled up the rabbit, flung it over his shoulder, and wiped his hands on the edge of his thin leather shirt. "Let's go." He gripped his knife, his hands still dirty with rabbit blood, and ran off.

The woman followed at a distance, glancing over her shoulder through her tangled black hair.

The hunter saw something move just beyond the trees.
A woman? Here?
Despite the pain in his side, he managed to stand, his breathing short and shallow.

"Help . . ." He tried to shout, but couldn't.

He'd never seen another living person out in the vast, lonely wilderness, far from any town, tower, or walls. He knew he wouldn't last long alone. In his condition, he'd barely make it to drink from the stream much less defend himself against predators.

"Wait . . . please." He gripped his side with both hands and forced himself to yell, "Help! I have food!"

He dropped to his knees in pain. A few quick breaths and he grabbed his pack and hobbled out from the obscuring trees dragging it along into the daylight.

The woman spotted him. There was a man with her. She caught up to him and grabbed his arm. She said something and they looked back.

The hunter staggered.

The man hesitated, watching, then began toward him with the woman following, both glancing from side to side. She was young, brown, and beautiful, but gaunt. He was dark and haggard, his hair matted. As they got closer, the hunter could see that the man's hands and skins were bloody. He held an obsidian knife.

Where's my spear? The hunter looked on the ground around him.

"What are you doing in the red woods?" the man growled as he approached.

"I was attacked." The hunter looked down at his pack. "I have food. Please help me." He gingerly opened it. "I'll get it for you."

"His head is bleeding," the woman said. "I told you he looked hurt."

The hunter felt his head and looked at his hand. It was bright red.

The woman winced. "That's a lot of blood. What did that to you?"

"Woman." The man tugged on her arm. "Are there others?" he barked.

The hunter looked in his pack and saw his daughter's little musical instrument. "No . . . there are no others."

The man moved toward him, his blade threatening. "Why are you in the woods?"

"I was hunting."

"Hunting what?" the man asked.

"You wouldn't believe me if I told you," the hunter replied. He looked for the dried meat in his pack, but he had difficulty focusing. "Please, help."

The wild man stared at him, tense and twitchy. His big brown eyes betrayed a sadness, like that of a scolded dog.

The hunter's tongue felt fat. He opened his mouth and moved his jaw back and forth trying to get his ears to stop ringing. He blinked his eyes a few times and opened them wide. He stared at the woman's face. Her features reminded him of his younger daughter.

"Tell us what you were hunting," the man demanded.

The hunter took a breath, grimaced at the pain, and said, "The shadow."

3

A Sign

She wondered what kind of man would dare hunt the thing that hunted them. The hunter was right, she couldn't believe it. Even if he were strong enough to somehow kill the shadow, he was too beat up to take it on now. She didn't want to leave him to the darkness, and her herbs could help the hunter heal.

Her man wanted to hear more.

They helped the hunter into the open where they had a clear line of sight for a good distance. They ate the hunter's dried meat while he managed to tell them about the chase, the dogs, and the darkness. While he talked, the couple exchanged glances. She waited for him to signal her to run.

"I need to lie down," the hunter said when he finished his story. He clutched his side and rested his head on his pack.

"Tend to his wounds," the man said. Then he whispered in her ear, "I'm going to get the trap I left and search where we found him." He slipped her his knife. "Careful."

The hunter was asleep when the man returned with his spear and the trap. He climbed a rocky perch above them to keep watch, the hunter's weapon across his lap.

Night came and the sky was clear, the air cool. As she cooked the rabbit over the fire, she became aware of the shadow's silence. *Why wasn't it wailing in the darkness? Did it have something to do with this man who claimed to hunt it?* She watched the hunter while he slept. The wet leaves still clung to his head, covering the healing herbs she placed on his seeping wound. His skin was pale and rough. Wrinkles spread out from the corners of his eyes. He was taller and more muscular than her man, but nobody the shadow would fear.

She wondered what else was in the pack under his head.

He blinked and opened his eyes. She looked away.

"Thank you for your kindness," the hunter said. "I've not seen anyone for some time." There was a long silence. "You remind me of one of my daughters."

The woman turned the other side of the rabbit to the flames and smiled. Her man wouldn't want her to say too much.

"He blends in, doesn't he?" the hunter asked, looking at the man.

"Blends in?"

"With the rest of the rocks." The hunter sat up, extended his hand to the man and raised his voice, "Why don't you come and join us?"

He must be starting to feel better, she thought.

The man didn't move. "See," the hunter said, "just like a rock. What's his name?"

She turned the rabbit once more, busying herself with its preparation. She thought about making up a name or just not answering, anything but admitting they couldn't remember. "I call him different names. It depends what I want from him."

The hunter chuckled. The man remained motionless. "Seriously, what's his name?" the hunter asked, squinting and touching his side.

"I can't tell you," she blurted.

"What? Why? He won't let you?"

"No, it's not that."

"Well, what about you? What's your name?"

She picked up a stick and poked around at the logs in the fire. The flames warmed her arms and her face. Fire, Wood, Ash . . . none of them sounded like real names. She hung her head and said, "He calls me Woman."

"Look up," the hunter said. "Look at me."

The hunter stared into her eyes—past her eyes. He seemed to be looking for something within her. "You don't remember your names," he stated matter-of-factly. He shifted and stretched his neck.

How did he know?

The hunter rubbed his ribs. He looked surprised. He touched his head. "What did you do?"

Did I do something wrong? Her heart started beating fast. "What do you mean?"

He took a deep breath. "My side, it doesn't hurt anymore." He took another deep breath through his nose and blew it out his mouth. "The pain is totally gone . . . it's a miracle. Who are you? Where are you from?"

She started to answer.

"Woman!" The man leapt from the ledge and walked to them. He pointed at the hunter with the spear and said, "Want to talk?" The man sat next to her by the fire. "I'll ask the questions."

The hunter nodded and crossed his arms, rubbing his side. He sat with his back to his pack. "Okay."

"The shadow. What do you know about it?"

The hunter looked down. "I know it's a killer," he said as his brow furrowed. "I know it's going to pay . . ." The hunter's voice quivered and he choked on his words. Tears welled up in his eyes, glistening in the firelight. She knew the involuntary display of feeling would make her man uncomfortable and an awkward silence followed.

When it seemed the hunter might be able to go on, she asked, "Pay for what? Who did it kill?"

The hunter sniffed. "It was late. I had just returned from a long hunt. As I approached our house in the woods, the dogs started going crazy." He paused, cleared his throat, and continued. "I knew something wasn't right. I opened the door . . . then I saw it . . . like a large man with crooked limbs, but black as pitch and empty. The shadow stood in the center of our home, filling the room with its twisted shape, bent over with its back to the ceiling."

"You saw it," the man said, more as a statement than a question.

"Worse than that, I felt it." The hunter looked at each of them in turn.

Her man looked at her.

"Yes," the hunter said. "It's a terrible void, isn't it?"

The man shifted. "What?" His voice wavered.

"It's like a deep hole you can't see the bottom of," the hunter replied, "threatening to pull you into it. It's . . . nothing."

The man stared.

"That's what the monster did to my family. It stole them, sucked the life right out of them. As long as I live, I will never forget its horrible presence . . . maddening. It was brooding over my wife, my boy, and my little girls. They were dead." He stared into the fire. "Still holding each other . . . so gray . . . like ash."

His words faded into silence, leaving behind the anguish of his memory. She wanted to say something to comfort him, but he seemed beyond comfort. She wanted to find out how he knew they couldn't remember their names. She wanted to ask about his wounds, but before she spoke, he went on.

"It took them . . . I didn't see it leave," the hunter said. He seemed to struggle with the words. "It just disappeared. But the dogs . . ." the hunter smiled, "the dogs must have caught its scent. I almost had it when the coward attacked me from behind and left me in the woods to die."

She looked at her man. His eyes told her he was impressed. He believed the story.

Anyone who would hunt the shadow must be special. Every time they got a look at it, all they could do was run. This man had even survived the shadow's attack. They would trade anything to keep the black hole away from them.

The shadow had pursued them longer than she could remember and she yearned to stop running, but its imposing, dark power would never let them rest. Time and again she woke in a panic in the middle of the night, long after the shadow stopped shrieking, but she knew it was still watching. She could feel its gaze on the back of her neck only to turn around to nothing. Even during the day, when she was foraging alone, a shadowy figure would often appear in the corner of her eye and then disappear when she looked in its direction. Those times were frightening enough, but when the shadow didn't vanish, its presence was a sustained shock. It was a punishing emptiness.

"We've seen it too," she stammered, glancing at her man. He didn't move so she continued. "It chased us from our home and burned it to the ground. It's still chasing us. The shadow never leaves us alone."

"How long have you two been on the run?"

Her man's eyes darted to her. Then he turned back to the hunter and glared.

"You don't know," said the hunter.

"No," she replied.

"Don't!" The man grabbed her arm.

"Leave her alone," the hunter growled, his voice penetrating.

Her man flinched and released his grip on her, then started to get up.

She touched his arm. "The rabbit is done," she said. "Let's eat." He jerked away, looked at her and scowled.

The hunter sat back.

She handed her man the skewered rabbit. "This will need to cool."

He stared.

"It's all right," she whispered.

He took it and she answered the hunter's question. "We've been wandering the wilderness for ages."

"Ages?" asked the hunter. "You two are young enough to be my children." He turned to the man. "Where are you from?"

The man sat, blinked, and turned his head away. He divided up the scant rabbit meat on a large, green leaf, burning his fingers and shaking them in the air as he did. He ate a piece and left the rest to cool.

"You don't know that either." The hunter stroked his beard. "You're lost in the wild, wearing crude skins. You don't know who you are or where you come from." He looked back and forth between them. "What about my wounds? How did you heal me?"

"Heal?" her man asked.

"He says his pain is gone." She moved toward the hunter. "Can I look?" A log hissed and popped in the flames, sending cinders rising with the smoke.

"Please."

"Lean your head toward the fire." His hair was crusted with dried blood. She peeled back the leaves and herbs covering his wound. There wasn't even a scar. She parted his hair for a closer look. "How?" Suddenly, she recoiled.

"What?" the hunter asked.

She thought she'd seen something move beneath his scalp. *Is it the fire?* She hoped the flickering light from the flames was playing tricks on her eyes. She looked again. Nothing.

She stepped back and looked at her man. "It's gone!"

The man got up and examined the hunter's head. "What kind of magic is this?" he asked.

"So you don't know," the hunter said. "It must be a sign."

"A sign?" she asked.

"Yes, to get our attention. I don't think our meeting in this godforsaken wilderness was an accident. We must have been brought together for a reason."

"What are you talking about?" the man asked as he returned to where he was sitting. He bent down and tossed the hunter a piece of the rabbit.

"You have nothing," said the hunter. "I've lost everything too. We have the same enemy. And now, we have one another."

Hope flickered within the woman.

"Thank you for your help," he said, "both of you," and then he ate his meat.

The man grunted, stepped toward her, and handed her some rabbit.

The hunter licked his fingers. "I'd like to return the favor."

"We need nothing from you," the man replied.

"You don't?" the hunter got up. He walked to the man and stared down into his eyes. "Don't you want to know why you're scared of the shadow, and I'm not?"

4

Names

The hunter could see the fear in the man's eyes, so he smiled. "Relax. I want to help you." The hunter put his hand on the man's shoulder. "Come, sit back down. Finish eating."

The man pulled away and turned toward a small pile of branches.

"At least hear me out," the hunter said as he took his seat by his pack. He looked at the woman. "Where I come from, people have names." The hunter turned to the man and asked, "How about I call you, Roark? It means 'rock.'"

"Call me nothing," the man said as he snapped a branch in half.

"Whatever you say," the hunter replied, "but Nothing is a strange name."

The woman giggled and the man glared at her. "I like it," she said. "It sounds strong. Fits you." She patted the ground next to her. The man placed the wood on the fire.

The hunter turned back to the woman. "And for you, my youngest little girl's name was Madeline. She was slight, but strong like you are . . ." The hunter smiled and tears pooled in his eyes.

"She was a wee little fairy with a big name. It means 'woman of the high tower.' I had hoped to make that name a reality one day, to build her a tower that would be a monument to our freedom. You would honor me by taking her name for yourself."

The woman smiled. "I like it."

The man sighed and tossed a log onto the fire. Sparks flew and drifted into the sky. He sat down next to the woman and ate.

"What about you?" the woman asked. "What's your name?"

"My name?" the hunter replied, staring into the fire. He closed his eyes and saw the faces of his murdered children. He would never hear them call out to him again. He looked at the young couple. He stared through them and into the past. The shadow left him powerless to protect his family. He failed as a father but he would avenge their deaths and put things right. "They called me Tatus. Where I come from, it's what little children call their daddies." They were so helpless. He struck his thigh. "I didn't have a chance to save them." Then his eyes met the woman's. "Madeline." He smiled at her and said, "I can't leave you two out here, endlessly running from that monster. Not when you don't have to be afraid."

"Why not?" the man asked, almost daring him to answer. "Why aren't you afraid?"

"Because I have faith," the hunter said. "I believe in a power greater than the shadow." The hunter pointed to the sky and looked up. "I serve him, so I trust him to protect me."

The man and woman glanced to the sky, then at each other. They looked confused.

"God," the hunter said. "The almighty."

The couple shook their heads.

"As I suspected. You wouldn't be running from the shadow if you had faith in God." The hunter smiled. "You have much to learn. If you have faith and you serve God, work hard," the hunter shook his fist, "his power will protect you." He touched his ribs, grateful to be free of the pain. "Yes, it was God who healed me."

"What do we do to get this power?" the woman asked. She looked up again. "Where is God?"

"Wait," the man interrupted, "how do you know all this?"

"I was born in a place called Ai. Everyone there serves God."

"Is that where he is?" the woman asked. "Why did you point to the sky?"

"God is everywhere, but he can't be seen. Trust me, I know how that sounds. I grew up with the stories my parents told about the shadow and the God who protects the town, but I never believed them." He turned to the woman. "My wife didn't either. We thought our people were slaves to superstition. We had enough, so we left. We went into the woods to hunt, live off the land, and build a life there." The hunter smiled and said, "We had children and dreams of forming a community of free people." His smile twisted into a grimace. "But, of course, the monster is real . . . and my family paid for my lack of faith. The shadow made a believer out of me."

The woman looked to the man, trying to read his reaction. He rolled his eyes and looked away. She turned back to the hunter. "Your town . . . they never saw the shadow? God's power kept it away?"

"That's right. My God is more powerful than the shadow."

"How do we serve your God?" the woman asked.

"We build," the hunter shifted and sat up straight. "Roark, what would you say if I promised you and Madeline safety and plenty of food?" The hunter stared into the man's eyes until he was sure he had his undivided attention. "We can trap the shadow and kill it."

The man scoffed and turned. "Ha! You are crazy if you think you can trap that thing. It can't be killed with spears or knives."

"Maybe not." He paused and waited for the man to look at him again. "I haven't had the chance to drive my spear into it . . . yet. But I promise you, it *can* be trapped."

The woman looked at the man, waiting for him to reply. She obviously wanted to hear more.

The hunter drove his hand into the ground and ripped out a handful of grass and crimson dirt. "It will be hard work, but I promise you'll have everything you need and never be afraid again." He held up his fist full of earth. "We'll make the shadow pay for what it did to us."

"You make big promises," the man said.

The hunter grinned. "I've got some big plans." He tossed the dirt aside and looked through his pack. He grabbed the music block. "See this?" he asked. "It's an instrument from Ai, a karimba. It plays music." He plinked out a few notes from one of his daughter's songs. The man and woman looked and listened. The hunter turned the karimba over to reveal a circular labyrinth carved into the wood. He caressed the design with his finger. "God gave us this pattern. It's a symbol of his power over darkness. The shadow hates it." He looked up and could tell the man was bewildered. "You'd call it magic . . . like my healing. My people built a fortress with walls in this shape. The king and queen live in a tower in the center while the people live within the perimeter, inside the outer wall. The labyrinth has protected Ai from the shadow for a very long time." He handed the karimba to the woman. "How would you like to make the shadow afraid of you?"

The woman smiled. The man looked at her as she examined the design. "Ai? We know this place," she said, "there are many walls and pale ones, like you."

"You've been there?

"We saw it once."

"We can build a tower with a labyrinth in this shape to protect it," the hunter declared.

"How can a symbol protect us from the shadow?" the man asked.

"It can't," the hunter answered, "not alone. If we want God to bless it, the symbol must represent a reality. It has to be infused with faith, hard work, sacrifice, and prayers. Follow God's ways, appease him, and he will give the labyrinth a supernatural power over the shadow."

"Why build?" the man asked. "Sounds like a lot of work for nothing. Just take us to your labyrinth town if this symbol is so powerful."

"Ai still stands, far to the east, but they're only content with building, generation after generation. They trust its pattern for protection alone. I think if we build a labyrinth of our own and get the shadow inside its walls, we can trap it. It's a bold plan, the people of Ai would never agree to it, but I believe God brought us together to give us justice once and for all. Then we'll be truly free."

"I don't know," the man said.

"Don't believe me?" the hunter struck himself in the side with his fist. "What about the healing? I'm telling you it's a sign! God wants this. Don't be stupid like I was with my family. Are you willing to risk Madeline's life with your lack of faith?" The hunter pointed at the woman. Fire burned in his belly. "Make no mistake, it will kill her. You too. It will stop at nothing until it sucks you into its darkness."

The man set his jaw. He looked to be on the verge of attacking.

"You're vulnerable, son. Look at you two. You're wandering in the wild in animal skins. This is no way to live."

"Tell me," the man demanded, "how come you haven't built a labyrinth for yourself?"

The hunter took a deep breath and raised his hands. "I couldn't do it alone, but now that we have one another . . ."

"How?" the woman asked. "How would we build such a thing?"

Her question told the hunter she was looking to the future. Her hope had grown as the fire died down. He smiled. "There's so much I can show you. There are kilns, with people who work them to provide bricks. There are cranes and tools that are common in Ai. Camels, beasts of burden . . ." He stopped at the blank look on their faces. "Just wait, you'll see. And food! We'll dig a well and plant gardens."

"You would do these things, for us?" the woman asked.

The hunter leaned back and looked up into the sky. "You would also be helping me, don't you see?"

She wrinkled her brow.

"I could have a family again, children to protect and care for."

Tears pooled in her eyes. "Children . . . I have no memory of a father."

The hunter reached toward her. "And you would be helping your man avenge the home that the shadow burned. You can put things right." He glanced up at the man at this. "Don't you agree, Roark?"

The man was silent, thinking.

"Maybe it's more than you two can handle," the hunter said. "We should sleep on it. You have been so kind. I'll take the first watch." He held out his hand for his spear. The man looked down at it.

The woman touched his knee and said, "Roark." He looked at her. Her eyes said, "Please." *Irresistible*, thought the hunter.

The man considered it, then sighed and reluctantly handed the hunter his weapon.

They slept that night, with the hunter keeping watch as the couple with new names lay together by the fire. Stillness surrounded them. The hunter sat and used a stick to adjust the burning wood. High above, a black form briefly snuffed the light of the stars as it circled overhead, unseen by the hunter. The infestation hidden within his body stirred.

He watched Madeline and Roark resting peacefully. *Things will be different this time*, he thought.

The blood worms whispered the hunter's thoughts to the dragon above. Wyrm sneered. "Not without me, they won't. You couldn't even save your own children." The blood worms spoke into the hunter's mind, mimicking his own inner voice, *What if I don't have what it takes?*

The hunter winced. *No. Never again. Please, God, give me strength. Don't let the shadow catch me unprepared again.*

The worms continued to stir up fear in the hunter long into the night. He shook off the thoughts with desperate prayer and surges of anger.

He watched Madeline's shoulder rise and fall as she slept. Then, it stopped. Her body was completely still. *Did she stop breathing?* He wondered if the shadow got to her without him noticing.

He tried to get up to shake her from her sleep, but the worms in his muscles paralyzed him. He couldn't even open his mouth or make a sound. Her color began to fade as he watched helplessly. Her body lay limp before him. The hunter panicked in silence.

As he looked up, the shadow emerged from the dark woods.

The hunter struggled to rise, but remained motionless, frozen in his helpless terror. The black figure slowly approached and bent down over Madeline. Her drooping body slowly rose in the air. As the shadow lifted Madeline higher, her eyes snapped open, they were as black as Wyrm's. She stared at the hunter.

"Help me. Please . . ." she begged.

Horrified and heartsick, he tried with all his might, but he couldn't move to save either of them from the shadow. It swallowed the couple in its nothingness.

And then, in an instant, the blood worms let loose their control of the hunter's mind and body. He sprang to his feet, screaming at the shadow.

It was gone. The night was still.

Roark and Madeline bolted upright, their faces veiled by fear and lit by the embers of the dying fire. "What is it?" Roark asked, breathless, his knife in his hand.

The hunter's heart pounded in his chest and his head ached. He blinked rapidly. A high-pitched buzzing made it hard to hear.

Madeline started to rise, but Roark held her back.

The hunter's hand shook as he wiped a tear from his cheek. He hated showing weakness. "Argh!" He slammed his fist into the ground to beat his trembling hand into submission. He continued punching the dirt until he could hold his hand steady. But he couldn't steady his heart or dismiss what he'd seen.

The blood worms crawled through the crevices of the hunter's brain, burning the vision into his mind. They would never let him rest. He had to keep Madeline and Roark safe.

"Forgive me," he said. His voice sounded strangely hoarse.

Madeline shivered.

"Just a nightmare. I only drifted off for a moment."

Madeline and Roark stared at him. He got up for wood to get the fire going again. "Don't worry. I will protect you."

"You need rest," Madeline said.

"No. I'm not sleeping again."

Roark stood up and climbed his rocky perch.

"Please. You can trust me," the hunter said, stoking the fire.

Roark looked down at him and then scanned the horizon.

"You can go back to sleep."

Roark jumped down and sat next to Madeline.

"Don't worry. I won't let any harm come to you," the hunter said as he took Roark's place atop the rocks.

Roark and Madeline did eventually sleep. And the hunter stayed true to his word. He kept watch over the couple until morning, and for many years after.

They came to call him Tatus.

5

Seeds

T he sun hung low in the sky, illuminating the massive wall
that divided the land and encircled the tower.

The shadow surged along the ground toward the brick barrier.
Nothing could be seen within its outline. The shape of the emptiness shifted as it moved, a flowing abyss that bent space and time
around it. The shadow reached the wall and crashed against it like
a wave hitting a rocky shore. Its nothingness churned in the air
and reformed as a dark figure standing on two hulking legs. Every
inch of the shadow was completely black. It had gangly arms that
ended in long, slender fingers. Thick growths hung from the shadow's head and swung in front of its featureless face as it walked
along the wall. It stopped and the growths draped over its knobby
shoulders.

A voice whispered from inside the void. "Freedom . . . it
is a frightening gift." The shadow reached inside itself and then
extended one of its lanky dark limbs to the wall, holding something similarly dark that distorted the world around it. The shadow

withdrew its hand, its pointy fingers leaving a small black hole in a space between the bricks.

"Our friend has fallen asleep, but soon he will awaken."

Tatus planted a seed the day he showed Madeline and Roark the labyrinth on the back of the karimba. He watered that seed with stories of what life would be like free from the shadow. He tended it with tools, supplies, cranes, and camels from Ai. The idea carved into the karimba took root and sprouted with each delivery of bricks he brought from the workers who ran the kilns. It took countless sleepless nights and years of hard labor, but Tatus's seed eventually grew into the large wall around the tower Madeline and Roark now called home.

Beyond the wall, Roark and Tatus had mapped out the pattern of the labyrinth with ditches and mounds of dirt. Tatus said the symbol would protect them as they built. A stone patio, rings of apple trees, and gardens wrapped around the tower.

The second half of a huge, bronze gate hung from a wooden crane inside the only opening in the wall. Ropes creaked as Roark labored beneath the mass of metal to guide the gate into place. Inside the tower, Madeline prepared to celebrate the safety their toil had won them.

It had been many seasons since they saw the shadow emerge from the distant forest, but from time to time they could hear its haunting cries far away in the night. They still felt it watching them.

Madeline sang as she climbed the stairs out of the cellar. "Come to your garden, love, and eat its pleasant fruits." She came up through the open door in the floor of the kitchen with a jar of preserved fruits. The ceramic containers Tatus brought from Ai were a godsend. The smell of roasting duck greeted her. Bread cooled next to a barred window and light from the setting sun streamed into the room. Dust danced in the golden beams. She took her jar to a table by the hearth and drank long from a jug of cider. The karimba on her chair begged her to plink out the notes to her song, but she still had work to do. She turned her attention to her apples and a basket of strawberries.

A noise above startled her and she glanced up the stairs that spiraled along the wall, through three levels of landings, to the bedroom at the top.

Silence.

Probably a raven. I must have left the shutters open.

Madeline wished she weren't frightened so easily. She wondered how long they would have to live without seeing the shadow before she could be free of fear. *Please forgive me,* she prayed. Madeline started singing again to calm herself while she sliced apples into thin wedges.

She carefully stacked the slices into a tower on a polished wood plate and built a wall around it with strawberries. "Perfect." She grabbed a strawberry and popped it in her mouth.

A horrifying crash of metal on metal came from the wall outside and Madeline dropped the basket of strawberries sending them tumbling across the floor. More clanging followed.

Oh, God. The shadow!

"Roark!" She darted to the tower's wooden door, put her shoulder into it, and pushed it open. Madeline burst onto the patio. Chickens clucked and scattered. Roark walked toward her, dusting himself off.

"What *was* that?" she yelled. "Are you all right?"

He looked up. "What? The gate? Come see."

She sighed, then growled. "Thank God. I thought it was . . ."

"Hey, relax."

She hated when he told her to relax. He didn't appreciate her love for him. Why was he so thoughtless?

"It's finished, Madeline."

She crossed her arms. *How long had he been at that stupid gate?* "Great," she said, turning back to the tower. "You can finally quit tinkering with it." She went back in to her work, leaving the door open.

Outside the wall, the shadow stumbled backward when Roark dropped the gate into place and slammed it shut, the metal still ringing. "The tolling of the bell," its voice whispered from the void. "This labyrinth will be a tomb for the living."

The shadow turned back toward the barrier. It slowly brushed its fingers over the rough, red bricks until it found a small crack near the last little black hole it left in the wall. A crooked arm emerged from the shadow and touched the crack, inserting a new tiny spot of darkness.

Roark stood in the doorway of the tower watching Madeline pick up strawberries from the floor. "The gate is a perfect fit," he said. "The wall is complete."

"You could help," Madeline said.

He knelt down and held her hand. "With this wall and Tatus's prayers, the shadow will never bother us again."

Madeline pulled away. "Good. Now you can help me."

Roark grabbed a nearby strawberry and placed it in the basket. He stood and walked over to the table by the hearth. "I put a lot of work into it, you should come see." He took a few slices off Madeline's apple tower.

"Hey!" Madeline barked, rising to her feet and slapping Roark's hand. "Those are for tonight."

Roark swallowed.

Madeline put the basket on the table and slapped Roark's hand again. "You scared me."

"What?"

"I thought . . . I thought the crane collapsed again."

Roark laughed. "You worrying about me?"

"I worry that some accidents aren't just accidents."

"Come on." He grabbed her wrist and pulled Madeline toward the door. "You worry too much."

He pulled her outside. She didn't resist. He led her down the wide path between the tower and the gate, past apple trees and around Tatus's well that provided water for drinking and a crude irrigation system. Beyond the well were rows of Madeline's vegetables.

"Look," Roark said as he finally let go. He pointed at the gate in front of them and followed the twisting metalwork with his fingers. "See the trees?" He watched for Madeline's reaction.

"Trees?" Madeline asked. "This is what was taking you so long?"

"It was Tatus's idea. He said I should surprise you with a design. Do you like it? One tree for you and one for me. Tatus showed me how to work the metal and make them look alive. See their budding branches? New life. Like us."

Madeline touched one of the metal trunks. A scowl passed over her face. "Strange . . ."

Roark bristled. "Strange?"

"I mean, I—it's beautiful, really, but was it worth risking our safety while you made trees?"

Roark shrugged. "Tatus said . . ."

"Is it strong?"

Roark grabbed the gate and shook it. It didn't budge. "And it only opens from the inside. Now we can live in peace." Roark smiled. "This is a big day, Madeline. The first ring of the labyrinth is finished!"

Roark took Madeline's hands. He pulled her toward him. "Tatus is going to be so proud. Let's celebrate before he gets back."

"I hope he brings honey bees this time . . . and more clothes. You need to get those hives started."

"Yeah, I know." He could feel Madeline's body tense against him. "What's wrong?"

"I don't know." She looked up at him.

Her sad eyes made him angry. "Madeline, look around. Why aren't you happy? We have everything we ever wanted."

"I know. Except . . . why aren't our prayers being answered?"

He let go of her hands.

Madeline stepped back and asked, "Wouldn't you like to have a little boy?"

"Of course I would."

"Or a little girl." Her face softened. "Or both. They would call you Tatus. He could help you on the wall and I could teach her about gardening. We'd give them the childhood we can't remember."

"Maybe now that we have a safe home . . . maybe that's what God's been waiting for."

"Maybe," Madeline said as she stared through the bronze branches in the gate and off into the distance. "Roark, it destroyed our home before. It could do it again."

"Why can't you just enjoy the peace we've earned? You know Tatus's plan as well as I do. He hasn't let us down so far and this wall is just the beginning." Tears were welling up and about to drip down onto her cheeks. "No, no, don't cry." He wiped her cheek and lifted her chin. "Look at me. Don't you trust me? I will do whatever it takes to protect you."

Madeline wiped her eyes and forced a smile. "Good, because I'm doing all I can just to feed you."

"Whatever it takes."

"I know." Madeline held Roark's hand. "It's just—it's so much work."

"Do you really like the gate?"

"Are you sure it will keep the shadow out?"

"With God's help, absolutely."

"Then yes, I like your gate."

He grinned. "I am Wall Builder! Gate Raiser!" He pulled Madeline close and kissed her. Her soft lips tasted of cider and strawberries.

Madeline looked into his eyes. "I am happy we have each other. Thank you for everything you're doing for us."

"That's more like it." Roark clapped his hands. "Let's celebrate! What's for dinner?"

"Go clean up and meet me in the apple orchard."

"Come on, what are we having?"

"It's a surprise. Something new."

"New?"

"My garden still has some secrets left." Madeline turned and tossed her broomstick skirt behind her. She flashed a coy smile at Roark, flicked her long black hair off her shoulder, and went to put the finishing touches on her meal.

Roark looked up at the gate and admired its construction. He knew its beauty and strength wouldn't do anything to stop the shadow if the gate didn't have God's blessing. He took a deep breath and prayed quietly, "God, please accept the work of my hands and give this gate and this wall your supernatural power. I pray that I have earned your protection." He looked through the gate and beyond to the labyrinth mapped out in the dirt. There was so much work ahead, but if it kept the shadow away, it would all be worth it.

Roark gathered up his tools and joined Madeline in the orchard. He lit the torches, poured himself some cider, and watched her lay out the dinner she'd been preparing all day.

The couple's laughter spilled over the wall. When the shadow heard it, it stopped leaving holes in the barrier and its darkness seemed to grow. Its outline bulged and everything around it was pulled closer toward its center. The shadow resumed its work with new intensity.

It circled the wall, touching it and leaving black holes in cracks, crevices, and at its base. When the sun had almost set, the shadow stopped to watch. The voice from the void gave a low chuckle, "When the morning comes we will rise, but now they delve deeper into darkness."

As the last sliver of light disappeared, the shadow turned and took a long look at the wall. "The seeds of your destruction have been planted," it whispered. Then it drew in a deep breath and shouted, "Come out!"

A thunderclap startled Roark and Madeline and it started to drizzle.

Madeline had finished her preparations and lay against Roark's chest enjoying her cider when the thunder hit. She jumped at the loud noise and spilled her drink. "Where did that come from?"

Roark looked up. "There wasn't a cloud in the sky a minute ago."

The drizzle became a downpour and Madeline rushed to collect her food.

"Come on, Madeline! Just leave that stuff. We're getting soaked."

"What are you complaining about? You could use a good soaking. Help me," Madeline begged.

"Funny." Roark grabbed their picnic blanket of stitched pelts and held it over their heads. He stood over Madeline as she grabbed the remains of her meal.

They fumbled over each other back to the tower, dropping wooden plates, cups, and food. When they finally made it inside, Madeline threw everything on the floor of their entryway. A plate of dirty apple slices wobbled to a stop as a basket of fruit emptied at Roark's feet.

"Ruined," Madeline grumbled as she struggled out from underneath the heavy blanket. She wiped her face and wrung out her hair.

"Hey, relax. It's all right." Roark let the wet blanket flop to the floor and touched her shoulder.

"Relax?" Madeline swatted Roark's hand off. "I worked hard to celebrate your wall, and it's ruined." She plopped down on the bottom step of the stairs.

Roark joined her and surveyed the damage. The fruit and vegetables, roasted duck, a loaf of bread, and Madeline's surprise dessert were scattered about on the ground in a growing puddle. "You're right," Roark grunted as he bent over, grabbed an apple from the floor and took a big bite. "It's ruined," he said around the mouthful, "Tell you what, I'll let you make it up to me tomorrow."

Madeline glared at him. "You can make *me* dinner tomorrow night."

Roark took another bite of his apple. "Sure. Gate Raiser, Wall Builder, Dinner Maker . . . whatever it takes." Roark grabbed a second apple off the floor and handed it to Madeline. "Take this. Don't let a little rain ruin our fun. I'll draw some more cider—that always cheers you up. Meet you upstairs. Let's get out of these wet clothes." Roark got up and offered his hand to Madeline. "Who knows, maybe tonight's the night."

"What about this mess?" she asked.

"I'll help you clean it up later."

Madeline took Roark's hand and he pulled her to her feet. She looked around, sighed, and gave in, "Fine. Pour a jug of cider. I'm getting drunk." She pulled off her wet shirt, flung it at Roark, and started up the stairs.

Outside, rain poured down the face of the wall and into the holes the shadow had created. Tiny, thorny vines twisted from the voids and started to grow across the bricks. The shadow laughed. Flashes of lightning illuminated the surrounding landscape, but the shadow remained cloaked in darkness. Thunder rolled through the inky plain below.

6

Trapped

A crash startled Roark awake. He looked out one of the small windows. Lightning shot through the sky. Thunder cracked and rumbled.

He started to drift back to sleep when Madeline exhaled a faint laugh. He turned toward her. She smiled, her eyes still closed. "We're pretty trees . . ."

Many nights, he awoke to find her hiding somewhere in the room or next to him holding some invisible object and mumbling nonsense. Her sleepwalking usually proved harmless, but one time he caught her leaning out the large tower window. Ever since, he tried to keep an eye on her when she talked in her sleep, just in case she started acting out her dreams.

He waited to see if she'd continue. She shivered and struggled against something. "Just leave me here," she demanded. "I can't . . ." She stopped breathing.

He nudged her. She gasped for air then rolled toward him and opened her eyes, jerking away. "Run!" she yelled.

He reached to shake her and she grabbed him by the throat. "Madeline," he croaked. He pulled her hand away. "Madeline! Wake up."

Sweat beaded on her brow. She continued to struggle and whimper, "The shadow. The fire."

"Shhh, Madeline. Wake up."

"Gone, gone. Oh . . . my roots. Our home. It's all gone!"

All of a sudden, she blinked back to consciousness and looked up, staring at him. "Roark?" She fumbled for a candle and held it up to his face. She stared into his eyes.

"It's all right. Everything's all right." He took the candle and placed it on its stand.

She slumped into his arms crying.

He held her and rubbed her back. "Same dream?" He didn't really want to know and was instantly sorry he asked. He needed sleep.

Madeline groaned. "We were in the glowing garden again. The shadow came and burned it, drove us into the wilderness." She took a deep breath. "But this time he was like . . . a giant snake." She turned to him and her face was ashen. "You had horrible black eyes. And somehow everything was your fault."

"What's that supposed to mean?"

Madeline shook her head. "I don't know."

"Well, look . . ." Roark pulled her close. He felt her clammy skin. "This is our home now. We're safe. You don't have to be afraid anymore. Tatus promised; the shadow can't hurt you here."

Another flash of lightning and then thunder. Night air whistled through the windows and blew out the candle. Madeline shivered.

She wrapped herself in a blanket of pelts and left the bed. The floorboards creaked under her bare feet as she crossed the room. Wind-driven rain hit her face as she stood by the large window and reached for the shutter. Fingers of lightning lit the sky and the thunder snapped high in the distance. Suddenly, she shrieked.

"The shadow is here! Roark, it's real. The nightmare is real!" She dropped to the floor and covered her eyes. The wind caught the shutter, throwing it against the tower wall with a smack.

Roark groaned. "Come on."

"The shadow is standing at the gate, Roark!"

Roark got up and shuffled to the window. He stared into the darkness below. "Everything is the shadow to you."

"Wait for the lightning. There, by the gate. Oh God, Roark, it saw me." Madeline grabbed Roark and hid behind him.

"I'm getting wet here. The lightning is just playing tricks on your eyes."

"No! I saw it!"

Watching and waiting for the lightning seemed to delay its next strike. It finally flashed and Roark stared at the gate through the rain. He saw what he expected—nothing. The light reflected in the water that pooled in the entrance.

"You had a bad dream. You're seeing things." He put his arm around Madeline and she quickly swatted it off.

"Don't treat me like I'm crazy."

"Fine. I'm tired."

"I saw the shadow."

"I didn't. Thank God."

Lightning hit again and Madeline hesitantly took another look.

"My wall will keep us safe. It can't reach us here in the tower. Don't torture yourself. Come, lie back down."

"It was there, Roark," Madeline whimpered.

He was angry, but too tired to show it, so he took her hand and wove her fingers together with his. "Let's get some sleep." He took a step and pulled Madeline toward the bed, but she looked out the window again. He tugged on her. "We're safe." She finally gave up and turned her back to the window.

They climbed under the pelts. Lightning flashed with a crack of thunder.

"It's getting closer," she said.

"Mmm."

Madeline tried to get comfortable. "I forgot the windows. Close them for me?"

Roark groaned, tossed the pelts off, and rushed to close the windows. Thunder rumbled as he returned.

Madeline lay on her back staring at the ceiling. "I don't ever want to see it again. Promise me that tomorrow you'll start on the outer wall. Tatus is right. We can't rest. We have to keep working if God is going to bless the labyrinth and protect us. One wall is good, more walls are better."

He turned his back toward her. "I'll build it just like Tatus showed me."

"Promise me that you'll start tomorrow."

He sighed. "I promise. Now get some sleep."

Silence.

He finally started to doze off.

"Why won't it leave us alone?" Madeline asked. "Why follow us? Why torture us? I know what I saw."

Roark growled. He turned over, trying to get comfortable.

Madeline started to pray. "We're sorry we stopped to celebrate. Please forgive us. We believe. Oh, God, hear my prayer."

He turned over again.

"Roark, you should pray with me."

"Sleep," he moaned.

Madeline kept begging God for forgiveness and safety . . . and children. The air in the room grew thick, clouded with her dread. It was suffocating.

No rest for Wall Builder, he thought.

Far above the tower, Wyrm tasted Madeline's fear in the air. Dark emotions were easy to draw out, and they were the only ones that nourished him. He extended his long black neck, opened his mouth, and slowly swung his head to drink in the gloom flowing from Madeline. The wall and tower had begun to serve their true purpose. In time, the prison would focus his captive couple's foulest feelings and flood the sky with his food.

Lightning flashed and, for an instant, his winged shadow darted across the clouds. Wyrm had to stay hidden to get what he wanted. Ultimately, the liar's death would be sweeter than any despair he could tease from Madeline and Roark. As the labyrinth took shape, it would become a symbol of his righteous power spread out beneath him, a great serpent coiled around his ancient tormentor in an inescapable embrace. The evil one would come for them, and then . . . justice.

He savored the meal his influence had cooked up. "Well done, my good and faithful servant," Wyrm hissed. Then he skimmed the last morsel of fear from the air and growled, "More."

"Thank you for blessing our work on the labyrinth, Lord." Tatus prayed as he made his way back to the tower, the wagon filled with supplies and bricks from the kilns. It creaked under the heavy load. Tatus and the camels that pulled his wagon were drenched from the rain. The road could be cruel, but it was his home.

The dragon's worms writhed within him and whispered in his ears, "More."

Tatus gripped the reins with one hand and pressed hard against his heart with the other. His head buzzed and that one word from the blood worms, "More," seized his thoughts and emotions, fixing them on the unfinished labyrinth. He closed his eyes and the worms gave him a vision of the shadow inside the wall. It had Madeline and it was attacking the tower. "Please, God, no," he prayed.

I have to save her, Tatus thought. *I have to kill it.*

He envisioned himself traveling through a labyrinth larger than anything he had previously planned. One brick barrier after another, each larger than the one before, encircled the tower. Between them, the winding wall of the labyrinth created the same pattern over and over, the symbol of power—control over evil—on an ever-increasing scale.

Yes, Lord, Tatus prayed. *If I'm going to trap it, we have to keep building. Then let it dare to enter the heart of your house.*

"Good," the worms whispered to Tatus. "He will never stop chasing Madeline and Roark. The day will come when he will enter the labyrinth to take them. Then the shadow will pay for murdering your family."

Tears welled up in Tatus's eyes and threatened to join the drops of rain on his face.

"Yes, I was with you that night, and I will be with you when you have your revenge. He will know your pain. He will suffer for his tyranny, trapped and killed in the labyrinth. Only then will the world be free. Then we will have peace."

"Thank you, Lord." The blood worms burned within Tatus, fueling a zealous rage.

7

Flies

T atus returned to the tower and Wyrm spied on Madeline
and Roark through the blood worms in Tatus's eyes. He used
Tatus to prod Roark to continue building and to stoke Madeline's
fear, ensuring a steady flow of dark emotions emanated from the
labyrinth. Beyond the food the couple provided, Wyrm delighted
that he could use them as bait to trap the shadow in a prison of his
enemy's own design.

Wyrm soared high above, unseen, as the labyrinth grew over
many years. The man who was once the hunter faded into memory
as a perverted puppet took his place. The serpent's spawn animated
Tatus, giving him unnaturally long life and extraordinary strength
for his work while keeping him boiling with anger and hatred for
the shadow. Ages passed and his blood worms watched Madeline
and Roark become shadows of their former selves. While their
bodies barely aged, the couple couldn't have children and their
spirits shriveled. The serpentine wall that served to protect them
eventually became their master, and their slavery hardened them
in a way wandering in the wilderness never had.

Madeline demanded Roark keep working on the labyrinth to keep them safe, but she resented his absence. She stayed securely alone in the tower as he labored far away on the labyrinth in a never-ending effort to perfect it. It was a long journey to the center, but the distance between Roark and Madeline grew long before walls separated them. The couple's heated arguments gave way to a cold efficiency.

Since it was such a long way to the center of the prison, Wyrm gave Tatus the idea for an exchange. Tatus insisted that midday on full moons, Roark would leave dried meats from Tatus's hunts on a large stone table in the labyrinthine path. In return, he picked up wheat, corn, and preserved fruits and vegetables from Madeline's gardens. They exchanged their goods, but exchanged few words. Before long they made the trade without seeing each other. Madeline was the first to come to the table and find it bare. Her anger and despair made an especially fine meal for Wyrm that day.

Roark eventually stopped traveling very far into the labyrinth at all. He went away to build their prison carrying the weight of the knowledge that no amount of effort would ever be enough to make Madeline happy.

Roark opened the door in the outermost ring of the labyrinth. He stepped outside for a break from his cramped world of mortar and bricks stacked to exacting standards. He'd been working since dawn. Tatus went hunting and told him not to stop building until the new section of wall was finished. The old man could return any minute, but Roark was so exhausted that he risked getting caught resting. He looked up into the cloudy sky and pulled a deep breath in through his nose. There were only a few hours of daylight left. The vast open space east of the labyrinth and the trees on the horizon beyond called to him. He asked out loud, "You'd come after me if I left, wouldn't you . . . hunter?"

Roark walked out into the open and turned around. With his back to the forest, he remembered how afraid of the shadow he was in the days before the labyrinth. He backed up until he could see over the looming wall and barely make out the tip of the tower off in the hazy distance. He imagined Madeline standing at their bedroom window and said, "I never wanted so many walls. I just wanted a home . . . with you."

He brushed his dreadlocks off his bare shoulders. He pulled his hair back out of his face to tie it behind his head, revealing a scar that ran from his forehead, across the bridge of his nose and down his right cheek. He rubbed his face and ran his fingers along the old wound. It reminded him what happened when he made Tatus angrier than usual. He went inside to get back to the bricks.

A wooden gate that had a door within it blocked the entrance to the labyrinth. Roark built the gate large enough to let Tatus's wagon pass onto the path between walls, and the small opening allowed for Roark to enter and exit without having to heave the gate open.

Beyond the door and inside the outer wall, the new section of the labyrinth waited. There was only one entrance, and there weren't any branching paths or dead ends like a maze. If Roark were to enter, go toward the tower, and then get turned around, he would just come out where he started. One continuous wall wound back and forth, folding in on itself like intestines. The path the wall created was over ten feet wide and it snaked in and out, ever closer to the center. With enough supplies, Roark could eventually reach the tower by simply walking forward.

Tatus said that when the time came for God to deliver the shadow, the unbroken path would invite it deeper into their trap. Since the path created the symbol of God's power over evil, the journey would digest the shadow's strength. Before it ever got near Madeline, God would disorient the enemy, focus and project its wickedness, using it against the shadow to create doubt, fear, and ultimately despair. Then God would give Tatus the power to kill it. But the shadow never came. The labyrinth obviously had the ability to protect them from it, but its ability to make the shadow vulnerable remained to be seen.

As Roark built the wall, Tatus walked the snaking path begging God to give the labyrinth its mystical and maddening power. "May confusion and fear be trapped within these walls," Tatus prayed. "Give me control through despair."

Roark thought of Madeline in the center of the labyrinth, barren and miserable. *Well, God answers your prayers, Tatus.*

A horsefly buzzed around Roark's head tickling his ear. He swatted it away with his trowel then used it to scoop mortar for his next brick.

He wiped sweat from his face and kept thinking of Madeline.
Roark, I miss you.

He spread the mortar. He could almost hear her voice.
I'm starting to think you love the labyrinth more than me.

The fly returned. Roark swatted it away. He picked up a brick, slapped some mortar on its end, and pushed it into place. Mortar squished out from underneath the brick and he scraped the excess away with his trowel.

I get scared here all alone, Roark. Don't you care about that?

"I'm building the labyrinth *you* wanted," Roark answered out loud as he shoveled more mortar from his bucket and heaped it on top of the wall. "You have no idea how hard I work for you! And when I'm home all you do is complain."

It's impossible to talk to you! I don't even know what to say anymore.

He slammed the next brick down and said, "How about 'Thank you'? Try that!" He scraped more mortar away.

Just go. Go sleep with your bricks, because you're not sleeping next to me.

The horsefly bit Roark's neck. He slapped himself trying to kill it and threw down the trowel.

"Talking to yourself again?" Tatus asked Roark from behind.

Roark turned around and mumbled, "Damn flies . . ." He froze at Tatus's appearance. The old man had shaved his head; his beard and even his eyebrows, revealing scabs on his scalp.

"You look like hell."

"Lice," Tatus said as he ran his hand over the new section of wall and grunted. "You're getting sloppy."

"How did the hunt go?" Roark asked as he sat on the ground.

Tatus bent over, grabbed Roark by the arm, and lifted him back to his feet. "Quit screwing around and get to the bricks. I don't care if you have to work by torchlight, you're not stopping until this section is done . . . and done right!"

"You may never sleep, but I still have to," Roark objected.

"Sacrifice and hard work, boy. How many times do I have to tell you? That's what it's going to take if . . . are you listening to me?"

Roark was staring at him. Without hair, he looked like a mangy animal. "Tatus, I've heard it all before. Look at all I've built."

"More," Tatus growled. "You have to keep building if God is going to honor our work and keep protecting us. Where is your faith? It is our destiny to free the world of the shadow, and we choose our destiny when we get to the bricks."

Tatus picked up a sledgehammer and swung, barely missing Roark's head. Bricks shattered behind him.

Roark stumbled backward, terrified. "Wha . . . are you crazy?"

"It's for your own good. This wall will never last." He started another swing but Roark grabbed the handle. Tatus kicked him in the gut sending him flying backward onto the dirt. He didn't stop swinging until the day's work lay in chunks on the ground. "Now you'll be at the bricks all night to make up for your laziness—unless you're okay with the shadow taking your home."

Tatus tossed the sledgehammer and walked away. Roark clutched his stomach, "This is no home," he wheezed. He could barely talk. "This is a prison."

Tatus stopped and looked back over his shoulder, his eyes afire. "Safety, food, and shelter are a prison?" Tatus turned and glared at him. "While you and Madeline live in comfort, I live in a wagon . . . for you! Hauling everything you need, and more. I haven't rested one day since we started this labyrinth!"

Roark got to his feet and bent over, his hands on his knees. "*You* haven't rested? God, what I wouldn't give for just a day away from this wall. The sick thing is I'm building it. I'm building my own prison out of bricks of . . . pain. And you, you're the God damned jailer."

Tatus pointed at Roark. "Watch your mouth, boy! You asked for this . . . one of the few bright things you've ever done. One day the shadow will come and you will thank me." Tatus stomped off.

Roark picked up a jagged piece of brick and stood up straight. Compressed anger burned inside him. His stratified emotions had turned to rock, but the pressure deep inside increased until a molten rage began to flow. With all his strength, he hurled the broken brick at the back of Tatus's head.

Tatus turned around and snatched the flying brick out of the air. He snarled then tossed it aside. Tatus walked out of the labyrinth to his team of camels and shouted, "Get to work before you do something else you'll regret! And be sure to lock the door so the shadow doesn't catch you off guard." Tatus climbed up into his wagon and cracked a whip in the air. The beasts lunged forward. "I'm going to the kilns. I'll be back with more water and bricks in a week. I expect some real progress."

Roark coughed as he stumbled to the door in the outer ring of the labyrinth. He tripped over his tools, stubbed his toe on a giant brick, swore, and slammed the door. Roark barred the entrance and slid to the ground defeated. He sat with his head in his hands seething.

He needed to calm down. Roark's leather bag called to him. It was never far away. He opened it and the sweet smell of its contents greeted him. He pulled the seeds from a bud and stuck them in the dirt. He had patches of plants growing all along the labyrinth's wall. After starting a little fire with his flint, he pulled out his pipe, packed a bowl, and lit up. His back to the wall, he took a drag, exhaled, and the smoke rose above the labyrinth.

Oblivion. It was the only way he could get any peace.

"Slave driver," he mumbled.

He looked at the pallets of bricks. "It was never enough for you either, Madeline . . . always afraid," he sighed. "Then you hated me for being gone . . . working to protect you. Now look at us."

He was loneliest at night; Madeline in the belly of the labyrinth and Roark far away at the outermost wall. He wondered if she really was miserable like him.

Roark took another hit and held this one in longer.

Buzzing above his head grabbed his attention. It was a small cloud of flies. He defiantly blew at them and engulfed the intruders in smoke.

He imagined that Madeline wished he would come to lie next to her and hold her like he used to. "I hope you're happy," he whispered. Something in him wanted to mean it, but he knew his hope was useless.

"I don't need her. I'm better off alone."

Roark looked up, past the flies and into the sky as a flight of ravens passed overhead toward the center of the labyrinth.

8

Ravens

The woman stirred in bed against the new day. She loved being unconscious. It stopped the pain of loneliness. If it weren't for her nightmares of being chased by the shadow through the glowing garden, sleep would be the perfect refuge. She turned her head to the empty side of the bed. Her man had long since left her. The late summer's unexpectedly cool morning begged her to draw the covers close and sleep in.

Outside the tower's open windows, ravens circled high above the labyrinth. Below them lay a sea of winding walls—ring after ring filled with the intricate pattern from the back of the karimba. The sun twinkled in reflection off something hanging from one of the bird's beaks. The others called out to him.

She rolled over and wrapped herself tightly in her blanket.

A raven fluttered to one of the open windows and landed on the sill. The woman spoke without turning, "What did you bring me today?"

Silence.

Curiosity won out over comfort and she rolled back over. The raven held a dingy silver necklace in his beak. When he saw that he had her attention, he flashed his wings, flapped and fluttered to the bed. She held out her hand. The bird delivered his gift, then another ebony flash and he disappeared.

"Wait, stay a while," she cried as she sat up in bed, but it was too late. She was alone again.

Her joints ached and her neck hurt. She stood and shuffled to the tower window. "Come back!" she called to the ravens. "We'll have breakfast in the garden!" The wind caught her voice and her entreaties tumbled to the ground. The birds were far off and flying away from her.

She hung her head and pictured herself soaring away with the ravens, leaving the tower behind, but thoughts of the shadow outside the labyrinth wouldn't let her enjoy that fantasy for long.

She yawned and stretched. *Why did they leave so soon?* She looked past the first wall that the man finished so long ago and strained to see the outermost barrier through the haze. The edge of the labyrinth couldn't be seen through the smog that always hung above the walls surrounding her home. She shook her head. "Impossible man." She looked down at her unkempt gardens. The plants desperately needed watering, but she barely had the motivation to tend to the plots of land that sustained her.

She turned her back to the wall and slid down to sit on the floor. *Where do they get their gifts?* She looked at the raven's trinket in her hand and polished it with her shirt. "Maybe I used to know where they came from," she said, holding up the necklace to catch the light. "It doesn't matter—their gifts are magical."

Uncounted years of isolation had darkened parts of her memory. She couldn't even remember her name.

She hung the necklace between her lips and got up. She extended her arms and imagined they were wings. Slowly flapping her arms, she stepped up onto the bed of pelts. Thousands of shiny trinkets hung on the walls around the small room: necklaces and charms and bracelets and pendants, some gold, some silver or bronze. They covered the walls and shimmered in the rising sun streaming through the windows. The trinkets comforted her. They reminded her that at least the birds still cared about her.

"What would I do without you, my loves . . . my ravens?" She hung her new necklace from a cracked brick in the wall, extended her arms again and pretended to glide toward the window.

She plopped onto the thick windowsill and sighed. Still no winged visitors. Staring out into the hazy sky, she wished she could see far enough back in time to recover who she was. "Maybe my name was Raven." She liked that thought. "I have no wings, but still, why couldn't I have a name that flies?"

She looked out at the labyrinth built to protect her. She wished her memories of the shadow had faded too. "Alone . . . at least the shadow will never reach me." But she was a caged bird. Safety for isolation, it was a bitter trade. And she'd make it again if given the chance.

"Yes. Raven. That will be my name."

At the center of the labyrinth, the wall was higher and covered in the thorny vines that plagued the labyrinth since its earliest days. Some vines were as thick as tree trunks and their thorns were spears. Their roots plunged deep, loosening the bricks and threatening to bring down the wall given enough time. Crumbled bricks on the ground were a common sight near the tower. Fewer and smaller vines plagued the wall further out.

Raven wondered if the man was still out there, building the ever-expanding labyrinth, pulling vines and making repairs. But she had forgotten his name as well.

She spent the endless stream of days working the ground. Talking with the ravens had become the high point of her routine, but as the day dragged on, loneliness gathered its strength for its nightly attack. It chipped away at her sanity like the thorny vines attacked the wall of the labyrinth. The unconsciousness of sleep was a welcome relief, but it was fleeting. The pain of daybreak was as faithful a visitor as the ravens.

She made her way down the winding stairs of the tower. She put her shoulder to the door, pushed, and it creaked open. The stone of the patio chilled her bare feet.

Thirst beckoned her to the well between her tower home and the gate that led to the rest of the labyrinth. She walked past the overgrown gardens and hung her head over the edge. She called into the darkness below, "Caw, caw!"

Her voice echoed back to her.

She let out another series of caws into the air above the well and scanned the sky for ravens. There were still none to be seen. She imagined the man could hear her and wondered what he thought of her raven calls. "He probably thinks I've lost my mind. Well, he's the crazy one . . . stubborn bastard."

She had started to wonder if maybe she only imagined the man—conjured him out of too much solitude—but she would never speak that thought out loud. That would give voice to her worst fear, that she actually was utterly alone, and beyond that, insane. If he didn't exist, she was crazy to think he was out there protecting her. If he did exist, she was crazy for doubting his existence. No, she wouldn't speak it. Still . . . if she had a man, surely they would have children, but there were no signs of them. The most powerful evidence that the man was real were the walls and the torment of the thought that his leaving was her fault. She couldn't make herself, the ravens, or the echoes in the well tell her heart otherwise.

She lowered the bucket and brought up some water. After a long drink, she splashed some on her face and turned her attention to her gardens. Many buckets later the plants were watered, but they still sorely needed weeding.

She gave herself fully to the task and within an hour, her back ached and she was cursing the dirt. When the old man first taught her how to work the soil and nurture new life, gardening had brought her so much joy. She straightened and rubbed her lower back.

"What was that he used to say?" she wondered out loud. "First the grain, and then the blade . . . one destroyed . . ." She struggled to remember the rest. She used to wonder at the miracle of a tender bud on a plant. She used to look forward to the harvest and sharing the bounty with the men. It had been so long since they had a meal together, she couldn't even recall their faces.

9

Darkness

Raven hadn't left the tower for days. She should have been bringing in her harvest, but instead she lay naked in bed counting the trinkets hanging on the wall. "Three hundred fifty five, three hundred fifty six, three hundred fifty . . ." She thought, in passing, that she should get to the gardens, wishing the relentless days would just stop coming. "Three hundred fifty . . . where was I? Three hundred . . . ugh. One, two, three . . . oh, never mind."

She sat on the bed for a while. Getting up, she caught a glimpse of her reflection in a dingy sliver of a mirror she broke long ago. Her tangled, long black hair didn't have a trace of gray. *How many years has it been?* Her body was haggard and drawn. The pained expression on her face and her dark, lifeless eyes startled her. She quickly looked away.

She willed herself down the stairs and out onto the lawn. "Get back to the gardens," she told herself. She hoped to get lost in her work and forget what she saw in the mirror. "You're not crazy. Just do what you normally do." She looked at her rows of withering corn, then up into the sky. She couldn't fathom why the ravens refused to return. Without the birds and their gifts to break up the monotony, the thorny vines of loneliness dug their roots in deep. She looked at the wall, cracked and crumbling, then down at her naked body.

Raven pictured what she would look like with black feathers. She raised her arms as if they were wings. "I'm a hungry raven. Fly to the garden!" Flapping her arms, she ran to raid what was left of her crops. She grabbed one of the few ears of corn. It was dry and flavorless, but she wolfed it down, leaving kernels all over her mouth and dropping on her chest. She cleared the cob and threw it toward the wall.

"Why won't they come and eat with me? Caw, caw!" she screamed. "Fly to me! Am I no longer worthy of your gifts?" She slapped herself in the face. "No, I'm not, am I?" She struck herself again and growled, "Fly away. I don't need you." She paced back and forth mumbling, "What's left? I don't know. Who do I have? Fickle birds." She clawed at her arm and bit it until it bled. "Wait!" she stopped, her own blood reddening her dry lips. "The dirt still loves me!"

Arms stretched out, she descended on her radishes. She dug up the red and white treasures, barely attempting to clean them as she shoved them into her mouth. "Yes, the dirt still brings me gifts," she said with a mouthful. "The dirt still loves me."

"Ha! A surprise? For me?" She plucked up an earthworm and admired it. "It's beautiful. You shouldn't have. Thank you." Then she ate it too.

After eating her fill of radishes, she rested under an apple tree and ate dessert. Her lips grew sticky with juice from her apples, and dirt from her digging stuck to her face and hands.

She looked up at her bedroom windows. "Where is he?" she asked. "Sleeping in again I bet. Lazy . . ." She dropped her apple, got up and stomped into the tower. "You're not leaving me to do all the work!" she yelled up at the bedroom, her voice bouncing off the walls. "Get down here!" She huffed, insulting the man all the way up the stairs. She pushed open the door and looked at the bed. It was empty. "Oh no, you're not getting away from me that easy." She turned, ran down the stairs and looked at the open door to the cellar. She growled. "Eating my preserves again, are you?" The cellar was empty too.

Her frantic search spilled onto the patio, into the gardens and right up to the great bronze gate protecting the center of the labyrinth. Lost in panic, she mindlessly opened it, pushing away the fear of what she might find . . . a companion who was never more than a figment of her imagination.

Thorny vines crowded the path and scratched her as she struggled past them. The labyrinth stretched on much longer than she imagined. She quickly became disoriented between the walls and lost hope that she could reach the exit. The desperate search gave way to exhaustion. Soon her bare feet were bloodied and bruised, and she grew very thirsty. She turned around and around, finally collapsing in despair on the ground among the rubble from the wall.

"God damn this labyrinth!" she shrieked. "And God damn yourself too!"

After what seemed to be hours, she trudged in the direction she thought she'd come, not caring if she even found her way back.

By the time she reached the center of the labyrinth, the sun and moon had traded places in the sky. She had spent the entire day lost in the walls. She quenched her thirst at the well and barely had enough energy to close the gate and climb the tower to her room. She dropped onto her bed and fell asleep.

The sun and moon traded places many more times.

Raven lay submerged in darkness in her room atop the tower. She dreamed she stood outside of a forest in a grassy moonlit clearing. A mournful, piercing noise filled the air. It was the haunting sound they used to hear coming from the woods back when they were wanderers. She covered her ears but she could still hear it. She turned to see if the shadow would emerge from the trees.

To her surprise, the noise changed and became singing. She dropped her hands and listened to the song in the night.

> "Light rolls away before the darkness,
> and the darkness from before the light."

Then a brilliant light filled the woods revealing the silhouette of her man slowly stepping from the trees. He walked up to her and kissed her. They looked at each other and laughed. The joy of their reunion brought her to tears. They reclined together on a bed of soft grass and held each other as the song continued.

> "It's time to lie down and rest in peace,
> as the bands of sleep fall on your eyes.
> Into my hands commit your spirits,
> and when the morning comes you will rise."

Raven awoke, her shirt wet with sweat and her face wet from crying. All was dark. She rolled over to put her arm around the man, but he wasn't there. The emptiness hit her with a wave of despair and then crushed her. She would always be alone. The shattering reality of her isolation and her helplessness to do anything about it were too strong.

"Why are you torturing me?" She sat up in bed, cradled her head in her hands, and wept. "Oh, please, God, send the man." She looked at the raven's gifts hanging on her walls and moaned, "At least send back the birds." With heaving sobs she pulled herself to her knees on the bed. "I can't do this anymore! I give up."

Then, from across the room, she saw it.

A way out.

Moonlight filled the room as she dragged herself to the large tower window. She climbed up into it. High above the labyrinth, she looked down, filled with a dark excitement. It would soon be over.

Through blurred vision, the beauty of the labyrinth's complex design lit by the moon struck her. It wound on and on, reaching into the night.

A light breeze caressed her cheek and then brushed her knotted hair off her shoulder. The endlessly folding wall would never let her leave, but she could make it out . . . right here and now. "He's been building this thing every day for who knows how long. It will go on forever." She strained to see the light of a fire at the edge of the labyrinth or on its winding path, but there was no sign of the man.

"No. He's not even real."

The sound of her words startled her. She'd actually said it. Speaking it, finally, she knew it was true. The thought had all the power of reality behind it. He had never existed. And she had never been loved.

She closed her eyes. *I have always been alone. I won't hold onto an imaginary past any longer.* She blurted out her next thought even before it fully formed, "What if I am a raven dreaming of being the crazy woman who feeds me?"

It all led to one answer . . . *jump.* Jump to wake from the bird dream. Jump to end her living nightmare. She was finally doing what she should have done a long time ago. She would soon be free.

"If you will not fly to me, I will fly to you," she said. And with that, the caged bird stretched out her wings and leaned over the edge of the window.

10

Hope Deferred

J ust as Raven was about to fly into the darkness, a light appeared
in the labyrinth. The peculiar radiance instantly caught her
eye and held her still. It glowed bright white, deep in the winding
walls far from the tower, but to Raven it seemed to spark within her
as well. The brilliance begged her to believe that she wasn't alone
after all. It stopped her from jumping and kept her transfixed on
its mystifying presence.

She sat on the windowsill, her feet dangling outside the tower.
Could it be the man? The source of the light hid below the top of the
labyrinth's wall. It was unlike anything she'd ever seen. A hundred
lanterns wouldn't shine with the same intensity. It didn't flicker
like light from a torch, but it moved, pulsating and sparkling in the
night. She couldn't tell if it was traveling into the labyrinth or out
of it. It moved slowly, then flashed as though calling to her, like an
old friend waving to get her attention.

"That's impossible," she whispered. Still, she wanted to believe
someone was coming for her. She dreaded the thought that the

light might fade into the darkness and leave her alone again. But as long as she watched it, she felt a faint assurance. She dared to believe she could be the light's intended destination. The wonder of it, to feel she was worth a visit from something so enchanting.

She tried to look ahead, to follow the path through the labyrinth to see where the light would end up. Doubt grew as she did. If it moved toward the outer wall she would never know what it was. A breeze blew through the tower windows and she realized she was holding her breath. She tried to relax and breathed deeply.

What could create such a light? "I know this, it's something . . . something other than gardens and walls," she said. "And that makes it a very special something."

The sky grew gray with the approach of dawn. The light had only moved a short distance as she watched, but somehow it was much closer! *Did it speed up when I looked away?* She stood on the sill and tried to predict its path again, but she couldn't follow the course through the twists and turns. Determined, she traced the labyrinth's path with her finger in the air until it went behind the tower and out of view. She held the edge of the window and leaned out.

Suddenly, a section of the sill cracked. Her foot slipped as pieces of brick broke away and fell to the ground. She clung to the tower and quickly pulled herself back in, but now the path was lost.

As the sun rose, the light in the labyrinth diminished until it vanished from view. Her ability to stay awake disappeared along with it. She felt exhausted, and without the light, she didn't want to endure consciousness. She went back to bed.

Her sleep was sticky and restless. Even so, by the time she woke up, the room was dark again.

Is it night or morning? She sat up, hung her head and massaged her neck. *Was the light a dream?* She hoped it was real. She needed it to be real. If there were no light, she was forever alone, a bird who needed to fly from her cage. *No, someone is coming for me!*

Heart pounding, she bounced out of bed with a fire reserved for lovers' reunions. She raced up the stairs to the roof of the tower where she could see the labyrinth in all directions. The heat of the day still hung in the air. She scanned the path, hoping the darkness would reveal her magical visitor, but she only saw walls lit by the rising moon.

No light.

She sat and waited until the night air sent her for a blanket. She waited atop the tower some more, then decided cider would make her perch a bit more comfortable. She returned to the roof with a pitcher and cup, some dried apples, and the karimba too. She once again looked for the light in vain. Eating and drinking made her sleepy, but she forced herself to keep watching and waiting.

"How long is the labyrinth's path?" she wondered out loud. "How many days will it take to reach me?" She sighed, and then tried to distract herself by plucking out a tune on the music block, humming as she did. She hoped to get lost in the music, maybe lose track of time, but she was too anxious.

She turned the karimba over. Her finger traced the pattern of the labyrinth carved into the wood. "What if the light is a trick of the enemy? But how? Light from the shadow?" The questions accumulated along with the items on the roof. "If the shadow is coming for me, I don't have a chance. I'd have to leap, unless I want it to swallow me." She shuddered at the thought of being pulled into the shadow. "Whatever happens, my days of living alone in this tower are over." At least she had that.

"Where are you?" she asked. "How long has it been?"

Eventually, expectancy gave way to disappointment. And disappointment soon became a fight with despair.

The light wasn't going to appear again. Loneliness gripped her.

She was so tired. "Have I waited all night?" She got up and paced, then found herself standing on the edge of the tower's roof, staring at the ground below.

She began to cry.

"Do I need to be on the verge of killing myself before you show up? Why am I waiting? I should just get it over with, jump and then I'll sleep forever." She looked up. "I should have known. Nobody is coming for me . . . no shadow or light or . . . man." Tears pooled in her eyes. "Even if he were real, I don't care anymore."

Raven hit herself on the forehead and slapped her face. "You're a stupid, crazy bird. Get on with it!" She hit herself again and grabbed her arm, digging her nails into her skin. "So stupid! What did you think? Grrrrrr!" She clenched her jaw and groaned through gritted teeth and tears, "Stupid!" She slapped her face again and again. "I hate you!" She scratched her arm and watched the blood rise and bead.

She waited until dawn, cursing and punishing herself for it the rest of the night.

The light never came.

She slept the next day away. As the sun set, she climbed the stairs to the roof again, telling herself it was to jump. The sky grew hazier. She tried to convince herself there was no light, that she dreamed the whole thing. But her hope betrayed her. Her hope hurt. She believed. There was a light—and someone who apparently didn't care, or at least didn't care enough to come. Not for her. "Did you change your mind about me?" she asked. She hated the light . . . and loved it too. She wished she had never seen it, but at the same time she desperately wanted to see it again.

She wondered if maybe the shadow saw the light and got to it before the light got to her. Maybe the enemy was tormenting her.

The horizon slowly swallowed the sun. Shadows stretched. She watched her own silhouette, long on the roof and falling into the darkness of the tower below. "I'm not waiting again tonight. I won't." Twilight passed and dusk ushered the first star

into the sky. Several times she told herself to jump. She wanted
to. But for some reason, she couldn't. She watched, and waited,
but the light didn't shine that night either.

Another day of sleep, another sunset. She dreaded the idea of
climbing the stairs to another night of torture, only to be disappointed again. Each lonely night spent squinting at the path con-
firmed she was not worth coming for. It was dark before hunger
got her out of bed.

After her evening breakfast, she went to the roof. She climbed
the stairs to the overhead wooden door and pushed it open. The
instant she stepped onto the roof she saw it: the light glowing on
the path closest to the tower. Her heart leapt in her chest. The
higher walls near the center of the labyrinth still kept her from
seeing the source, but there it was—the light, dancing on the
bricks.

"Hello! Hello?"

Silence.

The light slowly moved around the next bend in the labyrinth. She hoped it wouldn't disappear again and looked ahead.
Does its path lead to the tower? The wall wound on and on, farther
away. She lost the light's inevitable course and started over. On
her second attempt she kept her eyes on the trail through the
twists and turns, but she lost the path again in the dark distance.

She knew from the pattern on the back of her karimba that
the path could lead the light away from her, but closer at the same
time. It could go toward the outer ring of the labyrinth, and yet
actually it would be nearer to arriving at the tower than it was on
the innermost section of the path.

She still had hope.

The light fluttered on, illuminating the labyrinth like the
sun reflecting off water. Entranced, she whispered, "Look at you
dance." She giggled like a little girl.

The light brightened.

She stood wide-eyed. "Did I do that?" The idea made her giggle again, incredulous. Once more the light swelled. She looked closer and realized it was actually shining through the walls onto the paths next to it. *How is that possible?* she thought.

The light so thrilled her she wanted it to fly to her and bathe her in its beauty. She shouted out in excitement, "Who are you?"

This time there was an answer. It didn't come from beyond the center of the labyrinth where the light shone. It came from directly behind her.

"I am with you," a voice responded to her unspoken desire.

Startled, she spun around. There was nobody there. Her legs gave out and she dropped to her knees.

"I *am* crazy." She started to cry.

"Don't be afraid. I'm coming for you." The voice spoke from where she was standing just a moment ago. It was calm and reassuring, like a man's voice, yet childlike—a breeze setting leaves to dance.

Lightheaded and heart pounding, she tried to slow her breathing. "How can I not be afraid? I don't know who you are."

She got up and looked for the light where she last saw it. It was gone. She turned around again and found it on the opposite side of the labyrinth, far off in the distance coming toward her on the winding path.

She got the chills. "I'm dreaming. I must be. You're speaking in my mind. You're not with me or coming for me. You're coming *from* me."

Raven watched the light and waited for a response.

No answer. That was it. She had to be right.

The light kept moving toward the tower from the edge of the labyrinth. It twinkled, moving faster then slower and faster again, blinking around the bends as if playing peek-a-boo.

Mesmerized, she sat and whispered, "Is it a game? Even if you are just my mind playing tricks, you dance so delightfully. I wish I could catch you." She chuckled and suddenly remembered the way the man sometimes played, fanning her desire to respond and play along. *Is that what you're doing?*

She tried to turn her full attention back to the light, but the memory persisted. She was back in her bedroom, the morning sun painting the walls. His strong, rough hands, then the backs of his fingers on her cheek . . . on her neck . . . on her bare shoulders . . .

He stood. "I have to get to the bricks."

"Stay." She reached for him.

He pulled away and sat on the edge of the bed, his bare back turned toward her. "I'll probably be gone for a while." He bent down for his clothes. "We're working on the perimeter. No telling when I'll be back."

She pouted. "Stop it. This isn't nice. Come back to bed."

"You don't expect me to sacrifice our safety while I spend the morning in bed with you, do you?" He looked back at her with a smirk on his face.

She reached further and lightly touched his hip. His resistance crumbled. In one swift move he turned, put his hand behind her head, and kissed her. Looking into her eyes he said, "You know me too well."

She smiled. "You're so bad, you tease."

"You love it."

She pulled him toward her as a breeze blew through the window and across their bodies.

Wind whistled across the roof of the tower. She shivered, snapping back to the present. She took a deep breath and a song came back to her as she watched the light pulsating in the labyrinth. She exhaled the simple tune she'd written for the man, before their playfulness ended and he turned his back on her forever.

"O northern wind, rise,
come to me, the south!

Blow on my garden,
that spice may flow out.

My love put out his hand
to unlock my door,
I rose from my sleep,
my heart yearned the more."

She stood to sing on, her hope stirred by memory.

"My hands scented with myrrh,
longing, I find the door,
but my sweet love was gone
and my heart yearned still more.

Come to your garden, love,
and eat its pleasant fruits."

She finished her song, picked up the blanket, and wrapped it around her shoulders. She stood looking at the labyrinth, half expecting the light to disappear again. Her dark hair waved about her face. "If I'm crazy, so be it. If you are coming, then come. If not, then . . ." She looked below.

Watching didn't help her discern the light's path, and waiting didn't quicken its pace. She was a lone tree rooted in a dry wilderness, at the mercy of elements she couldn't escape or control. She knew nothing she did would quench her thirst. Powerless to satisfy her longing, she had no choice but to surrender to unfulfilled desire; a desire made all the more intense by the light's game of hide and seek.

She opened the door to the roof of the tower, descended the spiral stairs, and walked out into the night. She went to the large garden gate that led to the labyrinth, unlocked it, pushed, and heaved it open. The moaning of metal against metal filled the air. Her agonizing days of hiding locked in the tower were over. "Even if you're a trick of the shadow," she said, "I will face you." If she jumped to her death or gave herself to the darkness, it didn't matter anymore. She would take whatever showed up. Desperation to be held in the light pushed her beyond all fear of the shadow.

She looked into the labyrinth. The vines threatened to overtake the path. She was tempted to run to the light, but she'd been down the labyrinth's path before and knew there was no use. She leaned against the budding trees in the gate that were crafted so long ago, then turned and walked to the well to sit and wait for the light to come.

11

The Light of Love

Raven awoke to find herself lying on the ground wrapped in warm light. She looked at the stone of the well and watched a line of ants on their way up to its edge. She realized she must have drifted off to sleep and spent the night curled up outside.

What happened last night? Did I really leave the gate open? She rolled over and saw the strange light shining between her and the entrance.

She screamed and scrambled to the other side of the well. The sky was dark. The sun had yet to rise. It was the glowing light by which she was seeing. When she sat on top of the tower, she longed for the light to come, but now that it had come—brilliant in the center of the labyrinth—she felt exposed and defenseless in its presence. Raven considered running for the tower. She peeked from behind the well to see if the light was coming after her. "Leave me alone!" she cried.

"Don't be afraid, child," said a voice. It was the same breezy voice she heard on top of the tower, but now it was coming from the radiance in front of her. "The time of being alone is over. A new

day is dawning." The voice was now wind and water, gently blowing and flowing over her, washing away her fear.

She hesitantly stood and squinted as she looked directly into
the light, trying to make out its source or see a figure behind it. "I
can't see anyone there. Who . . . or what, are you?"

"I am Love," the voice replied.

As she stared, she discovered it wasn't a simple white light at all.
The swirling colors of a rainbow filled it, and its shape kept shifting.
First it greeted her as a multicolored star hovering in front of her.
A beam sprouted out of it and branched into ever-smaller wisps of
light until it was a towering tree. Its shimmering limbs swayed, and
for a moment, the light resembled a man dancing in the wind. Then
it flowed out in all directions—rivers of light from a single source.

Something in her wanted to jump into it—to swim in the light
and drink it in. She also wanted to run away screaming. She just
stood there, paralyzed, trying to remember to breathe. The world
was now an altogether different kind of place than she had thought.
The miracle of the light's existence meant anything could happen.
It radiated the terrifying beauty of that freedom—the exhilaration
of endless possibilities mixed with the vulnerability of being in
such a wide-open space.

She remembered the days of running in the wilderness from
the shadow. "You're not my enemy, are you?" It was more a realization than a question.

"No. But you have called me that."

I have? She backed toward the tower. "I don't understand."

The light followed. "Be assured, I only seek your good."

"My good? Why would you do that?" She continued backing
away. "You don't look like my enemy. You say you are Love—what
does that mean?"

"I am, and I will show you what that means," the voice replied,
clear as the morning sun, hovering even closer. "But I have another
name that you'll learn to call me." The voice giggled, sending out a

joyful burst of energy that blew through her body. She gasped and couldn't help but laugh at the sensation.

"Rest in my light," the voice of Love whispered in the wind.

She gingerly stepped back, but stumbled onto the patio surrounding the tower. "You're not my enemy, but I have called you my enemy. . . . The only enemy I've ever had is the shadow. Are you saying you are the one who's been chasing me?"

"Yes," replied the voice.

"How can that be? You're nothing like the shadow. You're so . . . bright."

The voice laughed and the light grew more brilliant. "The shadow is behind you now."

Raven's heart sank as she sensed a dark presence. She shivered and slowly turned her head. A giant shadow loomed over her on the tower wall. She shrieked, turned, and ran. She darted around the light and through the open gate.

Thorns sliced her arms as she struggled past vines and into the labyrinth. She made it to the first turn in the path before she dared to look back and see how close the shadow was. She couldn't spot it and rounded the bend. She turned back to the section of labyrinth that lay ahead and before she knew what happened, she ran right into the light shining in front of her.

The light enveloped Raven and drew her closer to its source than ever. Fear of the shadow evaporated in the peaceful warmth that surrounded her.

She slowed to a walk and emerged from the light into the center of the labyrinth facing the tower. "How . . . ?"

She froze when she realized what she'd actually done. The mixture of embarrassment and relief made her snicker. She had run from her own shadow, cast onto the wall by the light that was now behind her.

She walked toward the tower and the shadow shrunk. She waved her arms and the shadow did the same. She laughed and made claws with her hands above her head and growled. The source of her fear was now a silly amusement. She turned back toward the light.

"All of that is behind you now," explained the voice, "running in fear, hiding from the shadow in the tower, the ravens' hurtful gifts, those days are now over . . . because you changed your mind."

Raven scowled. "Hurtful gifts? Changed my mind? I don't know what you're talking about." She looked to the gate, then at her shadow. "How did I get back here?"

"Everything will become clear. It will take awhile for you to understand, just like it took time for you to surrender."

"Surrender?" she scoffed.

"Yes," the voice of Love let out a soft, deep sigh with a chuckle and continued. "When you came out of your tower and opened the gate. You sat there by the well, helpless and waiting for my arrival . . . you surrendered. And I'm so glad you did."

"I suppose . . . I was desperate. But I didn't know what I was surrendering to."

"When it gets really dark, just accept the light you're given, and you'll be surprised by how much you can see. You were blind and deaf until you became so weak that you opened yourself to my presence. Your rejection of me was the only thing keeping us apart."

It was all so bizarre. She didn't want to trust the voice and what it had to say, but she didn't want to return to the way things were either. She knew too well the darkness down that path, and she wanted to understand. "Well, I'm here. I have plenty of time."

"Exactly," said the voice. "Time is how you came to the point where you could see my light and hear my voice. Time is the beauty of a long road. We'll take it slow, I promise."

"Okay." She nodded. "Start with the shadow."

"When you turn away from the light, you see the shadow."

She looked at her silhouette on the tower wall.

"See, you no longer see the light, only its effects."

She turned toward the light, squinting. "Are you telling me the shadow wasn't real?"

"No," the voice said. "The shadow is as real as the light. Ages ago, you turned away from my light, the light of Love. When you did, all you could see was my shadow, the shadow of Love. No, the shadow is very real."

"And you created it? You're saying your light created the shadow that destroyed my home and chased me into the wilderness?" she asked, still unable to fully comprehend or believe it.

"Please hear me, child. I am Love himself. Whether you see my light or my shadow, you don't need to be afraid of me."

"Do you know what your shadow did . . . what it put me through?" Raven asked through gritted teeth. "And you tell me not to be afraid? If you made the shadow, then you are my enemy and I hate you!"

"I know you hate me. I know. And I understand why. But I am not your enemy, and you will see that once you choose to trust me again."

"But you created my enemy!" she protested. "How can I possibly trust you? I've been trying to recover from what you did for as long as I can remember. I nearly killed myself in this labyrinth. It's supposed to keep you out!"

The radiance flashed like lightning hidden in a cloud. A tree of light once again appeared before her, slowly cracking the sky. "This place wasn't built to keep me out, but to keep you in." The voice groaned, wind blowing through mighty branches. "The labyrinth is a trap, but it can't hold me." Then, in a flash, the light disappeared.

She turned around in the dark looking for it. Its sudden absence stoked the longing she felt watching the light from the top of the tower. "Where did you go?"

"Brick walls could never keep me away from you," the voice whispered behind her.

She turned and the light appeared out of nowhere—a shining orb filled with swirling color.

"You've not always been able to see my light or hear my voice, but I have always been here." There was a smile in the words. "I am free to go wherever I like, and I like to be with you."

Raven tried to make sense of what she saw and heard, but she couldn't. She thought It could be some kind of trick, but she refused to believe it was all illusion from an isolated mind. Better baffled than beyond hope. The light silently glowed on allowing her time to think.

She looked back at her shadow on the tower and remembered the darkness that drove her into the labyrinth. She watched the light dance and change shape. It was so beautiful that she grew painfully self-conscious. She looked down at herself in the light, unwashed, unkempt . . . scarred from years of self-abuse. Ashamed, she desperately needed to hide from the light. She turned away and looked down at the ugly scratches and bite marks on her arm. The dirty, self-inflicted wounds made her wince. She hid her arm from the light and looked up to see her silhouette's arm hidden as well.

Staring at her armless form, her thoughts wandered back to what the voice said about light and shadow. She paused, and then thought out loud, "Something's missing."

"What's that?" The voice replied.

"Who's casting the shadow?" She glanced at her arm, then back into the light. "You say you are Love. I see your light and I've seen your shadow, but where . . .? Does your light shine on someone who's casting a shadow?"

The light brightened, "I'm so glad you asked! Duron will be here soon."

Bursts of living color shot from the light of Love and swirled together in a whirlpool. The beauty shook her and she staggered backward in wonder. Warmth and comfort flooded the center of the labyrinth along with the sound of wind, water, and laughter all mixed together. Wisps of spiraling light flew from the middle of the vortex and gave her what could only be described as a hug. At first she stiffened against it, but then she relaxed into the light and feelings of safety and peace overwhelmed her. She belonged in the light. While Raven couldn't remember life before the shadow chased her into the wilderness, she thought, *This must be what it was like to have a real home.*

Then she heard the flapping of wings, and from the center of the light emerged a large white bird, like a raven. He hovered for a moment and then landed on the well. The light stopped swirling and went back to glowing like it had before. As it did, the sensation of home drained from her.

"Do it again!" she exclaimed. "That was wonderful."

The voice laughed, "It was wonderful, wasn't it? But if I keep shining like that, you'd never leave this labyrinth, and I'd like to make you as free as I am. Please allow me to introduce you to Duron.

Duron bowed.

"Duron is a gifted encourager. I thought he would enjoy bringing you a present from me. This is what has been casting the shadow."

She wrenched her attention away from the light and looked at the white bird. He was bigger than any of the ravens who used to visit her in the tower. His feathers glowed and shimmered with a light that seemed to come from within. "He's pretty. I haven't been afraid of his shadow all these years, have I?"

The voice laughed. "No, you've been running from the gift in Duron's mouth.

12

Madria's Gift

Raven could barely make out that Duron held something in his beak.

The light before her turned golden and glowed like sunbeams after the rain. "A long time ago, I promised you a matchless gift," said the voice of Love. "The time has come for you to receive it." The words sparkled.

Her heart beat faster. She loved gifts and she hadn't received one since the ravens stopped coming. *Does the enemy know that? Is it trying to win my trust?*

"This is a present meant only for you. It is the drop that finally overwhelms the dam and lets loose the flood."

Her caution was washed away by desire. "What is it?"

"It's a seed."

"A seed?" she drew back a bit. "That's a strange present." She let out an uncomfortable laugh and almost involuntarily put out her hand.

In a flash of white, Duron took to the air, hovered, dropped the gift into her palm, and landed next to her. He looked up at her and said, "We believe in you, our lady."

The words forced a smile onto her face. "I've only met a few special ravens who can speak."

"Duron is very special," the voice declared. "He's no common mimic. Duron is Lord of the Leukos."

"We sing too." Duron puffed out his chest feathers and then flapped back to the well.

She looked at the seed resting in her hand. It was small, but much heavier than its size suggested. It looked like a black pearl, a perfect sphere. Everything around it seemed to be drawn toward its center. "It's beautiful," she said as she held it up between her fingers. Looking into the orb, her reflection stared back at her with eyes full of wonder. It was like she'd been pulled inside the seed and was now looking out at herself.

She thought of her fear and distrust, her hateful words spoken to the voice of Love. She knew she was unworthy of such a gift. Raven teared up. She brushed her hair out of her face and said, "I'm sorry. I can't accept this."

"Only you can accept this. It is a gift worthy of a queen."

She wiped her eyes. "A queen?" As she examined the seed, she noticed a strange smell and held it up to her nose. It smelled foul and made her gag. "I'm sorry." She coughed. "I didn't expect the smell."

"Yes, you had the same problem with my water. But you can overcome that with the seed. When it fills you with light, my water will be like honey on your lips."

"If your water smells like that, no, thank you. I'll drink from the well."

"Drink your water and in a little while you'll have to return to the well and drink again. My water is life. Soak your roots in the water of light and you'll never be thirsty again."

"Roots?" She sighed. "Will you please just speak plainly and tell me what's going on? Have you come all this way through the labyrinth just to give me this gift?" She held up the seed. "Why?"

"I am speaking as plainly as I can, but you need experience, not explanation. That is why I brought you the seed, so you can see me. So you can see the one who's been casting the shadow over your past."

She held up the seed, the light reflecting off its shiny, black surface. "How will this help me see you?"

"It's filled with your memories . . . and so much more."

The voice seemed to be toying with her. "Who are you, really? My enemy? Love? What kind of name is that? Tell me who you are!"

"Oh, I long to, child. In time, you'll have answers to all your questions."

"Tell me now, or have you come just so you can leave me alone again, like you left me on top of the tower . . . ready to jump? Love," she scoffed, "you appear only to disappear."

"I have never abandoned you." The voice paused and then asked, "And what is your name?"

"Never mind that." Her arms stiffened at her side and she huffed, "Have you come to put me out of my misery? Have you come to poison me with your water? I'll never be thirsty again when I'm dead. Is that it?"

"I'm trying to slowly get you to accept who I am . . . and who you are." The voice spoke like water splashing and bubbling over rocks in a mountain stream, "I'm certainly not here to kill you; just the opposite. I'm here to give you light and life." The words were clear and refreshing.

She looked into the light. "You've cheered me with your company, and I'm grateful for that, but . . ."

"I have come to set you free from this labyrinth."

"Free?"

"I have been pursuing you and your husband for thousands of years."

"I have no husband," Raven objected.

"Then who is the man who left you so long ago?"

"A crazy bird's dream!" she yelled.

"No, he's real. And even though he has traded your gardens for walls, you are bound together. I want to reunite the two of you, even more than your heart yearns for him. You sang so beautifully about that longing in your song."

"What do you know about my heart?" As soon as she asked, she was scared of the answer, so she asked another question. "You heard my song? How . . . ?"

"I told you. I have always been with you. I know your heart's desire. I know you've endured great pain—the fire, the running, the toil in the labyrinth, the vines, the loneliness—it was all necessary so I could prevent an even greater torment. Now the time has come for you to join me in the fight for your freedom; and the freedom of the whole world. Join me in tearing down the walls of your prison."

"The world? This is crazy," she exclaimed. She started walking back to the tower and mumbled, "I don't want to destroy the labyrinth, it's my home. I just don't want to be alone."

"Don't try to hide from me again, you will only make it worse."

"I'm not hiding from anything!" She kept walking.

The light floated closer. "Do you wish to be free?" the voice asked. "I am here to help you. Believe me and you will see that you are a child of the light."

Raven kept walking. "I'm done talking to you."

The voice whispered in her ear, "Madria, please."

She froze. "Madria?"

For the briefest moment, the walls around her disappeared and the light beckoned her to become one with it. It would surround and fill her. She wanted it . . . but resisting came as naturally as breathing. The tower rose before her.

"My name is Raven. And I can fly from this tower whenever I please."

"That is not your name. You know that."

The words made her tremble. *Does the light know my real name?* She was laid bare and desperate to block out the fear that the light knew her better than she knew herself. She shut her eyes, clenched her fists, and turned before slumping onto the ground. She pounded the dirt. "What do you want from me?" Raven raised her head, tears falling.

The light glowed right in front of her. "My gift. Will you accept it?"

"What?"

"The seed."

She opened her hand and looked at it.

"Take it," said the voice.

She searched the light. "Wait? You mean eat it?"

"Yes."

"Why would you want me to eat this . . . this stinky thing?"

"I and the seed are one. Eat the seed and we will plant ourselves in your soil. We will heal you. You will give birth to the Tree of Love, and the water of light will flow from you, filling the world with life and Love. You will never be without the light again."

She shook her head. "I will give birth to a tree?"

"You won't understand until you leap into a new reality. Make a simple choice to eat the seed and you will bear its fruit."

She sighed and dropped her hands to her lap. "I nearly believed I *could* fly."

"It's much easier to trust me when you have nothing left to lose," the voice said. There was a soothing smile in the words.

She looked at the seed in the palm of her hand and wished she could see inside it.

"You were ready to jump to your death. Do you really believe that what I'm offering could be any worse than the nightmare you've been living?"

Raven thought aloud, "So either I leap from the tower or into . . . what?"

"Give up on death and I will give you my life. Take this one step from the darkness and I will guide you to freedom."

She wondered about the name the voice called her. It was scary to think of what the light would reveal about herself, but she had to know what would happen if she ate the seed.

"I was ready to die." She straightened and slowly rose to her knees. "But you've changed that."

The light brightened even more. It seemed to pull all sound into itself. The air stilled around her.

"I want to . . . I need to."

She took a deep breath, held her nose, and popped the seed into her mouth.

She winced. "Oh, that's awful."

"Wait. The light will take root and your body won't try to reject it."

She swallowed it. It was true. Soon, she felt warmth radiate through herself and all she tasted was sweetness.

Strange, she thought. *What could it all mean?*

The morning sun broke above the garden wall and the voice of Love giggled, "Ah. You can't imagine the joy you have brought to me. Thank you. Now, you may want to sit and rest a bit before . . ."

"Rest?" She took a deep breath of the morning air. "I feel really good. I mean, really, really good. And the taste still lingers." She laughed.

Duron started to sing in an exotic language she couldn't understand. He leapt into the air and hovered in front of her.

She kept laughing and spun around. She closed her eyes and stopped to feel the light on her smiling face. A breeze blew through the center of the labyrinth and tears of joy welled up in her eyes. "Was I ever alive before this moment? Was I ever sane?" She wiped the tears from her cheeks, then looked at her hands and wiggled her fingers. She crossed her arms and rubbed them, as if to give herself a hug.

A fresh song bubbled up from within her.

> "The light is growing in my soul,
> my spirit rejoices in my enemy's gift.
> For he has cared enough to come,
> I was helpless and now I am forever blessed.
> My mighty foe is good to me,
> and he is altogether different than I thought.
>
> His mercy is on those who trust,
> his sweet goodness chases us for thousands of years.
> The strong vines dig into the wall,
> their harsh roots are bringing down the proud labyrinth.
> Light shines brilliant on the helpless,
> the hungry are fed but the full are left empty.
>
> He helps his captive enemy,
> and he has shown me that I am not forgotten."

As she finished her song, the light of Love spun around her. The tower, the gardens, and the wall that surrounded them disappeared in a rising swirl of color, while all inside her was still and calm. She felt herself lifting off the ground. Raven closed her eyes and gave herself to Love.

13

The Tree of Love

The light held her swathed in comfort and filled with peace. She wasn't afraid of what would happen or sad about the past. She had no sense of the passing of time at all. Everything was right and good, a perfect moment of deep joy. She was safe. She was home.

She opened her eyes. Thousands of stars floated in a cosmic sea of color, and she swam with them. She wasn't only bathed in brilliance, it radiated from her. No shadow would be able to come near her without disappearing in the light.

The light of Love continued to shine all around and through her until she realized that she and the light were one.

Her breath was the wind rushing over plains and through trees. A river ran through her, giving life to the world. Oceans, deserts, mountains, and forests covered her. Roots reached into her, drawing nutrients from her soil. Life flowed through her and into the leaves of the plants that clothed her.

Birds flew across her body. Creatures of every kind lived on her land and in her seas. Drops of rain splashed on her flowers. Sunlight surrounded her and fed her fruiting branches as she breathed in the air that tickled her leaves.

A question erupted from deep within her body, deep down in her dirt. "Am I the earth?" she marveled.

"You and your husband are the conscious creation," the voice said, "the head of the body. You are the garden from your dreams, and you were made to be filled with light and Love."

"How is that possible?" It was all so glorious, but too much to take in.

The light gently lowered her into the flow of time and cradled her just above the ground in the center of the labyrinth. Duron soared high above in the expanse of a hazy afternoon sky. Her skin tingled. She turned her head to look at her arm. Her wounds and scars were gone. Her skin glowed with the swirling colors of a rainbow and pulsated with each breath. Her whole body seemed to be breathing; inhaling and exhaling light.

Filled with wonder, she asked, "What's happening to me?"

The voice was a summer breeze, "The seed has filled you with life and light," it answered. "Soon you will be able to see Love." She realized that the voice of Love was now coming from within her. "Everything is as it should be. Don't be scared. Sleep. I will care for you and keep you safe."

The light of Love embraced her with its warmth. She completely relaxed in its protection and drifted off into deep slumber.

The woman shimmered as she slept. The voice spoke to the seed within her, "Ilan, she has accepted your undying seed. We have reunited with her." Her belly swelled from beneath her shirt until it was bare and glowing like the moon. "You have filled her and drawn her into yourself. Your shoot will come forth, blossom, and fill the whole world with your fruit. Nali will flow once again.

It won't be long now. You will succeed where your brother failed. The Love Fractal must grow."

The voice sang in Duron's strange tongue, a joyful chant that became a deep tone ringing like a large chime. The song reverberated through the woman's sleeping body and she trembled in tune with the light. More tones, some high and some low, sounded and laced together in a supernatural chorus.

A tender green shoot with one gleaming leaf grew from her belly. The plant sprouted branches and more radiant leaves. Roots moved across her stomach, reaching from her body to the ground. Bark formed as the diameter of the growth increased. The woman was beneath a fresh arch of winding wood with a tree growing above it. The tree grew to be much taller than a man and just about as thick. The branches filled with luminescent leaves.

The voice's singing became laughter dripping with delight. The tree waved, fanning a fragrant breeze that swirled around her. The root structure quivered, cracked, and stretched upward, rising above the woman to form two legs.

Her skin stopped glowing and her belly was flat, without a mark on it.

The tree's larger limbs swayed and separated the radiant canopy. They morphed into arms with long, green fingers. The bark on the trunk of the tree thickened and grew features that began to resemble a torso and a head, and then it cracked and flaked away. As the bark fell to the ground, it revealed a smooth upper body with emerald skin and a face like a man with a leafy, blossoming beard. Lush vines grew from his head, hung to his waist, and then flowered.

14

The Two Trees

Raven flew far above a lush landscape, exhilarated by her great height and the cool air flowing over her wings. Her black feathers fluttered as she glided on, following the winding path of a great, radiant river.

She remembered the light in the labyrinth, eating the seed, and falling asleep in the comfort of Love's radiance. "Am I dreaming?"

"No," the voice of Love replied, "it's more like a memory. My light within you is giving you a vision of the past."

She looked at her wings. "So I really am a raven?"

"That's the form you chose for yourself, but it's not who you really are. Remember your experience of being one with the light? You don't really believe it yet. You won't know your true identity until you accept who I am. Look," the voice whispered, "the Tree of Love. This is your home as it once was."

She looked ahead and saw the source of the river. It was a tree. Enormous roots filled an entire valley and supported a towering trunk. Above, a shining canopy spanned several hillsides. Glistening water gushed from the base of the tree. A large opening glowed bright white, and all the colors of the rainbow poured out into the laughing river.

"The tree's name is Ilan," the voice of Love explained. "He's the Tree of Love because I live within him. He's my home too."

"Home . . ." Raven repeated wistfully.

"Yes," Love replied, "and I live within the river as well. Her name is Nali. Simply being together fills me and Ilan with so much joy that our happiness overflows from us as the great River of Love. Nali is the deep, abiding delight that Ilan and I share in each other."

Raven flew over Ilan. He was thick with luminous leaves, blossoms, and fruit. The light of Love flowed through him, illuminating a sprawling garden. Nali's brilliant water bubbled and fizzed as she danced through the fertile land carrying the joy Ilan and Love shared. Everything was bathed in the light of Love through Ilan and Nali.

"The Tree of Love, the River of Love, and I are one," Love continued. "Ilan and Nali share my essence and continually give my limitless life away, just as I constantly pour my life and light into Ilan and Nali. In the time not long after time began, each month Ilan would yield a different fruit. He sustained all the living things in the canopy with his bounty. Nali flowed through my garden feeding the land, plants, and animals with her water of light."

As Love spoke, Raven noticed a host of exotic creatures within Ilan's majestic canopy. Winged beings of light filled his radiant umbrella and it echoed with their singing. "They're beautiful. What are they?"

"They are the Leukos. They also made Ilan their home."

"And I lived here too?"

"Yes. Do you see the two little trees by the river?"

Raven turned and descended for a closer look. Far below, two saplings soaked in Love's light splashing on them from Ilan's leaves above. Each looked like a much smaller version of the Tree of Love. They had bark and branches full of glowing green leaves and brilliant blossoms too.

"I planted and nurtured them from their earliest days," Love said. "They haven't grown into their names yet, but one is Madria, the other, Ruak. I'm their daddy."

"Madria? That's what you called me by the tower."

"Yes, this is the beginning. Time drifted past the two trees unnoticed. They were immovable, peaceful, and perfectly at rest . . . until they saw the darkness in the river. Come, perch on one of their branches and you'll see. I'll show you how I used to talk with them."

Raven swooped down and fluttered to a landing. The air was thick with the scent of flowers. Leaves twinkled as they twisted in the breeze, and her feathers reflected their light.

The voice of Love giggled. "That's funny, you landed in Madria's canopy."

"It's dazzling," Raven exclaimed.

"Yes, she is. Listen, do you hear that?"

Raven cocked her head. She heard rustling leaves and babbling water, then something else in the distance. It was laughter . . . child-like and infectious. It came from Ilan. She snickered. "Is the tree laughing?" she asked.

"Yes," Love exclaimed. "Isn't it wonderful? When I get tickled about something or other, he joins in. My laughter fills Ilan and causes him to gently tremble and sway with an amusement all his own. When that happened in the early days, wind proceeded from Ilan's massive branches, lush with his shining leaves. The happy wind of my laughter blew through the canopy, breathing new life into its inhabitants, then swirled around his trunk and through the leaves of the little trees below."

Raven heard the whoosh of wind in the distance. It blew through Madria and Ruak and their leaves danced with delight. It was enchanting. She couldn't help but laugh too.

"I used to speak to Madria and Ruak in the wind from Ilan. I would also speak with them through Nali. Their roots went deep and reached out to drink her cheerful water of light. Nali pooled my thoughts and emotions in the water and shared them with the saplings. They talked with me through Nali in the same way, but she provided more than a way to communicate. As the children's roots drank from the pure River of Love, she filled them with my very life. Through the water of light within them, Madria and Ruak experienced the rapturous joy Ilan and I share. As the two trees communed with me through Nali, she connected Madria and Ruak too. They spoke to each other through her water of light that carried their thoughts, feelings, and shared memories of many days filled with goodness. Each perfect, still moment from the past flashed in their minds like fireflies in the woods."

"That's . . . incredible," Raven replied. "It's hard to imagine what that would be like."

"You can experience it for yourself if you would like. Leave behind this idea that you are a raven and enter into the past to experience the world as Madria did."

Raven looked at her ebony bird body. It paled in comparison to the beauty surrounding her, and all that Love described. Wings gave her the ability to fly away, but she no longer wanted to. She ached to feel the water of light within her, flowing through roots connected to Love's garden. "How?" she asked, spreading her wings. "How do I let go?"

"Do you wish it?"

"I do."

"Then it is done."

The two trees awoke and stretched their roots to Nali for a morning soak. Her water of light flowed into them, their branches outstretched, their leaves shimmering and taking in the light of Love that enveloped them.

Do you see it? Madria asked telepathically through the water.

Ruak searched the water of light looking for Madria's strange discovery, a point where their memories went black. He explored further and further back in time—warm days, wind making their leaves dance, cool nights, rain running down their trunks—each moment filled with Love. *There it is, upstream.* Ruak replied in the water of light. *Darkness. How have we never noticed that before?*

I'm not sure. Look! It's downstream too.

What?

Madria felt Ruak's excitement and watched his thoughts flash. *Look ahead.*

Ruak tried to see beyond the present moment. All was black there too. *Where did it come from?*

He watched connections light up between Madria's thoughts in the water. *You think it has always been there?*

Maybe we've just never noticed it. Maybe we've always been surrounded by some kind of . . . nothing.

Ruak struggled with Madria's ideas. *A nothing? What's a nothing?*

Madria's curiosity in the water grabbed Ruak's attention. She was focused on the darkness behind them. *What is that thought you're forming?*

Or . . . I wonder . . .

What?

. . . if there was a time when we weren't here.

Not here? That's silly.

Madria stared into the darkness ahead. *If we appeared, will we disappear too?*

Madria, stop it.

Nali's water of light began to bubble with joy inside the two trees. Their leaves sparkled and their blossoms opened. A breeze descended from Ilan and blew through their branches. "Good morning," Love spoke in the wind.

The light of Love embraced Madria and Ruak. Their leaves quivered with delight.

Daddy, we've seen a strange nothing! Madria happily exclaimed.

What is it, Daddy? Ruak asked. *Tell Madria we're not going to disappear.*

Love's laughter filled Ilan. "Slow down," Love whispered in the breeze from Ilan's swaying canopy. Then Love's presence in Nali washed away all their questions. *My little saplings, how you've grown.*

Love's pleasure permeated Madria and Ruak, and their canopies brightened.

You're not going to disappear. Love spoke through the water of light within them.

Ruak's roots dug a little deeper and he swayed in the wind.

Still, Madria's right, you weren't always here.

Madria's leaves fluttered.

Until now, you two have only experienced what's happening in the light of this moment and in the shining memories of moments we've shared. You've never cared to look beyond right now or before your first memory. The darkness behind you is filled with the past, and the future is in the darkness ahead.

Show us what's in the darkness, Daddy, Madria blurted.

Love laughed again. "Madria, you are a delight," said the wind. *Tell you what, I will show you the past and you two can reveal what's in the future,* gurgled the water.

Questions came flooding back into Ruak's mind. *What do you mean? How will you show us? How can we see into the darkness?*

You can see the future by choosing it, Love replied. *All I am and have is yours, except one thing . . . freedom. I will be happy to give you freedom too if you would like. Then you can decide what the future holds.*

What is freedom? Madria and Ruak thought at the same time.

Freedom is the ability to uproot and go wherever you want. There's so much to experience. But I will be perfectly happy if you stay rooted too. Know this, whatever you decide or wherever you go, I will always be with you.

I would like this freedom very much, Madria thought.

Then you shall have it, declared Love. *And you, Ruak?*

If it is something you would like for us, yes. As long as we can still root here by Nali.

Of course. You will be able to do whatever you like whenever you like.

What about the past? Madria asked.

A gentle breeze tickled the saplings' leaves. "Look into the darkness and you will see," said the soft voice of Love from Ilan. "Then I will make you free."

15

Love's Laughter

Madria and Ruak stared intently into Nali's water of light flowing into their roots and through their collective consciousness. They searched their flashing memories all the way back to the nothingness before their first moment together planted by the river. Love spoke in a gust of wind, "Once upon a time before time, there was only the Love Fractal."

And then they saw it, light shining in the darkness of the past. Ilan blazed in the middle of nowhere.

Nali filled the saplings with Love's thoughts and experiences through the water of light. *We have always been one. We have always been the Love Fractal.*

Suddenly, Madria and Ruak found themselves floating in the mystery of an eternally repeating pattern of joyous being, selfless giving, and grateful receiving.

They saw that Ilan had always grown from Love's radiance. Before the beginning, waves of light perpetually flowed from Love into Ilan's roots, filling his trunk, branches, and sparkling leaves. Madria and Ruak realized that while Nali had always been the joy

Love and Ilan share, she had not always poured from his trunk. Love, Ilan, and Nali were full of life and perfectly happy in their singular brilliance—older than the mountains, forever young and free from the constraints of time and space. They were never alone. They always had one another. They were forever in Love.

The two trees watched as the Tree of Love filled with glowing white blossoms. The flowers became beings of light and they burst into song, their harmonies echoing through the canopy. They so delighted Love that he granted them eternal life and named them the Leukos. Then he gave them wings formed from their petals and set them free to sing wherever they wanted. The Leukos enjoyed singing for Love so much, they pledged to stay in Ilan's canopy forever. All of them, except one.

One of the Leukos did not want to live forever. To him, freedom was a lie and eternal life a curse. This one flower refused to sing and refused to live. He wilted and fell from the Tree of Love's branches to decompose in the nothingness.

Like all living things, the Love Fractal grew.

Love spoke to Ilan and Nali, *Let us fill the void with our joy.* Ilan and Nali lit up at the thought of sharing the life of Love they so enjoyed. Love laughed. His laughter in the water of light tickled Ilan's roots and reverberated up into his branches and leaves of light. Before long every inch of the Tree of Love started to tremble with a massive giggle that grew into full-blown laughter. Ilan cackled and swayed with delight. A great wind from his expansive canopy's movement swirled and carried Love's laughter out into the nothingness. Love inhabited the wind. Love was the wind. His happy vibrations created new fractals; patterns made of repeating versions of themselves. The universe, the galaxies, planets, mountains, clouds, waves, vegetation, and animals of every kind were all fractals born of that night's tree-trembler.

Ilan's wind blew for days, sending lights sparkling and spinning into endless self-similar patterns. They filled the darkness and sailed out into nowhere. Some spheres of light coalesced into larger lights, and some larger still. Others split off, cooled, and dimmed. Gales of laughter echoed across the surface of one of the orbs, raising fractal peaks from its ocean of light. Ilan's roots dug into the jagged rocks breaking them up into rich soil, which in turn gave birth to every kind of plant imaginable. Each new shoot grew and reproduced after its own kind. Fractal seeds were caught up in powerful gusts that carried them in all directions to settle in the dirt further than the eye could see. The base of the Tree of Love split, letting Nali flow as the laughing River of Love. She fed the seeds with water of light and caused them to sprout into fish, birds, and animals of every kind. One of the large lights began to move through the sky. As it did, its rays fed the lush freshly planted garden. The great light passed out of sight and another lesser light rose above the Tree of Love.

Love blew through Ilan's branches, around his trunk, and out into the garden. He slowed to a breeze, hovered over a small patch of dirt, and said, "The Love Fractal must grow." Then in a deliberate instant, he spun into a whirlwind, pulled dust up into himself, and disappeared leaving behind a tender sapling. One of the little tree's leafy branches stretched, peeled off, and fell to the ground. It sprouted roots of its own that dug into the soil, uprighting the branch to form a second young tree.

The saplings waited by Nali, but didn't know what they were waiting for until her water of light touched their roots. As soon as they drank, the two trees were illuminated. They knew they were made to be filled by the River of Love. They also instantly knew their names.

Madria and Ruak emerged from the past. It was still morning. They looked into the water of light to see their first moment of life with Love. The darkness before that memory was gone. It was filled with the Love Fractal. The darkness ahead remained.

16

Freedom

L ove surged through Ilan, filling his roots, trunk, and branches
with Nali's creative power in the water of light.

The intricate root structure of the great tree stretched upward,
creating arches that grew into a grand entry hall, adorned with
elegant twisting patterns of wood. Opposite the mouth of the River
of Love, roots wove together forming a soaring entrance into the
ancient tree.

Above, Ilan's immense trunk began to slowly twist. As it did,
bark bulged and grew to reveal the winding levels of a tree house.
The organic architecture made it hard to tell where the tree ended
and the house began. Inside, living rooms took shape and a wide
variety of flowers blossomed right out of the walls. Sweeping
hallways and staircases connected bedrooms, kitchens, and dining areas, all wrapped around Ilan. A network of more rooms
filled the branches of his glowing canopy—libraries, parlors, and
countless suites.

Ilan became a castle-cathedral filled with Love, and that made
his tree house a true home. It was ready for Madria and Ruak.

"And now," Love spoke through the wind and the water of light, "I give you a gift only true Love can give. Madria and Ruak, I give you freedom!" Love laughed and a broad, round apple orchard sprouted in a valley untouched by Nali. The intricate labyrinth of saplings grew in concentric rings, emanating from a single tree in the center. The largest circle had a diameter as wide as Ilan's trunk. Nali poured into the valley and wound through the labyrinth, watering the trees before she ran on to the edge of Love's garden. Soon the water of light fed giant apple trees in winding rows. Red, green, and yellow fruit dotted each ring of the labyrinth in turn, coloring the dazzling design. The splendor sang.

Inside the tree line that made up the first ring of the labyrinth, that one tree towered over the others in the orchard. Its trunk twisted out of the ground, thick and knotted, and immediately split into branches that snarled together to form a cramped cage. The weaved wood came back together again above the cell to form a single trunk that supported a fruiting canopy. Love named this twisted prison the Tree of Trust, and inside it he placed the decayed flower who didn't want freedom or life.

Love overflowed with joy and he swirled within Nali and in the wind above the saplings. The water of light filled Madria and Ruak with the same energy that transformed Ilan into their new home.

The trunks of the two little trees swelled and their branches became leafy arms. They divided at the base to form legs and feet of roots. Their rough bark cracked and flaked off leaving behind smooth, green flesh.

Love giggled.

The saplings trembled and more of their bark cocoon fell to the ground revealing a treeish young couple, lush with glowing leaves, heads bowed and crowned with blooming wreaths.

Love couldn't contain himself any longer. He flew toward his children and blew into them. Madria and Ruak took their first breaths and opened eyes that shone with the light of Love.

The sun sparkled in the dew that covered Love's garden. The air was crisp and filled with Nali's babbling. The Leukos sang above.

Madria looked down at her legs planted in the ground. She lifted one of them and her roots came right out of the dirt. "Ha!" She took her first step and pulled her other leg up from the earth.

As she uprooted, Madria could still sense Nali flowing within her. The water of light shared Ruak's thoughts and emotions. Astonished, he stared at his leafy arms and hands. He touched the supple bark that remained around his waist. Before he realized what he was doing, he spoke, "Madria?" He lifted his head and they saw the light of Love in each other's eyes for the first time.

Without a word, Love called out to Love. The water of light within Madria and Ruak began to draw them together. It was irresistible, a river overflowing its banks. They had to touch.

She smiled and reached out to him, "Ruak."

As soon as Ruak thought about joining her, he uprooted and was on his way, gliding on his roots. He held her hand and they felt the sensation of skin touching skin for the first time, their palms pressed together with branchy fingers entwined. Glistening tears dripped from the corners of their eyes.

The water of light continued to flow and they silently walked toward the River of Love. Their roots tingled and lit up as they stepped into Nali. The feel of her flowing over their new flesh made them giggle. They waded in the water and soaked up pure delight.

Madria fell back into the water of light with a splash.

Ruak laughed. "I can feel your happiness in the river, Madria."

"I know," she said with a smile. Madria floated away on her back, wiggling her roots in the air.

Ruak splashed toward her. Nali's joy was infectious. He dove beneath the water of light and emerged to find Madria standing completely still with a stunned look on her face. Her eyes were ablaze as she stared into the sky behind him.

"Look at that!" Madria exclaimed.

Ruak turned and gasped at the first sight of their new home in Ilan.

Ilan's canopy gently swayed and a fragrant breeze surrounded Love's children. They each smelled his blossoms for the first time. The sweetness was intoxicating. The breeze became a wind and stirred Nali. The multicolored water of light bubbled and rose in a fine mist. The wind and the water swirled around Madria and Ruak, leading them out of Nali and to the entrance of the tree house. There, with the great arch of winding wood above, shone the pure light of Love.

"Welcome home," Love spoke from the brilliance.

"Daddy!" the children squealed. Madria and Ruak ran to Ilan and right into the light. Inside Ilan, embraced by Love's warm presence, they had once again entered a mystery—they were welcomed into the Love Fractal. Love, Ilan, and Nali eternally existed as one, and Madria and Ruak were created from the overflow of their joy. The children were now and forevermore part of Ilan, made in his image, filled with Nali's water of light, and united in Love. Love had become one with his creation and set Madria and Ruak free.

17

Choices

Many days filled with goodness passed over Madria and Ruak. They spent the mornings soaking their roots in Nali, filling themselves with her pure, life-giving water of light and communing with each other and Love. They often took long walks in the light of Love and then ate Ilan's fruit for breakfast, followed by afternoons working in the garden and lunches on the lawn with wide assortments of fresh fruits and vegetables.

Everything Madria and Ruak needed was a gift from Love's garden, and yet they labored with Love to reveal the earth's bounty. They worked hard, but their work wasn't drudgery. It was like opening a present with layers of enchanted wrapping. From transplanting a seedling to waking up and finding a flowering bud promising fruit, each step in the process had its own beauty and filled them with wonder and anticipation. But the best part was that all of the work was done in the light of Love.

They always did something different after dinners. The children of Love had inherited his creativity, and he took great joy in the games they'd craft from treasures found in the garden.

Sometimes they would curl up by the fire to listen to one of Love's stories, filled with strange creatures, and heroes and heroines on grand adventures. Love said that as he told his tales, the characters and animals actually leapt into existence, inhabited distant lands, and populated the world.

Madria and Ruak found it odd that the people in the stories were never treeish. From the children to the adults, nobody had any roots. Their daddy didn't mention one glowing leaf growing from common folk or kings. When the children asked why, Love said, "Well, that's because they haven't met you yet. One day you will show them how to be treeish: to trust me, to eat from Ilan, and drink from Nali." Love's answers always left them with more questions.

One clear night, Ilan lifted Madria and Ruak in his branches to the top of his canopy so they could gaze at the sky and listen to Love sing the names of the stars. The star song was never over because every time their daddy sang it more lights appeared in the night, and their names needed to be sung as well. Many nights the children would fall asleep right there, high above their garden home, but not that night.

The couple stayed awake until Love stopped singing. They reclined on a bed of Ilan's leaves in their daddy's silent presence.

All was completely still until Madria spoke. "Daddy, what's beyond the stars?"

Ruak smiled, rolled over, and put his arm around her.

Ilan gently swayed, his leaves quivering with joy all around them. Love whispered in the breeze, "Your questions are delightful. Keep asking them and one day you'll see for yourself what's beyond the stars."

Madria and Ruak's eyes glowed like the moon.

"Enjoy your freedom, the whole universe is yours to explore. Start searching here in my garden, and in time you'll find the answers to all of your questions."

The couple continued to silently take in the beauty of the heavens. Madria tried to imagine what she would find when the last star was behind her. Nothing? Maybe the Love Fractal would be there too, brilliant with her daddy's happiness and ready to make a new kind of world.

The light of Love began to sparkle around them. The stars seemed to dim in his radiance. The light jumped from branch to branch at the top of the Tree of Love, twisting in the air.

Madria and Ruak giggled and sat up.

"Daddy, what has you dancing?" Madria asked.

Love spoke from the twirling light, "I can't contain myself! It fills me with so much joy to give you all that I laughed to life." The light of Love flashed in the sky, popping and crackling. "You were born to be king and queen of everything you see, and beyond!" Ilan's branches danced in the wind, and the water of light within Madria made her feel like dancing too.

"It is time for each of you to choose the future," Love declared.

Everything returned to stillness.

Love whispered, "While it's important you know I've given you the whole world to do with what you will, it's more important you know that I have given you myself. It would delight me to see you learn to give yourselves to each other. If you do, and you work together as one, you will fill the world with the Love Fractal."

"What do you mean?" Ruak asked.

"I'm giving each of you a matchless gift."

Madria's heart leapt. "I love gifts!"

Love laughed. "Soon your curiosity will lead you away from Ilan and you will follow the setting sun to an apple orchard. In the center of the orchard, you'll find a special tree, the Tree of Trust. It's an apple tree just like all the rest, and its fruit tastes no better or worse than the others. However, this tree *is* different."

Love paused, and then spoke in a gust of wind from Ilan's waving branches, "Ruak, I am giving you Wyrm."

"What is Wyrm?" Ruak asked.

"Remember in the vision of the past," Love replied in the light, "before you grew in the garden—the Leuki who didn't want to sing?"

"Yes."

"He is Wyrm, and he is no longer a being of light. He rejected freedom and chose death. He separated himself from my light and decayed in the darkness—rotted from the inside out. He is filled with worms—evil through and through. The trunk of the Tree of Trust is woven to form a prison for him."

"A prison?" Madria asked.

"A prison is an instrument of peace." Love explained. "It's a place of justice. It contains evil so that it doesn't destroy all that is true, good, and beautiful. Death's freedom would mean your captivity."

"And death? Evil?" Ruak asked. "I don't understand."

"I would like to spare you two the knowledge of such things. Trusting me is so much better than knowing the difference between good and evil. In fact, judging which is which has driven Wyrm mad. Ruak, I am handing Wyrm over into your hands. If you choose to accept this gift, all you have to do is go to the tree in the center of the orchard and take him by the tail. If you do, don't hesitate. Deal with him quickly."

Ruak looked down, his brow furrowed. "But . . . why?" He looked up into the light. "Why are you giving me this thing that destroys beauty?"

"Ruak, if you take Wyrm by the tail, he will die and become a staff of power over evil, my scepter to use as you rule all creation. I won't vanquish Wyrm for you. I want you to taste the glory of that victory. This is a gift worthy of a king. I'm offering to make you sole protector of the world I have given you. Will you choose to accept this responsibility?"

Madria listened in silence, filled with anticipation. *What kind of gift is fit for a queen?* she wondered.

"Sole protector?" Ruak asked.

"Yes, guardian of the garden. Only a true son of Love can take Wyrm by the tail. Trust my light within you, I've given you everything you need to defeat him."

Ruak nodded and his leaves glowed green with the light of life. "I want to . . . I do." He looked out over the moonlit garden. "So pretty," he whispered. "Why would any creature want to destroy something so rich and good?"

"Wyrm wouldn't accept my gift of freedom and eternal life. He doesn't understand how freedom is possible in a world where he is forced to exist. Rather than trust me, Wyrm thinks I am a liar. My very presence insults his intellect and sense of superior virtue. I've offended his dignity. Wyrm believes that only the darkness of death is true freedom, and he will try to set this world 'free' if given the chance. Since he is powerless to overcome my light, I granted him death at your hand. Ruak, you will be giving Wyrm his heart's desire if you take him by the tail."

Ruak rose to his roots. "I'll do it. I accept."

"My son." Ilan glowed brighter, as did Nali far below. "Wyrm will be waiting for you in the Tree of Trust."

Madria couldn't wait any longer and almost asked about her gift, but Love continued.

"I must warn you both, Wyrm is dangerous. Fiery poison drips from his mouth. He has infected the Tree of Trust. Taste the fruit from that tree and his blood worms will infect you too. You will change."

"Change?" Ruak asked. "How?"

"In the worst way, son. Your desires will be bent to Wyrm's will. You will long for home, but run from me. You will hunger and thirst, but you'll refuse to eat from Ilan or drink from Nali. Without the water of light within, you will wither: dry up, shrink, and become leafless like the people in my stories, less like Ilan and more like the creatures in the garden. Eventually, you will go dark and forget everything . . . even me and our life together with Ilan and Nali."

Madria and Ruak stared into the light of Love, speechless.

Love continued, "I know that's a lot to take in. Just remember this, you are welcome to eat the fruit of every other tree in the labyrinth, but don't eat from the Tree of Trust. If you do, you'll turn away from the light of my life, and you and all the earth will dwell in my shadow."

"How is that possible?" Ruak wondered.

"A king is his kingdom."

Madria was about to burst. *What about the queen?* she thought.

The light of Love surrounded her and lifted her to her feet. "Madria, will you dance with me?" She lit up at the thought and the Leukos started to sing. Madria began to float in her daddy's light atop the Tree of Love. Ilan's glowing leaves and branches reached up to meet them as they danced.

"Madria, the gift I am giving you is priceless beyond your ability to comprehend," Love whispered in her ear. "I am giving you the undying seed of Ilan."

She smiled and closed her eyes, lost in Love's embrace. Madria's leaves shimmered in the night as daddy and daughter glided effortlessly across the canopy.

"The seed is not something that can be grasped like Ruak's staff," Love continued. "You must wait to receive it. I will lead you to your gift and, at the perfect time, it will be revealed to you. If you choose to accept it, you will bring so many free children of Love to soak their roots in Nali that you'd be able to number the stars before you counted all of them."

"I accept! I accept!"

Love laughed and the sweet smelling wind from Ilan's swaying branches swirled around them as they danced.

The Leukos finished their song and the light of Love led Madria back to Ruak. "That was beautiful to watch," he said. Ruak reached out and she held his branchy hands.

Love danced around them. "Trust each other with the gifts I'm giving you, just as you must trust me to receive them. You, the earth, the garden and even the stars are one, just as Ilan, Nali, and I are one. In you, I have joined with my creation through the water of light. We are the Love Fractal, and the Love Fractal must grow."

18

Doubt

Madria and Ruak found the labyrinth and wore a path between Ilan and the orchard. They carried baskets full of apples back to the tree house, and their daddy taught them how to make ciders, sauces, and pies. They candied and carameled them and made apple butters, breads, dumplings, and cakes. The variety of recipes was matched only by the variety of apples. Each ring of trees in the orchard produced a different kind of apple with its own unique mixture of sweet and sour. Some were juicier and some were crisper, but they were all delicious.

While Love nourished Madria and Ruak with his goodness, Wyrm starved in his prison. He fed on fear and despair, but these things didn't exist in Love's garden.

Besides producing fabulous fruit, the orchard labyrinth's serenity provided Ruak and Madria with hours of enjoyment. Madria liked to lie on her back under the trees and stare into the network of leaves and fruit above. As the sun peeked through the branches, she closed her eyes to see its light through her eyelids, while feeling its warmth kissing her face.

Sometimes the couple spent time with each other simply strolling on the labyrinth's winding path, or they'd play hide and seek with Love, darting in and out of the trees. Love would hide his light until his children found it. Sometimes he'd make it easy for them. Many times Madria and Ruak just gave up and begged for him to come out. Once in a while it was so hard to find his light that they lost interest and wandered off. It thrilled Love to sneak up on them when they least expected it and hear the squeals of delight as his light burst before them.

All this time, Ruak never walked the labyrinth's path the entire way to the center. From time to time he would set out to take Wyrm's tail, but there was always a reason to turn back. Once he left too late and ran out of daylight before he reached the Tree of Trust. More than once, he made his way to a new ring of trees with apples he hadn't tasted, stopped to collect as many as he could carry, and returned to the tree house. Many times it was his fascination with the labyrinth itself that distracted him from his task.

Madria asked Ruak why he hadn't gone for his gift. He said he was in no hurry—that he would get around to it. But Love knew Ruak had a question that only he could answer for himself.

Madria waited and waited for Love to reveal her gift, but he never did. The longer she had to wait, the more it bothered her that Ruak was waiting when he didn't have to. She often searched Ruak's thoughts and feelings in the water of light trying to understand why.

It was clear to Madria that evil remained a mystery to Ruak. Despite Love's explanations and their discussions about freedom, Madria didn't understand either. She was content to let it go, but Ruak struggled to fathom why Love would create a creature who wanted to destroy all that in which he so delighted. Once he began to question Love's motives, it wasn't long before he wondered what difference it would make if Wyrm stayed trapped in his cage forever. *Daddy made Wyrm, why not let him deal with evil?* he asked himself. The idea shocked Madria when she eventually found it deep within Ruak, drifting among all his other questions. Ruak was barely aware of the thought himself.

Love could see what both Madria and Ruak couldn't. Ruak's questions about Love concealed Ruak's question about himself. Did he really have what it takes to face evil and rule all creation? It was a seed of doubt that hadn't taken root, so Love waited patiently for Ruak to remove it. Love also knew Ruak would take hold of his gift when he was ready.

However, it was Madria who made delaying any longer impossible.

Nali flowed through the orchard labyrinth, giggling and glistening with the light of Love. Madria sat under an apple tree, her back against its trunk with her legs outstretched toward the water of light. The long walk through the labyrinth to the Tree of Trust left her spent. The River of Love looked so refreshing, but she didn't dare dampen one dry root. She hadn't soaked in Nali for days. The thirst was almost unbearable, but she was determined not to even touch the water of light. Her roots instinctively reached out to connect with the life of Love coursing past her, but she pulled her legs away and wrapped her arms around her bent knees. "No, he needs my help," she thought out loud.

"Who's there?" The words came from an unfamiliar voice behind her.

She poked her head out from behind the apple tree and looked toward the Tree of Trust. It was just as her daddy described it, a towering tree with a tangled trunk grown in the shape of a cage. Deep darkness filled the wooden prison. It was like the nothingness she saw in the water of light before her first memory, a completely still void. There was no sign of Wyrm. She didn't know exactly what she was looking for, just that whatever Wyrm looked like, he would be in the cage and he would have a tail to grab. She wondered if maybe the darkness *was* Wyrm.

"Have you come to help me?" the voice spoke again from the Tree of Trust.

She stood and the world around her dimmed. Her vision blurred. She lost her balance and steadied herself against the tree trunk in front of her. She was dizzy from thirst, but the thirst wasn't only physical. An emptiness was growing within her that ached for the fullness of Love's presence in the water of light. She missed the sensation of his joyful way of simply being. Without Love's peace filling her through Nali, Madria's thoughts, memories, and desires seemed . . . confused. She wondered if it was all worth it.

A hot craving in her chest focused her attention on Ruak's gift. That was the reason she was torturing herself, cut off from Nali. Ruak couldn't know what she was doing. She couldn't risk him seeing her thoughts in the water of light, not if it was going to be a surprise. She was hiding from him. She was hiding *for* him. If Ruak wouldn't come for Wyrm, she would bring Wyrm to Ruak. She had to do it now. The thirst was too much to endure any longer.

But where was the gift? It had to be wrapped in the darkness within the tree. She looked again at the cage, rubbed her eyes, and took a few deep breaths. She waited until her head was clear enough to walk, then crept toward the Tree of Trust.

"Will you grant me death?" the voice asked, stopping Madria in her tracks. The black, scaly tip of a tail emerged from one of the small openings in the cage.

"Will I?" she wondered. What would happen if she grabbed the tail? Would Wyrm become a staff she could deliver to Ruak? She had to try.

"Only a true child of Love can take me by the tail," the voice said. "That's what Love told me."

Is that what Daddy said? It was hard to recall without the water of light within her illuminating her memories. She tried to remember the exact words.

The voice interrupted her thoughts, "Are you a child of Love?" The question didn't make any sense. "Are there children who don't come from Love?" she replied.

"Then do it. Don't leave me exposed to your father. Let me disappear into the nothingness forever."

The end of her suffering was in sight. All she had to do was grab the tail. If it worked, she could give the scepter to Ruak and then soak her roots in Nali. With his gift in hand, maybe then Love would deliver hers.

She inched closer to the Tree of Trust. The foliage above cast its shadow over the knotted roots in her path. She climbed one of the largest roots, and Wyrm's tail was within reach. She stretched toward it. The gift was almost within her grasp when, in an instant, Wyrm pulled his tail back into the prison.

"No!" she shouted. She had to have it. Burning desire consumed her. Without thinking, she stuck her arm in Wyrm's cage and groped in the darkness.

Ruak walked through the orchard labyrinth. He dug his roots into the ground and stood completely still, becoming part of the intricate design. Time slowed to a trickle as he basked in the beauty of his daddy's creation.

Wandering off alone and planting himself among the trees in the orchard taught him how the labyrinth worked. It intensified everything Ruak brought to it. If he came to it with the tiniest drop of peace, he would soon be carried away on a river of tranquility. In the labyrinth, a spark of joy quickly became blazing exuberance, and a seed of hope grew into a tree of quiet confidence.

Ruak extended his roots toward Nali as she streamed through the orchard. He closed his eyes and imagined he was still a simple tree. *I wish. . . .* His empty belly interrupted him mid thought. He wanted breakfast. He opened his eyes and the light of Love greeted him.

"Ruak, Madria is in danger."

Ruak couldn't make sense of the words. He looked into the water of light and couldn't see Madria's thoughts or even feel her presence. "Where is she?"

Love spoke from his radiance. "You can still save her, but there's no more time to spare." The sound of Love's voice comforted Ruak, as always, but his words did not. "Wyrm is growing. He's a mindless eater once he finds food. You have to go to the Tree of Trust before it's too late. Grab him by the tail and use the staff of power to help Madria."

"What happened?"

"Madria made a bad choice, but it's nothing we can't fix."

"What did she do?"

The light of Love flashed. "Ruak, listen to me. There is no more time for questions. All that matters now is that you know you can do this. Feel the strength of my light and life within you. Remember, don't hesitate for any reason. Go to the center of the labyrinth. No matter what you see there, just walk up to Wyrm and take him by the tail. Now go. It is time for you to protect your kingdom."

Ruak's leaves glowed white-hot and he ripped his roots out of the ground. Instead of running along the path of dry ground between the flowing water of light, he cut straight to the Tree of Trust. He splashed through Nali, and then scrambled up her bank and through the next ring of trees, then back into the water of light. Ring after ring, he made his way to the center of the labyrinth with speed he didn't know was possible. As he ran, his mind swelled with images of what he might find when he got there.

Am I ready to prove I am a true son of Love? Ruak's seed of doubt sprouted. Soon he was deeper in the orchard than he had ever been. What Ruak found when he arrived at the Tree of Trust wasn't anything he could have envisioned.

19

Worms

Ruak passed through the trees that made up the first ring of the labyrinth and he saw the towering prison up close for the first time. Above, the most beautiful golden fruit filled the canopy. Below, Madria lay in the dirt next to the twisted wooden cage. Ruak froze.

"Madria!" He called out.

She didn't move.

Hissing came from inside the Tree of Trust.

"Madria!?" he yelled again as he ran toward her. When he got closer, he could see that one of her light green arms was blackened and ripped open. Ruak dropped to her side. Madria looked like she was sleeping. "Oh no! What happened? Madria, wake up," he whimpered. His hand trembled and his leaves rustled as he reached out to nudge her awake. "Madria, please . . ."

"Son of Love," a voice crackled from behind, "take my tail." Ruak turned around to see Wyrm peering at him from inside the Tree of Trust. His body filled the cramped prison. He was polished ebony, twisted in knots. Scales glistened on his snout pressed against the cage. Wyrm's eyes were dark pools. He hissed again and exposed a mouth full of black fangs. "What are you waiting for?" Wyrm snapped.

Ruak fell backward at the display. Wyrm stuck his tail out of one of the holes in his cage and shook it at him.

Madria moaned. Ruak turned around to see her coming to. "Madria!"

She looked at him, then down at her arm and cried.

"Madria, what happened?"

"Oh, Ruak. I'm so sorry."

"What did you do?"

He helped Madria sit up. She cradled her wounded arm and said, "You were taking so long. I thought . . ."

"Thought what?"

Madria hesitated. "I thought I could help."

"You're a liar just like your father," Wyrm growled from his cage. "She was jealous. She couldn't stand that she had to wait for her gift, while you got yours now."

"You don't know anything about us!" Ruak yelled over his shoulder.

Wyrm hissed. "She told me everything. Admit the truth, child."

Madria didn't reply. She couldn't even look Ruak in the eyes. She just sat there, head bowed, holding her arm and rocking back and forth.

"Madria?" Ruak questioned. "Did you put your hand in his cage?" He looked at her wound and winced. Up close he could see that the discoloration on Madria's arm was actually thousands of tiny black maggots. They squirmed in and out of the gashes and under her skin. "He bit you." Ruak pulled away.

Madria tried to pick the maggots out of her wound, but there were too many.

"My blood worms course through her," Wyrm hissed. "She's already dead. Leave her. Come, free me from your father's tyranny."

Ruak looked into Madria's eyes. The light of Love was gone. "No, no!"

"Oh, your fear is so sweet," Wyrm whispered. Ruak turned to see the creature's mouth pressed up against his cage with his black tongue licking the air.

"Madria, we have to get you home."

"More," Wyrm roared before letting out a chilling shriek. Fire erupted from the cage. The Tree of Trust began to burn. "More!"

Ruak grabbed Madria. "We have to go. Dad will know what to do."

"No," she objected. "I am not going home like this. You can't tell him."

"What are you talking about? Why would you think Dad doesn't know you're hurt? He sent me here to help you."

Madria looked over at the Tree of Trust on fire. Ruak saw Wyrm's tail still sticking out of the cage as the creature gulped the air. He was growing inside his blazing prison.

"Do it," Madria growled while staring blankly at Wyrm. "Kill him."

Ruak looked over at the tail, then back at the maggots writhing in Madria's wound. *The staff of power. I can't. . . .* His heart thumped in his chest. *I can't wait anymore. I have to do this now.* He stood, but his legs were weak. "You're right, Madria. I'm not taking you home." He walked toward the cage and said, "I'm going to do what I should have done when we first found the orchard."

Wyrm laughed. "Yes, little sapling!" His tail quivered. "Do it. Free me from your father's maddening presence. Curse the liar Love!"

As Ruak moved closer to grab the tail, the heat from the burning tree was almost unbearable. He endured it until his leaves caught fire. It was the first time he ever experienced pain and he was shocked by the sensation. He stumbled backward and flopped onto the ground, rolling around in the dirt.

Wyrm's burgeoning black body pressed hard against the inside of the trunk. "Get me out of here." Another blast shot from the tree. His fiery breath weakened the wood that contained him and it started to splinter under the pressure.

Madria screamed and Ruak looked to see her roots in flames. "No!" He got up and kicked dirt onto her roots trying to put out the fire, but she kept burning.

"I told you to leave her!" Wyrm yelled as Madria screamed in pain. The weight of the canopy above the cage could no longer be supported. The tree buckled. Ear-piercing snaps and pops exploded from the center of the orchard labyrinth as the Tree of Trust came crashing down to the ground. Wyrm's full length spilled out and coiled around what was left of the burning tree.

The flower that fell from Ilan's canopy had become a serpent. Wyrm's head rose from the flames, he screeched and blew fire into the air. The snaking evil reached upward, bulging and shifting. Swarms of worms burst from beneath his scales and formed two dark masses on each side of his body. Then, like sails in a stiff wind, Wyrm unfurled his ebony wings.

Ruak finally snuffed out the fire on Madria's roots. He dragged her to the first ring of the labyrinth as Wyrm took to the air.

"Madria, put your arm around me!" Ruak demanded as he reached down to pick her up.

"Just leave me here."

"I'm not leaving you!" He lifted her off the ground, but as soon as he did, Wyrm landed in front of them with an earth-shaking thud.

"Where do you think you're going, little sapling? You're supposed to take my tail." Wyrm extended his head to Ruak and stared him down.

He looked into the great serpent's eyes and saw they were full of the blood worms that infected Madria's arm. Wyrm hissed, revealing his fangs dripping with black ooze. The drops hit the ground and smoked. They bubbled and coalesced and more black maggots emerged, squirming toward Ruak. He turned and ran carrying Madria toward Ilan.

"No!" Wyrm snarled.

Ruak made his way toward the edge of the labyrinth. Madria grew heavier with each ring he managed to pass. He looked back and there was no sign of Wyrm. Ruak turned to press on. Suddenly, flames engulfed the apple trees ahead. Wyrm landed in front of the blaze, gulping at the air and growing larger as he did. Ruak turned around and ran. Wyrm followed, flying just above the treetops and torching apple trees in Ruak's path.

Ruak's strength finally gave out and he collapsed in Nali's water of light, dropping Madria on the ground beyond. The remains of the Tree of Trust burned before them. He wept as he realized Wyrm's fire had forced them back to the center of the labyrinth.

Wyrm flapped his wings above the couple, blocking the light of the sun, his shadow growing around them. He growled, "Grab my tail, little tree, or I'll burn your roots too."

Madria screamed. Ruak cowered in Wyrm's shadow. The seed of doubt had grown into paralyzing fear. He looked up at Wyrm and sobbed.

Wyrm landed, coiled around Ruak, and held him under water. The water of light singed the serpent's body, his scales bubbling and sizzling. In an instant, Ruak was swinging upside down with his roots flailing in the air. Wyrm took to the sky, dangling Ruak's head just above the ground. He shrieked and Ruak screamed in pain. His roots lit up like a torch. He twisted in Wyrm's grip as the flames overwhelmed him.

"Burn, burn son of Love! I will feed on your fear until you give me what I want." Tornadoes flew from Wyrm's wings as he hovered above Madria. "I have liberated you from Love's lie," he said to her. "There is no freedom in a world where you are forced to exist, forced to choose when he knows your choices before you make them. Your daddy knew you would burn." He set her on fire again and fanned the flames with his wings.

The dragon rose higher and higher above the labyrinth with Ruak in his grasp. "Liar," Wyrm shouted into the air. Then he dropped Ruak next to the burning Tree of Trust.

Madria's head ached. Smoke stung her eyes as she regained consciousness. She lay on the ground, her skin tingling. The bite on her arm throbbed and she looked down at it. The blood worms were closing the wound. She sat up to find the black maggots all over her, eating her scorched flesh. In a panic, she swatted them away. Her skin had lost its green hue and her body was as brown and dry as a withered branch . . . but her burns were healed.

The charred canopy of the Tree of Trust lay on the ground with its fruit scattered in all directions. The mangled wood that used to form Wyrm's cage splintered from the tree's smoldering stump. Thick smoke hung in the air. All was dark. The light of Love was gone.

"Why?" she asked. The pain of her burns had vanished, and only a scar remained on her arm, but she ached on the inside. "Why did you leave me?" She was alone without Love, cut off from her father. "Come back!" she screamed into the haze.

She heard the faint sound of crying in the distance through a high-pitched buzzing in her ears.

"Ruak?" she croaked.

Madria turned to see Ruak standing next to the River of Love. Wyrm's fire left him leafless and with only his arms and legs branching from his body. His roots were gone, burned from his feet. Nali's flowing light was gone too, replaced by a vein of black water coursing through the orchard. Madria managed to get up and immediately fell to the ground. She looked past her trunk and limbs. "My roots," she whimpered. There were only little black nubs where her roots used to branch out.

Ruak stood hanging his head and panting. "My roots!" he exclaimed. "I can't draw the water."

Madria got up again and haltingly walked toward him on her burnt stumps. A foul smell from the river made her gag.

Ruak knelt down by the river and cupped the wet darkness in his trembling hands.

It disgusted her to think of drinking the black water. "Ruak, don't!" She grabbed his arm.

Ruak stopped and turned his head. "Our roots are gone." His breathing was labored and shallow. "The flames have dried up the water of light within me. I'm withering. I need Nali."

Madria crumpled in exhaustion on the riverbank. "How could that be Nali?"

"What are you talking about? Of course it is. Drink. We'll need strength to make it back home." Ruak lifted the water to his mouth.

"No, Father can't know. If that really is Nali, and you drink, he'll see what you did. We can't go back."

Ruak looked at her with panic on his face.

She looked down at her arm. Even the scar was gone, the bite was completely healed. Her eyes darted to her feet. Her roots weren't growing back. *Nali.* Madria looked to the black river, then back at her rootless feet. "The water of light is gone. I have no roots." She realized the horrible reality. "I'll never feel Nali flow into me again, ever . . . never again!"

Ruak let the water drip from his hands and struggled to his feet. He staggered backward into the river. "The water of light isn't gone, Madria. Nali is right here. Can't you see?"

"Where is our father? Why didn't he stop this?"

"He . . ." Ruak looked at Madria's disfigured body and choked on his words.

"Why would he leave me to be burned?"

"He . . . wanted me to . . . I was supposed to protect you." Inky tears dripped from his eyes. "But I couldn't. I'm sorry, Madria. I was scared."

The ache within her became enflamed. Her breathing quickened. Her entire body burned inside. A strange power surged within her and before she knew what she was doing, she was standing in the river choking Ruak. "If you just did what you were told, none of this would have happened! He should have given me the staff."

"Stop," Ruak strained to talk. "We have to . . . home."

The water around Madria's feet began to gurgle and her skin burned. She looked down and her legs were smoking in the black river. She released Ruak with a push and fell backward onto dry land.

"Look at what you did to me!" she shrieked.

Ruak stared at her legs. "What's happening?"

"You are blind to the truth. Nali is poison. Can you see that now? You did this."

"But I . . ."

"How will you face Father? We have no roots! Wyrm is loose in the garden. It's all your fault!" She turned and crawled toward the Tree of Trust. *We're on our own now,* she thought. She looked at the golden fruit strewn on the ground. She picked up one of the apples and stood.

"What are you doing?" Ruak asked.

"I'm going to eat one, and you are too. The worms can heal us. Our roots will grow back."

"Are you out of your mind?" Ruak stumbled out of the river on his stumps.

Madria took a bite. The fruit was sour and black inside its golden skin, but crunchy.

"Stop!" Ruak grabbed her arm and spun her around.

Madria swallowed and glanced where her wound used to be. "Look."

Ruak gasped. "The bite. It's gone." He let go of her.

"See?" She stepped back. "My burns are healed too. It's the worms." She bent down, picked up another apple and handed it to him.

Ruak put his hands up. He stared at her, wide eyed. "I don't want to wither. Didn't Dad say we'll forget?" He turned his head, his brow furrowed as he struggled with his thoughts. "I can't remember. Was it . . . go dark? I have to go back."

"Back to what? Father's disappointment? A cage made just for us? Look at us!" Her entire body shook uncontrollably. "Look at what you've done. Do you really want his light shining on your burnt body?" She grabbed his hand and put the fruit in it.

He looked down at the apple, then back at her healed arm.

"Would forgetting all this really be so bad?" Madria asked. She took another bite, and then another. "The worms have given me eyes to see the truth. You have to believe me, Nali is poison." She devoured the apple as she talked. "Father has abandoned us. You said it yourself, he left it all up to you. We're on our own now." She threw the core on the ground and looked up at Ruak. "Eat, you fool. Eat and you'll be healed. The worms will give us the strength to leave and find a new home. Father won't have to know what happened."

Ruak wiped the tears from his face. He stared at her and then looked away in disgust. "No, Father will know . . . but I can't." He shook his head. "You're right, I can't live knowing what I've done."

Madria's shaking hands cradled his and lifted the fruit to his mouth. "Darkness will be a relief. Eat and forget."

"You're right, I can't face him. We can't go home." Dark tears filled Ruak's eyes as he raised the apple to his mouth.

20

Death

The sun hung low in a smoky sky. Ilan towered above the lush, misty garden below. Wyrm swooped down out of the haze above emerald hills and shot toward the Tree of Love. After his escape, he torched everything in sight. Love had not set him free into the nothingness of death, so he flew into a blind rage. Anything living had to die. All the world would burn before him, the way he did in Love's presence. Now the liberation of the Leukos was at hand.

The dragon leveled out just above Ilan's canopy and fire exploded from his mouth. Ilan wouldn't burn, but the Leukos and the other creatures living in the Tree of Love's branches scattered to hide. "Repent," he roared. "Follow my light to true freedom and feed on death!"

Wyrm flapped his wings to turn for another pass, but something seized him. No matter how hard he tried, he couldn't stay in the air.

"Wyrm," a voice whispered in his ear.

It was Love pulling him toward the ground. "Is this more of your freedom?" he asked as he struggled. "Tyranny!" he yelled for the Leukos to hear. "Witness the lie of Love's liberty!" He looked down to see Nali's scalding water flowing from Ilan, black as night. He writhed in the air until he landed with a thud in front of the gaping entrance to the tree house. The shadow of Love within Ilan's entryway held him there with a dark power. "Love," he sneered. "Is it not enough that I am tortured by your very existence? Must I be forced to stare into your abyss?"

"I've been expecting you, Wyrm," Love's voice echoed from Ilan.

"Of course you have," he growled. "Let me go!"

"You chose captivity and I gave it to you," said the voice from the darkness. "Will you now accept freedom?"

Flames flickered in Wyrm's throat and smoke billowed from his snout. "You can't force life on me and then call it freedom. You promised to lift the curse of immortality and give me peace in the darkness of death."

"You will die at the hand of Ruak. He will take you by the tail."

"Your son is a coward."

"His fear has given you another chance, Wyrm. It's not too late. Will you please trust me? Come home to Ilan. Eat his fruit and live. You can help me heal Madria and Ruak."

Wyrm laughed. "You must be desperate. Stop with the charade. You know what I will choose. You know I would rather die than suffer the indignity of confessing your lie is the truth. Until then you can watch as I set your creation free in the flames of death. The king and queen are mine now, and with them, their kingdom." Wyrm coiled up, then glared at the black hole in Ilan's trunk. "Unless you'd like to prove yourself a liar and take back the world you gave them. Just kill me yourself, or must your children do your dirty work?"

"The children's freedom was real," said the voice from the mouth of Ilan. "I do not lie. The world is rightfully yours. I gave it to them and they surrendered it to you. I have been grieving their absence from the moment they ate from the Tree of Trust."

"I almost feel sorry for you," Wyrm mocked, "but you knew this would happen. You were a fool to let them choose their own destiny." Wyrm snarled. He rose from his coil and spread out his wings. "Your beloved creation vomited you out. What the hell were you thinking?"

"I was thinking you and I could make a deal."

Wyrm laughed again. "A deal would require that you have something to bargain with," he gloated. "What do you have that isn't already mine?" The dragon cracked his tail like a whip. "Your king has given me the key to your kingdom, and once it has burned to the ground, my worms will force your son to relieve me of my existence."

"I have that which you want most," Love said, "more than death itself."

"And what is that?"

"Justice. You believe I have done wrong by giving you life. While I don't agree, I have honored the true freedom I gave you and answered your complaint by granting you death instead. Beyond that, I now offer you payment for bringing you into existence. You may have my life."

"Ha! Impossible," Wyrm hissed and turned away. "Another lie." Love's words intrigued him, but he didn't want to show it. He stared blankly into the distance and asked, "And just how exactly do you propose I go about killing you? I can't even kill myself!" He wagged his tail at Ilan. It was ripped into shreds.

"It will take some time," Love replied, "the children chose a long and difficult road, but there is a way."

"Go on."

"I can become like them," Love declared.

Wyrm growled. "And what will that accomplish?"

"I am life himself," Love continued, "death has no power over me, but my children? My children can die."

Wyrm smiled and looked sideways toward the entrance to Ilan. Black smoke billowed from his mouth and nostrils. "Yes . . ." the dragon roared. "Your children can die."

"You will have to await the fullness of time for my arrival in treeish flesh, but when I come, the source of life will die. You will have your justice."

"And how do I know this isn't another one of your lies?"

"Madria and Ruak and all the earth are yours as security. They remain cut off from the water of light. They will no longer breathe the air stirred by Ilan. But when the appointed time comes, you will give the world back to my children. Set them free to do as they please and take me. Until then, withdraw your worms from Madria and Ruak. I will not have you twisting their thoughts and emotions. Life will be hard enough without you torturing their minds. Keep your distance from my children and don't even let them see you. I, however, get to visit them whenever I like."

Wyrm looked up at the towering tree, then stared into the darkness within Ilan. "I want your death to be excruciating."

"I wouldn't expect anything less from you, Wyrm."

"And what about my death? What can I expect about that?"

"It will come as I promised. If you won't believe me, what have you lost? But if I fulfill my end of the deal, I give you what you could never take for yourself."

Wyrm lifted his head and said, "Then it's a deal."

"It's a deal. Now leave. I am going to draw your poison from Madria and Ruak."

Wyrm spread his wings and took to the air. "Of course. Enjoy your visit with my children, 'Daddy.'" The dragon laughed as he hovered, kicking up dirt and rocks with his wings. "Thanks to you and your saplings, I have a world of fear to feed on."

Wyrm ascended. Love watched the winged serpent disappear back into the smoky sky.

The sun had set and rose again since Ruak left for the Tree of Trust. Love cast his thoughts back in time and remembered his children swimming in Nali, upstream near Ilan. He could see their bright, innocent faces as they laughed and splashed each other with the water of light. Madria and Ruak were made to live in union with Love, receiving his life through Nali, and the scene in his mind filled him with delight. Then a vision of his children shattered the memory.

Madria and Ruak were rootless, cut off from the light of Love and withering. The joy of sharing his life with his children disappeared. Though they no longer had roots, Love could still quench their thirst if they would simply drink from Nali, but he knew they would refuse her water of light. After eating from the Tree of Trust, the blood worms within Madria and Ruak corrupted their senses. They could no longer experience Nali as she really was. The water of light was as dark and foul to them as it was to Wyrm. Love's children were dying of thirst while walking next to Nali's pure, luminous life. It overwhelmed him. Apart from him, they would live in darkness relying on their own inner strength to survive, blinded by this perverted potency.

Love longed for the day he would once again welcome his children back home in the Tree of Love. Ilan moaned and creaked at Love's pain. Nali's shimmering water of light slowed until she stopped flowing from Ilan altogether, leaving behind a dry riverbed.

Love thought about the consequences of giving his children freedom, and he remembered considering the immense price he would one day have to pay for it. But for all the heartache he felt and all he had yet to lose, he knew that the joy of reuniting with Madria and Ruak was worth it.

Love lingered long within Ilan as they shared their last day together. Love knew what he had to do, as did Ilan and Nali. They were united in a singular purpose, but Ilan would suffer and die. Love had to lose his home to bring the children back to theirs.

As the sun set, Love promised that Ilan's suffering wouldn't be without its reward. He spoke to him through the water of light. *The day of mourning is here, Ilan, but if you lead Madria and Ruak back to us, they will fill you with children. Their freely-given adoration and devotion will be yours. We will be one forever.*

"For the joy ahead of us," whispered the wind from Ilan's branches, "I will endure this."

For the joy, Love said to Ilan.

It was time to reveal Madria's gift.

A deep groan rose up through Ilan's roots. The Tree of Love began to shake violently. Soon the entire garden quaked. The opening that fed Nali became a fiery, gaping hole. The gash grew until Ilan's trunk split wide open. The light of Love exploded from him. The blast left Ilan's leaves dark and he burned from the inside out until fire engulfed him. He smoked and swayed, fanning the flames with a great wind the likes of which hadn't been seen since before the beginning. The wood of the tree house cracked and great bursts of snapping branches pealed through the air. Its kitchens and pantries and dining areas and living rooms and bedrooms and all their contents came crashing to the ground.

The creatures who lived in Ilan's canopy scattered to save their lives. The Leukos wailed in confusion and pain as they flew away, leaving their home ablaze below.

Driven by the wind, the fire spread. Before long, the entire garden was swallowed by an inferno. The firestorm grew until it reached the great orchard labyrinth. Every last apple tree was reduced to a charred stump.

The blaze burned and billowed as Love left his home behind to draw the blood worms from his children.

21

Love's Promise

Madria and Ruak walked along the orchard labyrinth's path until Nali dried up. Once they could cross the riverbed without the black water there to burn them, the couple ran straight out of the labyrinth and left their father's garden. They headed deeper and deeper into the wilderness, farther away from home than they had ever been.

The day smoldered away, the sky afire. The infested fruit hadn't healed their roots like Madria claimed it would. The couple plodded along on their stumps while Madria cursed Ruak from behind. Their memories faded with each step, but they still remembered enough to blame each other for their predicament. She went on and on about how it was his fault they could no longer glide forward on their roots. His gut burned as he fought the urge to turn around and beat her into silence. Forcing her to be quiet seemed like the only option. Still, it was a troubling compulsion, he didn't want to hurt her, but at the same time she deserved it—she wouldn't shut up, and none of this would have happened if she hadn't tried to take what was rightfully his. The tension kept him moving on even though he was exhausted.

"Why? Will you just answer that one question?" The very sound of Madria's voice got more and more infuriating. "You didn't believe you had what it took, did you? Well, it looks like you were right."

Ruak couldn't stand it anymore. He stopped and turned toward Madria, his fist in the air. "Shut up! Just shut your mouth!"

Madria flinched. She looked pitiful, small, withered. Her lush leaves were all burned off, revealing dark skin devoid of its usual glowing green hue.

He lowered his fist and looked down at his arm. The worms had healed his burns, but his skin was now as brown and dry as Madria's. Dead hair had started to grow where live leaves used to sprout.

They had covered themselves with crude clothes made from the garden's plants. Their dimmed, shrunken bodies were grubby and hidden, and their heads poked through holes torn in giant leaves. But, despite their efforts to appear treeish, Ruak and Madria now looked more animal than plant.

"Just be quiet." Ruak rubbed his temples and then looked ahead at a forest of evergreens. The giant pines were silhouetted against the setting sun, pitch black with long shadows that reached out toward his feet. The air was cool, and for an instant he thought of the after-dinner walks with his father in the garden. Then the memory vanished.

He turned to Madria. "I'm hungry," he said.

"The apples are gone. You ate the last one."

Ruak heard rumbling in the distance and looked up, past Madria toward their home behind her.

"If you don't find us another source of water soon, we're in trouble," she worried.

He stared off into the distance.

"Ruak! Are you listening to me?"

"What is that?"

"Water, Ruak. We need water."

The rumbling grew louder. "Do you hear that?" he asked. The earth began to tremble and then heaved beneath them, knocking them to the ground.

"Look!" He pointed to Ilan towering over the garden in the distance. A pillar of fire rose around the Tree of Love until their home was engulfed in flames. The fire was spreading fast. "Our home is burning!"

Madria stared wide-eyed.

"What could start a fire like that?" he asked as he watched the fire grow, lighting up the horizon.

"It's coming toward us!" Madria shouted over the quaking earth. She tried to get up, but couldn't keep her balance. She staggered toward the pine trees.

"Madria!"

He looked back toward the burning garden and saw a black hole in the fire, the flames bending toward its center. Ruak stood mute. Madria screamed behind him. The hole grew, branching in all directions and threatening to pull him into its nothingness. His legs gave out and he dropped to his knees. The shape of the dark power shifted before him, changing until it looked like the shadow of a tree-man walking on his roots.

"Run!" Madria yelled from the evergreens.

Wind set the trees swaying and the countless needles and branches moved back and forth, letting out a grand, *Shshshsh. Shshshsh.*

The ground stopped shaking. Ruak pulled away from the shadow, got up, and ran for the forest. He darted past Madria cowering behind one of the trees. He stopped, turned around, and grabbed her by the arm. "Come on!"

They only took a few more steps before thunder cracked behind them. Pain rippled through Ruak and he collapsed. His skin crawled and his body stiffened. Madria fell to the ground next to him, gripping her chest. They both shook uncontrollably. Horrified, Ruak watched as worms poured out of Madria's mouth. He gagged. He couldn't breathe. His stomach churned and his throat swelled. His mouth was forced open from the inside and the black maggots burst out of him too.

Madria went limp and passed out. Ruak was barely conscious. He watched as the blood worms writhed away from them toward the shadow lurking at the edge of the forest.

There was no escaping its pull.

He curled up and hid his face in his arms. "Father," he whimpered. "Don't leave us here to die. Make the shadow go away." Then everything went dark.

"I'm here, child," Love said as he watched Ruak lose consciousness. "I will never go away. I would never leave you orphans." The children's fear hung in the forest.

The blood worms swarmed out of the woods, sprouted little wings and took to the air, a buzzing black smoke rising. They flew guided by a singular mind. Suddenly, bursts of song shot through the dark cloud. The Leukos swooped down upon them. They circled the flying worms, their voices stunning them.

Love looked on. He gave the Leukos the gift of freedom and he knew how they would use it. When Ilan burned, the Leukos lost their home in his canopy. Without the Tree of Love to sustain them, they needed a new source of food. The destruction convinced them they were abandoned by Love and the Leukos turned to Wyrm.

The blood worms were forced into a ball and the Leukos took turns shooting through it. It was a feeding frenzy. As they ate the worms, their singing changed. They began to croak and caw. Their bodies changed too. Wyrm's infestation snuffed their light, and black feathers grew on their dimmed bodies. By the time the

Leukos cleared the sky of the last flying worm, they were no longer luminous beings, but ravens, dark as death. Having been fed by Wyrm, the black birds left Love to scavenge for the serpent.

"This is the beginning of sorrows," Love said to the Leukos as they flew away. "It will take a very long time for the worms to make you weak enough to see my light again." Love turned to his unconscious children.

The light of Love entered the forest and hovered above Madria and Ruak. He watched over them as they slept. "Everything is going to be all right," he said with a still, small voice. "I have yet to reveal my true nature. I will show you how the Love Fractal grows. I will follow you through all of time to once again make my home in you, and when you grow old and die and are buried in the ground, you will once again spring forth with new life in the light of my garden."

The light of Love brightened. "Oh, the joy we will share. Our reunion, my beloved children, it will be the grand finale, my eternal gift to you. I will make everything new. The day will return when I will once again fill you with the water of light. I will plant the source of Nali within you and you will never be without me again. I will once again hear you call me Daddy, and I will wipe away every tear from your eyes. There will be no more death, sorrow, weeping, or pain. They will all pass away. You will not only be free, you will freely choose to trust me forever. And together, with all of my children, we will live happily ever after in the Love Fractal."

Love knew his promise was lost on Madria and Ruak. However, a promise from him, even if that promise goes unheard or forgotten, is sure to come to pass.

The light of Love dimmed and became smaller and smaller until it was just a flickering flame from a lone candle. Love sang as his light went out above his children lying on a bed of pine needles in the forest.

"Light rolls away before the darkness,
and the darkness from before the light."

Madria and Ruak stirred at the sound of Love's lullaby, but
to them it wasn't singing. Instead, they heard shrill screeching—
unintelligible and shocking.

"It's time to lie down and rest in peace,
as the bands of sleep fall on your eyes.
Into my hands commit your spirits,
and when the morning comes you will rise."

The children woke up disoriented and covered their ears.
They looked around in confusion for the source of the maddening
noise, and then ran away into the woods. Night had fallen and they
slipped into the shadows under a purple sky flooding with stars.

Their memories dried up within them along with the water of
light. It happened just as Love said it would. The darkness in their
minds and hearts eventually erased their life together with Ilan
and Nali. To Madria and Ruak, the light of Love, the Tree of Love,
and the River of Love never existed. They no longer remembered
Wyrm and the Tree of Trust. They even forgot their own names.

Love had to let them go. Even though he freed them from the
worms, it was too late. They hardened while cut off from the water
of light. The seed of distrust had taken root and they would not be
able to see the light of Love until they were weak enough to want to
be rescued. Now the suffering on the path they took would have to
teach them to trust again. Love ached, longing to chase after them
and hold his son and daughter in his light, but their fear of him
wouldn't let that happen. They turned away from his light and so,
to them, he was now the shadow; a dark, punishing presence that
chased them from their home. But without the light of Love, there

was no home, only the twisted idea of home that was left in the children's minds.

22

Beauty from Ashes

The fire raged until there was nothing left to burn. It completely consumed Love's garden leaving behind a scorched wasteland. No birds or animals or insects could be heard, only the howling wind whipping up lonely clouds of swirling cinders. Then the rain came. The sound of the wind gave way to the patter of raindrops on the ash covering the ground. Smoke choked the air and darkness blanketed the land.

Ilan's smoldering stump filled the entire valley. Having burned from the inside out, he left a great chasm, a gaping mouth surrounded by jagged, black wooden teeth. Sooty tears fell where Nali once flowed from the great Tree of Love. As the heavy raindrops hit the fine ash in the riverbed, they created miniature versions of the crater Ilan left in the earth.

Far off in the distant future, ravens circled high above a very different landscape; a landscape with a forest and a vast plain beyond. A great lifeless circle marred the plain, but it wasn't the scar of Ilan's stump, it was the circle of the brick labyrinth Love's children built.

Below the birds, the light of Love appeared as a brilliant sphere at the edge of the woods. Streams of white light shot through the trees. The outer wall of the labyrinth stood far off, hard and cold. To Love, the barrier and the tower in its center were a chilling monument to his children's fear. Tearing down their prison wouldn't do any good. They couldn't see the truth. They would run again. Forcing them out would only prolong their suffering. No, the pain of the imprisonment they chose had to do its freeing work. Wearing them down required the slow work of the vines that were planted in their wall.

Now the birds who comforted his daughter had to go.

The light of Love slowly emerged from the forest and stopped. "Duron," Love whispered.

More ravens appeared in the sky and their caws filled the air. The flock grew until hundreds then thousands of birds became a dark cloud that cast its shadow over the trees and field below. The circling ravens became a whirlwind, and from the center of that swirling mass, the biggest, most regal raven descended to the light. He was three feet long with a wingspan over six feet. His chest puffed out and his black feathers glistened with reflected light. The ebony wonder of nature landed with a thud, tripping and falling over himself. He writhed on the ground while ravens shrieked above.

Love spoke again from the light, "Wyrm, free him."

The large raven stiffened, then shook. A low guttural rattle swelled within the bird, followed by hideous croaking and then silence as the shaking continued. The raven's beak opened wide and the dragon's blood worms poured out onto the ground. They swarmed and coalesced into a black snake of writhing maggots. The creature sprouted wings and flew off into the forest while the raven quivered on the ground. The bird managed to turn his head away, burying it in one of his wings, and choked out, "What is happening to us?"

"Duron, Lord of the Leukos, don't be afraid. Look into my light. I come to you now in the fullness of time to give you another chance . . . if you will receive it."

The raven peeked from behind his wing. "Our name is Corvus," his voice cracked. He buried his head again, weeping. "There is no hope for us."

"As long as there is life, there is hope," Love said.

Corvus hesitantly looked again. Flowing beams of light sprouted from the sphere until it became a glowing tree dancing in the wind. It bathed everything in its brilliance. Corvus lifted his head. The ravens continued to swirl wildly above. "Your warmth is so familiar. Who are you?"

"I am the one who set you free. Now your days of scavenging can be over."

The great bird's head dropped. "We have to eat," he croaked. "Wyrm's world, Wyrm's rules. We have no choice."

The tree of light began to vaguely resemble a large man. It reached within itself and swung its arm in an arc, casting sparkling little lights into the air. They floated to the ground all around Corvus. "You always have a choice," Love said. "Your choices are like these seeds. So small, yet one contains a forest, another, vineyards or a field of flowers. You are surrounded by towering redwoods and seas of golden grain." The light reached down and picked up one of the shimmering seeds. "I hold eternal life in my hand, a never-ending succession of living orchards. But until this seed dies in the ground, we will not see a single bud. It starts with a choice." The light dropped the seed. "Life gives way to death, and through death life is born."

"What does that have to do with us?"

"When you choose one seed, you renounce many others. Long ago you chose a seed that has yielded a bitter harvest, but it is not too late. You don't remember now, but you once trusted me to feed you. Trust me again. Turn your back on Wyrm's seed and choose new life." The tree of light reached into its shining canopy and produced a tiny, gleaming orb. "Take my seed and the Leukos will blossom again. You will no longer be Corvus. Your name will be Duron."

Corvus's wings shuddered, his eyes searched the light. "The Leukos? We don't understand. Why? Why would you do this for us?" he asked.

"Because I alone remember how alive the world was before it withered, and I want to see it live again . . . with you singing in its skies instead of Wyrm's shrieking. Wouldn't you?"

Corvus looked at the glowing seeds scattered all around him. "Is such a thing really possible?"

"Yes. Your flock can bloom again as white ravens." The light offered the seed to Corvus. "All you must do is choose it. You are, of course, free to follow Wyrm, but why? You now know the darkness of death."

Corvus stared at the seed, mesmerized. "We have grown so tired of scavenging. We do not sow or reap, but instead of nourishing us, the worms have left us weak. We suffer."

"You are the head of the flock, and what you do now can heal their body."

"If you are sincere in your offer to feed us and you promise we will be free from Wyrm, we would be grateful."

"I am, and I promise." The light grew brighter and Love sang in the language of the Leukos, wooing the raven closer.

Corvus quivered. "So beautiful," he said, his voice trembling with emotion. The bird slowly approached the light and bowed. "We want . . . to trust you. . . ." He was barely able to speak. He rose, stared into the light, extended his neck, and took the seed in his beak. Then he jerked his head back and swallowed Love's peace offering.

The light flashed. "Corvus is dead," Love's voice thundered. "The raven rebellion is over. Long live Duron, Lord of the Leukos."

Duron stepped back and extended his wings. Power burst from the light and he watched the darkness in his feathers disappear like smoke in a rushing wind, leaving them a pure white.

The black cloud broke into chaos. Amidst caws and shrieks, the ravens expelled the blood worms en masse. Their feathers instantly turned white. The black maggots flew from them and swarmed like a cloud of locusts, then retreated.

Hissing came from the trees. Duron turned to see the snake that was pulled from him and, in a frenetic flash of white, hid behind the light. The winged serpent took to the sky to join the other worms and they flew away as one.

A radiant cloud of white ravens descended, surrounding Duron. The light moved among them feeding the flock with luminous seeds. "Eat," Love spoke from the radiance. "Once you have regained your strength, you will begin to remember what it means to be the Leukos. Soon you will be able to sing again."

Duron followed the light as the birds all ate. "Your light is so comforting," he said, his voice no longer croaking. "We feel . . . home." He wondered at the beauty of his brothers and sisters. "The Leukos?" He joined their feast.

All of a sudden, Duron looked up at the light. "Yes, we are the Leukos. We are the Leukos! And you . . . you are . . ."

The light stopped scattering seeds. "I am Love."

Duron gazed into the light as if looking for another memory. "This isn't the first time you set us free, is it?"

"No, it's not."

"How can we thank you?"

"Enjoy your freedom, my friend."

Duron stretched out his wings again. "We will." He marveled at his white feathers. "Thank you. Thank you!"

"You are most welcome, and someday you will know how much joy you've brought me. I wish that for you . . . and for all my sons and daughters. Duron, tell me, how does a father give his children everything he has without destroying them with it?"

Duron stood still. "Is that something we should remember?" the white raven replied.

The light scattered more seeds. "No, but if you like, you can help me reveal the answer."

"The Leukos are at your . . ." Suddenly, Duron stepped away from the light. "No! There was a fire. Our home! We remember now. That horrible fire." Duron stumbled backward. "Ilan is dead! You destroyed our home."

"No, Ilan is alive."

Duron tilted his head, his chest feathers rising and falling with his panting.

"Come and see. I have a very special gift I would like you to personally deliver to the woman in the tower. Until then, she must be left alone. No more visits."

Duron hesitantly walked after the light. "But . . . we have been her only friends. Without our help, she will die of loneliness. She needs our gifts."

"Your gifts have been keeping her from accepting mine. Sometimes, helping hurts and hurting helps. Don't you see that now after suffering the worms for so long?"

Duron walked in silence as Love finished feeding the flock. Then Duron asked, "How did our suffering help us? The worms were killing us. We were so helpless for so long."

"If it weren't for pain's blessing, you would never have been weak enough to see my light, and you wouldn't have eaten my seed so quickly. It took time for your anguish to blossom into a choice for freedom. No, don't even fly within sight of the labyrinth until you deliver my gift. Her suffering will lead to her salvation."

"But how can you allow that?"

"I know her, Duron. Like I know you. She is Madria, your queen."

Duron stopped and looked wide-eyed into the light, then at the shining flock of white birds feeding on the sparkling seeds. "We see," he said as he stared. "We rebelled . . . such a dark and painful journey."

The light dimmed. "It is for those who choose to stay on it. There are brighter days ahead for Madria once she sees another way. But you must not let the desire to simply end suffering blind you. Your generosity can be used against you and those you intend to comfort."

"We will do as you say. Where is your gift?"

"Not far, but you will have to travel quite some time to reach it." The light swelled and began to swirl, bursting with all the colors of the rainbow. It spun into a vortex with a still center.

"Come with me and I will show you," Love whispered in the wind. "Fly into my light."

The white raven hesitated, then crouched, flapped his wings, and flew into the heart of the brilliant vortex.

Duron appeared from the still center of Love's swirling light. He flapped and fluttered above the charred landscape. "Where are we?" he asked.

"I brought you back in time," Love said, his light pushing back the darkness. "This is where Ilan once stood . . . before he burned."

Duron looked down at the gaping stump of the Tree of Love. "But . . . you said that Ilan is alive."

"He is. Listen."

They hovered there waiting above the smoking remains of their ancient home. Suddenly, singing broke forth from beneath the ash and burnt chunks of wood.

"Beauty from the ashes.
Joy for the mourning.
Freedom for captives.
A new day dawning."

Shafts of light reached out from Love's radiance above the stump. The dazzling vortex of light grew in the sky. The sound of wind and water and laughter filled the smoky air.

"Prisons will open.
The dragon will pay.
Healing for the broken.
Love's on the way."

Love was a cyclone of living color. He pulled ash up into himself uncovering a tiny, brilliant orb in the center of the hole left by Ilan. A rainbow burst from it and shot out in all directions. The little sphere continued singing.

"Love is upon me.
Good news I will bring.
Light is within me.
Love's praises they'll sing!"

"Duron, come and see," Love's voice echoed from the small, shining sphere below.

Duron landed and examined the clear orb, mesmerized by the swirling colors within it. "What is it?"

"Madria's gift; the undying seed of the Tree of Love . . . our home. Ilan lives on. He is the answer to my question."

"How?" asked Duron.

"Yes," Love replied. "How does a father give his children everything he has without destroying them with it?"

Duron stared at the seed.

Love continued, "He lays down his life for them and hopes they will see that the giver is the gift. Duron, go back. Take the seed of Love to my daughter in her labyrinth prison. If she chooses me instead of the world she inherited, then she will have both and live."

Duron picked up the seed in his beak. He flew back into the center of the blinding whirlwind, back to the queen who had forgotten who she was. The light of Love received him and disappeared in a flash.

23

Awake

Duron's singing teased the woman from her sleep. She opened her eyes and found herself lying on the ground in her labyrinth prison under the canopy of a tree. The light of Love shone bright all around her and on the tower beyond. Tears wet her cheeks. It relieved her to realize the visions of the past had stopped. They were given to make her whole, but the intense emotions they stirred threatened to pull her apart.

If it weren't for Love's presence, she would have tried to dismiss all she saw as simply a dream. If she did, she would have soon sunk back into despair. Without Love's rays comforting her with the warm sensation of home, the tower would surely have tempted her to fly from its height. But she couldn't go back to being Raven. Love's light assured her that she wasn't a lonely dreamer.

Still, she couldn't bear to accept the name Madria for herself. She would rather be a nameless prisoner than the treeish daughter of Love who set evil and death free. Madria was someone from another world, another time. It was better to focus on the here and now. If she didn't, the weight of all that was lost would crush her.

"How long was I asleep?" she asked.

"Only a few hours after you ate my seed," the voice of Love replied from the light.

She looked up. Dark clouds filled the sky and hid the sun.

Duron's song ended and he landed on one of the branches of the tree that stood next to her. She remembered the white raven bringing her Love's gift, and now she knew where it came from, but she couldn't remember a tree being in the center of the labyrinth.

"How did that get here?" she wondered.

Love giggled and said, "He isn't a that, he's a he."

Only then did she notice that the branch on which Duron perched looked very much like a man's outstretched arm. Instead of a trunk, the tree had legs covered in bark up to its waist. It had a bare chest with green wood that looked like smooth skin, and a man's face above. It was as if one of Love's treeish children had stepped out of her visions into the center of the labyrinth.

"Ruak?" she asked without thinking. She crawled backward on the ground. "No, he withered. Couldn't be."

The voice of Love replied to her unspoken fear, "Peace. Be still. This is my son . . . Ilan. He is filled with the light of Love. Hear him." In an instant, the light shrunk and vanished in a blinding flash. The implosion created a burst of wind that blew into Ilan. As it did, his eyes opened, he smiled, and took a deep breath.

Without the light, all was veiled and dim. The encircling wall with its thorny vines seemed closer, darkening the center of the labyrinth and threatening to suffocate her. That familiar loneliness returned. Bricks loomed above. She clutched her chest and gasped for air. Clouds and haze churned in the sky making the tower appear to sway like it was going to fall on top of her.

She frantically looked around for the light, but it was nowhere to be seen. "No! Don't leave me." She trembled as emptiness welled up inside her.

Ilan stood at a distance with his leaves lighting up in the gloom.

"What did you do to the light?" she cried bitterly. "Bring it back!"

After being in the light of Love, she couldn't imagine life without it. All safety and comfort and peace were gone. She remembered the visions of the garden and thought of Madria walking away from her home.

Fear gripped her. She stood up and stumbled backward, still trying to catch her breath. She ran to the tower and slammed the door behind her. She pulled down the beam that locked the door and sat down on the stairs. She took a deep breath, slapped herself in the face, and exhaled. "Am I still sleeping?" She pinched her arm. "Is it all a dream? Wake up!" She slapped herself again. "Am I just a crazy bird?"

She heard leaves rustling in the wind outside the door. There was a knock and she screamed. She moved up a couple stairs, paused and listened intently.

"Please come out. It's me. I won't hurt you." The words were muffled by the door. "You don't have to hide. You won't like what you find in there." It sounded strangely like the voice from the light of Love.

"Go away. I want to be alone . . . unless you can bring back the light."

Childlike laughter echoed outside the tower. "You'll never be alone again, the water of light is bubbling up within you now. Come, open the door and we'll have something to eat. You must be hungry."

She looked at the barred tower window, then back at the door. "No. I've had enough of this craziness!" she yelled. She ran up the stairs. "My room, my comfortable room. I know you well. No lights, no seeds, no tree-man." She slowed as she noticed a strange smell the higher she got, but she chose to ignore it. She climbed through the opening in her bedroom floor and closed the door behind her. She sat down with her eyes closed and sighed with relief.

Oh, that smell!

She put a hand to her mouth as she noticed a low buzzing sound. Her stomach dropped. The walls were smeared with red and black, strewn with animal entrails, rotting produce, moldy bits, and maggoty meat, all crawling with flies and hanging everywhere. The raven's gifts were gone. The necklaces, bracelets, and pendants were now bone and small animal skulls dripping with hairy flesh and blood.

She retched and flung open the door. She stumbled down a few steps then pulled the door closed above her. It slammed shut sending flies billowing into the air. She ran down the stairs and stopped, unable to make sense of what she just saw.

There was another knock at the door and the voice beyond greeted her with delight, "Did you change your mind? Come, eat."

She half-coughed, half-gagged and said, "I've lost my appetite. What happened to my room?"

"The light within you has given you new eyes. You've been accepting the gifts and hanging them on your walls all these years. They gave you comfort, keeping you content with slavery."

"The ravens," she said.

"They only served to soothe you into remaining the labyrinth's prisoner. Their comfort was killing you. That's why I lured the ravens away. There's nothing in there for you anymore."

She looked up the stairs at the flies buzzing around the closed door to her room. "You've turned my world upside down. I don't know what to do with myself anymore."

"It is time for you to leave your prison behind." The voice spoke with such compassion.

She looked at the locked door, then back up at the flies. "I don't suppose I have a choice."

"That's not true. You simply see your options more clearly than ever. You can't go back to the way things were, but it's scary to go forward into the unknown. You can be sure of this: there is joy in the freedom ahead that is greater than you can imagine. Yes, you will have to mourn the passing of your younger self, but there's no new life unless the seed of the old one is buried in the ground. You've always had that choice."

She touched the smooth new skin of her arm and marveled at how young it looked. "I suppose you're right. Maybe I don't feel like there's a choice because I've already made it."

She lifted the barricade that locked the tower. The door creaked open and she was greeted by Ilan's smiling face and the fragrance of the blossoms in his branches and leafy beard.

"Come out of your cell and I will show you how to live free." His jade eyes twinkled as he spoke. It was the voice of Love she'd been hearing all along, now coming from Ilan's mouth.

"Love . . . is that you?" She took a cautious step back, trying to make sense of what she was seeing, but there was no use.

He extended a branchy hand to her. "Ilan."

"Ilan? But how?"

Ilan's smile grew and his dazzling eyes brightened, "It's me, Love, and you too. I am your son, the Tree of Love."

"My son?"

"The gift. It happened the way Love said it would. I grew from you and the seed you ate . . . while you were sleeping. Believe me, it was much easier on you that way."

"This is madness!"

"It really is. Why are you still standing in that nasty tower? Take my hand and we'll go look for your appetite in the garden. There's nothing to fear."

She hesitantly took Ilan's outstretched hand. It was strong, but with the soft texture of a dense moss. "You have a sly way about you, the way you get me to want to do what you want me to do."

Ilan lightly raised her hand to lead her out of the doorway. He walked gracefully, his roots reaching out and pulling him along.

He guided her as if he were leading her to dance. "May I see your gardens?"

"There's not much to see." As they approached, the pungent scent of decaying plants stung her nostrils.

She pulled back.

Ilan turned toward her.

"I don't want to show you the gardens," she objected. "I've spent enough time in the gardens. I want to see the light. I want to go back into the light."

Ilan smiled. His leaves brightened and his eyes lit with a flash. "Follow me," Ilan replied. Warmth and the inviting scent of Ilan's flowers surrounded her, pushing away the stagnant air of her garden. Before she knew it, she was once again being led by his tender touch.

24

Remembering Roark

More clouds rolled in as Ilan guided her to the rows of trampled and withered crops. Fruit decayed on the ground, covered in mold. Bugs gnawed on what was left of the plants' leaves. She looked up at the green vines that hung from Ilan's head, lush and filled with flowers. Having such an enchanting visitor made her aware of just how bad things had gotten. Ashamed, she said, "I haven't been doing much gardening lately. I've been . . . distracted."

"It will be okay," Ilan replied. He looked up toward the garden wall. "I have just the thing to cheer you."

Wanting to offer something, she thought of her apples. "There's still some fruit on the trees that I haven't . . ." She stopped mid-sentence and looked at Ilan. "I hope that's not an offense?"

Ilan laughed, "No. We trees joyfully share the life within us. Instead of fruit from the trees, perhaps you will allow me to entice you with the fruit of the vines."

"I haven't planted any vines."

"I know," Ilan said as he touched one of the brown, thorny pests that plagued the wall of the labyrinth since its earliest days, "but I did . . . a long time ago." The spot he touched glowed bright green and began to spread. Light flowed through the vines revealing that they were lush, leafy stalks. Large clusters of green and purple grapes hung on the vines, swollen to the size of plums.

"Where did they come from?" she asked, wide-eyed.

"They've been growing here all along," Ilan explained. "The fruit is quite sweet, very juicy, even intoxicating. The grapes have aged on the vine. Their juice has fermented and turned to wine." Ilan called out to the vines, "Come feed your queen!"

The vines stretched and lowered their fruit toward the ground. It was irresistible. She plucked one of the green grapes and took a large bite. "These are amazing," she garbled through a mouthful.

Ilan laughed as she continued to devour the fruit. "It looks like we've stumbled across your appetite. When you're done with that one, try one of these." Ilan pulled an entire cluster of grapes from the vine. "You're going to like these purple ones."

"These green ones are delightful." Juice from the grape ran down her chin. "Thank you so much."

"My pleasure." Ilan popped one of the purple grapes from the cluster and handed it to her.

She plucked another green grape, and another . . . and one more, and held them in her shirt. She ate Ilan's grape, slurping up its juice. Her arms and cheeks began to warm. "Mmmm." Her body tingled all over and she laughed. "These are miraculous."

"They are good, aren't they? I think I'll have one as well. On second thought, maybe two!" Ilan lifted his purple cluster of grapes above his head, looked up, opened his mouth, and bit one off with a pop. Then another. "Mmmm." He looked over at her and she was devouring another green grape. He laughed and said, "Slow down; they're filling."

"Let them fill me. I need a faster way to get these into my mouth! They're so good."

Ilan popped a green grape in his mouth and looked up at the dark clouds. "It looks like rain. Grab one or two more grapes and give me the pleasure of sitting with me under my branches."

"I'd like that," she said as she stuffed more grapes in her shirt. She walked with Ilan, sat down next to him, and let her stash of fruit roll onto the grass in front of her. "I can't remember the last time someone joined me for a picnic." She took another bite and laughed. "I'm sitting with a sparkling tree-man having a meal of magical grapes! Ha! If you would have told me this morning that this is how the day would end, I would never have believed you."

"That's why you had to experience it for yourself."

The woman nodded and continued eating, feeling more and more giddy as she did. "I'm glad I ate your stinky seed."

Ilan giggled. He ate a couple grapes and asked, "Would you allow me to shine a little more light for your next step?"

"Sure, why not?" she asked as she chewed and slurped.

Ilan touched her shoulder. "Ruak needs you."

"Ruak . . ." she repeated wistfully and looked up. She closed her eyes and remembered running in the wilderness with her man, nameless and terrified of the shadow of Love. She thought about how they held each other's ears as Love sang over them in the wilderness. Then she recalled something she hadn't thought of for a very long time, the day they found the hunter hurt in the woods. She opened her eyes. "The old man . . . he called him . . . it was something like Ruak."

"The wine in my grapes is helping you to remember."

"It's on the tip of my tongue. What was it?"

"He named him Roark," Ilan replied.

"Roark! Yes, of course." She laughed. "Roark was his name." She took a deep breath through her nose and exhaled. Her whole body relaxed. "But he's not Roark, he never was." It was as if she had cast off a weight she didn't even know she was carrying. "He's Ruak." She looked up at the tower. "How have I been so blind?

All those years alone. . . . Thank you. Thank you for helping me remember."

Ilan smiled. "And now you can help Ruak."

"How?"

"Share all you've experienced with him."

"Ha! That's impossible," she objected. "He'll never believe me."

"After all you've witnessed do you really think anything is impossible?"

She looked up at Ilan. "What do you want me to do, just tell him I gave birth to a tree? And what about the shadow? How am I supposed to explain that? I'm not even sure that I understand."

Ilan's leaves brightened. "The light of Love has always shone on me, and when you turned away from his light you only saw the shadow I cast. But now I'm here in treeish flesh so all people can see Love's light through me."

"How could it have been you chasing us in the wilderness? You just got here."

"When I grew from your soil, I entered space and time, but I've never been bound by them."

"If I tell him you cast the shadow, he'll never believe you aren't our enemy. He's spent his entire life protecting us from the darkness. He won't listen to me."

"We'll need to give him time," Ilan replied, "and the freedom to reap what he has sown." Ilan plucked something from one of the branches that grew from his upper back. He held it up between his crooked fingers and showed it to her. It was glowing and it looked like a fig, but smaller. "Belief is just a choice to act on what you hope to be true. Evidence follows. Offer him this."

"What is it?" she asked.

"It's my fruit. A seed for Ruak like the one you ate," Ilan said. "He'll need to eat this if he wants to live."

She looked at the seed. "That doesn't look like the seed Duron gave me."

"Yours was one-of-a-kind and older than time itself. This seed will fill him with light, but it will not grow into another tree like me. I'm one-of-a-kind too!" Ilan smiled. "After all, I'm treeish flesh *and* Love. My fruit is as I am."

She took the last bite of the last grape and it started to rain.

Ilan lowered a hand to the ground. "Come, I'll shelter you from the coming storm. Rest in my branches, like you did in Love's light."

She smiled as cold raindrops wet her hair and rolled down her cheeks. "Sounds wonderful." She leaned against his large, mossy palm. Ilan gently picked her up with another leafy limb and cradled her close to him like a little baby. More branches grew from Ilan and sheltered her from above. She noticed he was trembling.

"You're shaking. Is something wrong?"

"I have longed for this day," Ilan replied. Glowing water dripped from Ilan's eyes. He dug his roots into the ground and grew taller, lifting her higher into the air. The light of Love radiated from his leaves and wrapped her in the now familiar comfort of home.

"It is you," she said as she delighted in his embrace.

Ilan slowly swayed back and forth. Duron fluttered out of his luminous leaves, landed next to her, and nestled into her arms.

"Soon you will be free of this labyrinth," Ilan said as he wove his limbs and leaves to enclose her in a cozy little shelter within his canopy.

The sky opened up and she reclined on Ilan's leaves, warm and dry as she listened to the rain fall all around her. It was so peaceful.

Ilan became still and silent as she considered all that happened and how she would escape from the center of her self-imposed prison. Her thoughts were soon interrupted by snoring from below. She snickered. Ilan had drifted off to sleep as he held her in his strong arms.

25

Temptation

Coiled in a dark cave on a high cliff, Wyrm looked beyond the entrance to the rising sun. The evening's rain breathed new color into the landscape below. Burning back life was a never-ending chore. Each day was just like the one before it and every morning made him angrier than the last. He hated that he was forced to endure the monotony of existence, unable to make it stop. He couldn't escape by taking his own tail and the sun taunted him, reminding him that no matter how much power he had, he was impotent to keep the light from shining on another tedious day.

Only breakfast could pull him from his hole. Still, while he had more to eat than ever, the food just didn't satisfy. It filled him, but it didn't excite him like it used to. He had tasted it all before, over and over again through the ages. Regardless of the variety available to him, it had all become so dull, but he was burdened by the ever-present compulsion to eat.

"Eternal life," Wyrm sneered. He growled and slithered to the mouth of the cave. He dove, wings wide, and caught a warm updraft that carried him away from the cliff. He flapped and flew on toward a great plain. He ascended higher to feed.

Beneath the dragon, labyrinths dotted the land as far as the eye could see. They were in various stages of construction. Some were just getting started. Others were larger and well formed. Like the stumps of old trees, the ones with the most concentric rings told the stories of ages gone by.

He had amassed an army of worm-infested slaves to run his network of brick-making operations that fed the labyrinths littering the plain. They moved through the forest along the rivers where mud and trees were plentiful, clearing large sections for their drying huts and kilns. The trees became fuel and the land was left scarred and barren as resources were exhausted and brick production moved further on. The slaves were driven beyond human limit by the blood worms that raged within.

Many of the labyrinths were isolated, but some grew closer together, competing for space and resources. The stories of havoc created by the meeting of two labyrinths would fill volumes. Battles fueled by pain, paranoia, and rage flared wherever the prisons met, and Wyrm would gorge himself on the suffering and fear. He took great pride in these clashes of self-protection and twisted longing.

One labyrinth stood apart from the rest, alone beyond the forest and far from the view of the nearest prison. It was a very large stump that told his favorite story.

Wyrm let loose a piercing screech and shot toward the labyrinths below, a single arrow with an abundance of targets. Billows of misery rose from the towers and winding walls of each prison, polluting the sky with food for the despair-hungry dragon. He leveled off just above the soupy filth that hung high above the land. He extended his long black neck, opened his mouth and took in his morning meal of the dark energy—a yawning sea creature filtering food from an ocean of death.

Wyrm tasted the bland emotions of a young man lost in the drudgery of daily life, and then swooped away toward the next labyrinth. A small adjustment to the angle of his wings and he flew into the bitterness of a woman who had convinced herself that she wasted her commitment on a man who never lived up to her expectations. He drank in her pungent brew and moved on to the stale sadness of an old man who accomplished everything he set out to, but still felt empty inside. The sharp grief of a young couple who had just lost a child was a fine morsel. He would work to infect them with his worms and come back after their pain drove a wedge between them. Their passionless marriage would make a decent meal once their grief mellowed a bit.

He came up to breathe and belched. It was the same old fare and he was still hungry for something sweet. He turned and flew off toward the lonely, ancient labyrinth on the other side of the woods. As he got closer, he was perplexed to find the air over his prized labyrinth quite a bit clearer than the rest, and he could no longer smell Madeline's despair. Then he saw a tree planted in its center.

He winced. The scene looked eerily familiar. It reminded him of his ancient prison in Love's orchard labyrinth.

"What in the hell . . . ?" he growled. Finding out would mean flying closer to the tower, and he couldn't risk being spotted by Madeline. "Damn deal." He silently glided high above.

The tree stood as tall as the tower and its roots were choking its base. "How did that grow here so quickly?" Madeline was nowhere to be seen and he still couldn't sense her presence, so he dared to get closer and find out what was happening. He dove again at top speed and slithered to a landing by the tree. It was snoring. Wyrm hissed. "A son of Love?"

His vine-covered head was bowed as he slept with his beard resting on his chest. The leaves of his beard danced in rhythm with his snoring. Branching arms extended from his shoulders and back. They stretched high above his head and their foliage formed a thick canopy that soaked in the rays of the late morning sun. A light breeze blew from his swaying branches as he breathed in the gloom coursing through the prison and exhaled clear air into the center of the labyrinth. The tree was a son of Love, no doubt about it, and he was stealing Wyrm's food.

"Your leaves stink, thief," the dragon snarled. The serpent slinked around him examining the tree-man's body. Wyrm matched his thickness. The dragon passed over his roots and wound around his legs feeling the strength of the dark green bark that broke up into patches around his stomach muscles. There was no sign of Madeline. *What did he do with her?* Wyrm wondered.

He took to the air again with furious flapping to hover above the intruder and look at his green umbrella of leaves.

The commotion woke the tree-man. He stirred, groaning and creaking as he stretched his limbs further into the sky. A deep rumble grew within him and he slowly spoke, "Oh that's just what I needed, forty winks in the light."

Wyrm landed. "I thought Love's children were dead." He sounded more desperate for information than he would have liked. "I have been around the world and I have not seen roots walk this fading rock for a very long time."

The son of Love laughed and said, "I'm here to change all that," then his roots extended deeper into the ground in the center of the labyrinth and toward its wall. As they did, his grip around the tower tightened and a large crack appeared at its base. He looked Wyrm up and down. "You've grown. You must be eating well."

The dragon saw the damage being done to his prison and his blood boiled. He glared at the tree-man and his rage grew. "Who, may I ask, are you?"

"I am Ilan, the Tree of Love."

Wyrm's thoughts darted through the dark ages of his reign, all the way back to the beginning. "Ilan, huh?"

"Yes, I am Love in treeish flesh. My roots go down deep into Love and he fills me with his water of light. I am in the light of Love and the light of Love is in me."

"Nonsense," the serpent scoffed. "What light?"

Ilan laughed again. "You've always been blind to the truth."

"You call nonsense truth? You certainly sound like Love."

Ilan yawned. "I'm sure you'll remember that we had a deal. I have come to set the children free."

Wyrm hoped that it really was Love, that he finally got around to becoming kindling like his sad little saplings. He had to know. "If you are Love, be my guest, tear down the tower. Destroy the labyrinth. Set your leafless children free. Your life for theirs. Isn't that what you said?"

"I won't move until Love says it's time. Until then, I wait. I will only walk where his light shines on my path."

Wyrm felt the power of his rage burning within and black smoke billowed from his mouth and nostrils. "More nonsense! If you're really Love, how can you say you'll wait for him?" Ilan's commitment to stay put would disrupt the proper functioning of the labyrinth for who knows how long. He slowly slithered closer as he spoke. "How do I know you're really Love himself? What's stopping me from setting you ablaze, ripping you out of the ground, and throwing you from the top of that tower?" The dragon lifted his black body and reared back, prepared to strike.

"Try it, Wyrm," Ilan replied. "Love and I are one. You cannot have my life until I lay it down. Like I told you when we spoke alone after you escaped from the Tree of Trust, death has no power over the source of all life. I am who I am."

Wyrm lunged forward and a column of flame shot from his mouth toward Ilan. Fire engulfed his trunk, but he wouldn't burn. A sickeningly sweet-smelling wind swirled around Ilan and cleared the air of Wyrm's smoke.

Wyrm pulled back and stared. "So, it is you." The smell from Ilan made Wyrm gag and cough. "The mighty Love has become one of his pathetic creations, Ilan, son of Love." He coiled into a knot just outside the shadow of Ilan's canopy. Love's power gave him pause. He had to try another angle. "Why keep the children in this living hell one moment longer? Haven't you made them suffer enough, or do you actually enjoy torturing them?"

Ilan glared at Wyrm with dark eyes that gripped the dragon. "That's a lie."

"Prove me wrong," Wyrm dared. "You say you must lay down your life for their freedom, then do it. Sacrifice yourself."

"Now is not my time. Love sent me and told me to plant my roots here and wait, so I wait. I will trust him. I am rooted in Love, and I will stay rooted in him with his water of light flowing through me."

Desperate to find a way to get to Ilan, he blurted his next thought. "Where is the woman?"

Ilan winced. "Leave her out of this."

"I will not. Until you're dead, she's mine." The dragon rose and extended his wings. "I have every right to know what you've done with her. You abandoned her to me." He beat the air in an effort to clear it of the smell from Ilan's canopy.

"You're wrong, Wyrm. Love brought me to her, and to the rest of the children. The fact that I'm planted here is proof that they are not forsaken, so bite your forked tongue."

"Tell me where the woman is," Wyrm demanded. "If now is not your time, then it is still mine. This is my world, unless, of course, you're going back on your . . ." The dragon lifted his head with a sudden realization. "Are you stalling?"

Ilan stood motionless.

"Are you scared?" Wyrm's tongue flicked with pleasure at his insight. "You're scared of death, aren't you? Ha! Maybe you'd like to alter our deal? If you really are the son of Love, there is another way."

The dragon uncurled, slithered, and flopped his tail in front of Ilan. If he could get Ilan to take his tail, it would be plain for all creation to see that Love lied when he said Ruak would do it. "It's a gift only a true son of Love can grasp. The staff of power can be yours, and I will finally be free of my miserable existence." He turned away from Ilan and lifted his tail. "Take it and all that was given to me will be yours. Unless you prefer to prolong the children's lonely agony." He wagged his tail at Ilan. "And the best part? You won't have to suffer yourself. Succeed where Ruak failed. Take your victory, become lord of the labyrinths, and let the animals out of their cages."

Ilan's leaves rustled. "Do it!" It was the woman's voice. "Let me out of here!"

She was inside the canopy struggling to part the branches.

Wyrm took to the air, eyes black and burning. "Yes! There you are!"

Ilan twisted to turn her away from the dragon and whispered to her, "I know you want this all to end now, but—"

Wyrm couldn't hear the rest. "Did you tell her why she's in prison?" he cried out. "Love is a liar, Madeline!"

"What?" she asked from behind Ilan's leaves. "What did he call me?"

He hovered over Ilan, dangling his tail in front of him. "Your daddy knew you would try to take my tail yourself. Love set you up. Then the tyrant abandoned you to me for doing what he created you to do."

Ilan's branches shook again. "Is that true?" she asked. "It is, isn't it?" The desperation in her voice gave Wyrm a clue as to where to attack next.

"Enough!" Ilan raised a branch and swatted Wyrm away. The dragon tumbled through the air. "Love has not asked me to take you by the tail. That privilege was promised to Ruak. I will not fall for your tricks."

Wyrm frantically flapped his wings to right himself in the air and smiled. He did it. He got to Ilan through the withered woman. "Madeline, the meaning of your name proves you are cursed," he continued. "From the moment of your birth you were destined to be punished . . . tower woman! It was always your fate. You were born to rot in this tower with the rest of the trash for bringing fear and death into Love's creation."

"Away with you, Wyrm! I will not listen to your lies any longer. Need I remind you that you're risking breaking our agreement by showing yourself? Keep your distance."

"I am your humble servant," Wyrm mocked. "If you wish me to leave, I will leave." He ascended higher wagging his tail in the air and shouting, "But I urge you to consider my offer, it still stands. My tail is yours for the taking. End the children's pain, son of Love. Don't let the world rot . . . like Madeline did!" The snake said the name with a condescending sneer and flew away laughing.

26

Accepting Madria

Ilan's leaves quivered and reached up to catch the tears falling from his mother's cheeks. Each salty drop of despair fell and disappeared in a fragrant little flash of light as it was absorbed into his gleaming canopy.

She curled up and covered her head in a futile attempt to hide. Wyrm was gone, but his words had cut into her heart and still burned. His condemnation rang true. Love knew everything about her, past and future. The visions showed her that he wasn't bound by time. Of course Love knew what she'd do before she did it, and he let her ruin everything. She believed Wyrm, that she was destined to be locked up in the tower. His accusations helped her accept that she used to be the daughter of Love, but she was no longer treeish. She was cursed from the beginning, born to be a rootless animal as punishment for not trusting her father. The hardest part to bear was that she deserved his wrath.

Ilan opened his branches. He held up a hand to let her out of his canopy and lower her to the ground. She stayed curled up on his leaves weeping bitterly. "It's true. It's all true. This labyrinth . . . this world . . . it's all my fault."

"Please listen to me," Ilan pleaded. "Everything is going to be all right."

"It's all my fault that we lost our home," she sobbed as she lay on Ilan's branches. "I didn't want to believe that was really me in the visions, but Wyrm is right. I belong in this prison. I was Love's daught . . ." her voice quivered and broke. "He gave us everything and I destroyed it."

One of Ilan's smaller branches raised his mother's head and another extended a lone leaf to wipe away her tears.

She stared into his twinkling leaves above. "I never should have tried to grab Wyrm's tail. It was the bite on my arm that caused all the fear. It's too much to . . ." She pulled away. "I was better off in the dark not knowing the truth."

"Truth is dangerous in the hands of a liar," Ilan replied, "and Wyrm is the fount of deception. The truth can make you free, but it can also be used to bind you in darkness when truth is laced with lies. Wyrm wants you to give up hope, but listen to me; you were not made to be locked away. You were created for freedom. The dragon is just trying to feed on your misery. Why don't you come down from up there, sit next to me, and I'll make you something nice to eat? A cheery breakfast will starve that despair-hungry snake."

"I don't deserve it," she objected as she wept. "You should pluck me out of here and stuff me in that fly-infested tower."

Ilan shuddered as if a sudden gust of chilled wind set his leaves rustling. "Oh, don't talk like that. You don't really believe that, do you?"

"It's my fate for doubting Love, just like Wyrm said."

"No it's not," Ilan declared. "Choice reveals your destiny . . . and your true name. No, don't believe what Wyrm says about fate."

She sighed. "They called me Madeline . . . 'woman of the tower.' I remember now. Wyrm's right."

"Madeline is a glorious name for those who are meant to have it. Not all towers are like the one you've been living in. Look at me, I am a strong tower of Love, born to be a place of refuge for his children. How wonderful to be a woman of Love's tower. However, Wyrm gave you that name through the one who called himself Tatus. He used it to make you feel loved, to gain power over you."

"Tatus," she said pensively, "the old man . . ."

Ilan cradled his mother and raised her out of his branchy shelter. He set her in front of him, lifted her chin, and bent down to look into her eyes. "He had no right to name you. He certainly had no insight into who you really are. There is only one who can give you that."

She felt Love's warmth radiating from Ilan's leaves. "Love."

"That's right."

"But Love has shown me who I am; a prisoner. I deserve to be locked away in the tower."

"Do you believe that I am in Love and Love is in me?"

She watched the light of Love dance in Ilan's eyes. "I can't help believing what I see."

"Then look at me and see that Love doesn't give you what you deserve. I have come so you can see Love's true nature . . . and yours too," Ilan explained. "If you have a hard time believing my words, watch my actions. Just so, I have watched your actions and I know your name. If you don't accept that name, you will never be free, even if I picked you up and carried you away from this labyrinth. Love named you Madria. It's a name you hadn't grown into . . . until now."

"What do you mean?"

"Madria means 'mother.' It's the name given to the woman who chose to bring life into the world," Ilan smiled and his leaves flashed, "and light into darkness. You made it possible for Love to be reunited with the world he laughed to life. I am that reunion, and I came from you. You are not only my mother, but also the mother of all who will eat my seeds. Your choice to trust has set events in motion that cannot be stopped."

She turned her back to Ilan. "It was also my choice that sent the world into darkness." She started to cry again.

One of Ilan's glowing leaves floated down toward her from his canopy. She reached out and it landed in her hand. The leaf brightened. Greens, blues, and yellows flashed within it, and then it dimmed. She looked at the dead leaf in her hand. She touched it with her finger and it turned to dust. A fragrant breeze swirled from Ilan's branches and blew the remains of the leaf away.

"Don't be sad about the leaf," Ilan said. "There are more where that one came from. And don't despair over the choices you made. Our daddy will weave them together with his to make something beautiful." Ilan's entire canopy lit up with color.

Ilan's warm light embraced her. "Our daddy?" she asked.

"Yes," Ilan said. "You'll always be his little girl, just as I have always been his son. Nothing can change that. Once a child of Love, always a child of Love. He sent me here so you would never doubt his care for you again." Ilan touched his mother's shoulder. "Love makes choices too. He knew giving you freedom would plunge the world into his shadow for a short time. He knew Ruak would be paralyzed by fear at the Tree of Trust. He knew Nali would stop flowing and that I would burn to reveal my seed. He knew you would end up in the labyrinth scared of him. But Love did all those things anyway, and that should give you some comfort."

"Comfort?" She spun around. "Why?"

"Because Love is good. Simple trust in that truth is all that was ever required."

"If he's good, why would he allow all that pain?"

"Giving you freedom was a greater good than the absence of suffering, especially when Love can create beauty from all the pain. You'll see that when I set you free. Until then, rest in knowing that everything we all chose, as much as it hurts, is leading to a revelation of Love and his selfless generosity toward his children. Don't fall into Wyrm's trap. Trying to discern good and evil drove him mad. There are some things you won't be able to understand until you get home. Love is beyond comprehension, but I offer you communion with him through trust. Will you choose to trust Love?"

"That's asking a lot."

Ilan stood up straight, towering over her. "All I'm asking you to do is rest in me like you used to. Soon you'll see the greatest gift Love could give to the world. Love's true nature is only revealed in response to that which is unlovely."

She dared to hope. A tear slid down her cheek. "He's not mad at me?"

"Not in the slightest," Ilan replied. "Just the opposite. He delights in you." Ilan laughed and swayed.

She drew in the smell of his blossoms and laughed too.

"So, what do you think?" Ilan asked. "No more listening to the dragon? No more despair? Will you accept the name Madria?"

"Mother?"

"Yes," Ilan smiled. "The mother of the living. There's a world full of people stuck in labyrinths just like this one. Wyrm feeds on their misery. Let's get out of here and sow the seeds of Love. We'll start with Ruak. He too must become who he already is." Ilan laughed. "We need to help Ruak grow into the name Love gave him. What do you say, Madria?"

She thought about all she saw in the light of Love and remembered the good days with Ruak. She gave in and smiled. "Yes, I am Madria." She looked at the open gate, then down at Ilan's thick roots in the dirt. "Well, shouldn't we go now? Give me your seed and let's take it to Ruak."

"That won't be necessary," Ilan said. "He'll come to us."

"What?" Madria exclaimed.

"Yes. All we have to do is enjoy each other's company. Nali will take care of the rest. She'll break us out of this labyrinth before you know it. Now, how about some breakfast? Please allow me to wait on you while we wait to be set free." Ilan smiled and bowed to Madria. "At your service, my queen."

27

A Father's Faith

Alone lantern lit the trees that reached across the forest road. Branches overlapped and entwined to form a tunnel that stretched on into the night. Tatus's wagon groaned with the weight of barrels of water, pallets of bricks, food, and other supplies for Roark's work on the wall. The team of camels plodded along with their burden in tow. It was a familiar trip for Tatus—he had travelled the lonely road from the kilns countless times. The rhythm of the camels' padded feet and the rocking of the wagon soothed him. He closed his eyes and nodded off.

Barking and baying echoed in Tatus's mind. The hounds sniffed and scratched at the door to the log home he built for his family. He went for his spear, but it became his daughter's karimba in his hand. He looked at the labyrinth carved into the back of the wooden music block, then up at his home. All was dark inside. It was late. He walked to the door and put his hand on the latch. It was freezing cold. He threw open the door and felt himself being pulled into the house as he saw the crooked shadow consuming his wife and children.

Suddenly, the camels stopped and the wagon creaked to a halt. Tatus woke up to see the harnesses on the beasts swinging, their hammered metal parts clanking. "Never sleep," he mumbled. "Never rest." He shook his head and snapped the whip. A flurry of noise erupted from the harnesses as the camels lunged back and forth. They bellowed and wouldn't budge.

"Damn it!" Tatus clambered down the wagon's ladder.

At the last rung, thunder exploded in the night and a sharp pain seized his heart sending him to the ground. He gripped his chest and felt something crawling beneath his skin. His stomach dropped and his body convulsed. His throat closed, choking him. Whatever was inside him was forcing its way out through his mouth. Tatus contorted as black maggots burst out onto the ground. Wave after wave erupted from him, and then stopped in an instant. He gasped with all his might, terrified and weakened, and then he crumpled. The burning rage that had been Tatus's strength was gone and he wept in a broken heap on the dirt road.

Tatus cried like a little boy just realizing he's hopelessly lost in the woods. His uncontrollable emotions only made him more terrified and ashamed. He put his hands behind his head and buried his face in his arms. In utter helplessness, drained of all pretense and potency, he whimpered, "What's happening to me?"

"You are finally feeling something besides anger," a voice replied.

Tatus looked up and a brilliant light burst out of nowhere to push the darkness deep into the forest around him. "My God!" he cried and lay prostrate on the ground.

A soothing voice spoke from the radiance, and addressed Tatus by his given name. "Erik, ever powerful, don't be afraid." Beams of children's playful laughter reached out to kiss Tatus's cheeks and warm his face. "I am not your tormentor. I have come to free you from his worms so you can see what you have chosen. The snake has had your ear for long enough."

"Who are you?" Tatus shuddered. It took every ounce of his strength to drag himself away from the light. "How do you know my name?"

"I am Love, and I know you better than you know yourself. You have a choice to make. It could be your last, but it could be your first choice in a new life, so listen carefully. Stand and look at the blood worms I pulled from you."

Tatus felt himself rising. The light swirled with color all around him, giving him strength to stand. The maggots writhed in an inky, putrid mass on the ground. Waves of stench from the undulating swarm hit Tatus and made his stomach churn.

"Wyrm," the voice of Love spoke in the brightness, "show yourself."

The blood worms morphed into a serpent, sleek and black. It slithered into a coil and extended its head into the air. Wings sprouted from its back. The little dragon looked Tatus up and down.

"I'm dreaming. This isn't happening." Tatus slapped his face. "There's no way that just came out of me."

"I am sad to say that you are wrong," said Love. "Listen to him, I'm sure you'll find his voice all too familiar. Wyrm, speak."

"What if I don't have what it takes?" The snake sounded just like Tatus's own inner voice.

Tatus trembled.

The little dragon whispered, "I am a pitiful excuse for a man."

Tatus's wife and children appeared in his mind. He believed the serpent's words completely.

"I'm a failure as a father," the snake shook his head. "The shadow will take Madeline and Roark too. And I call myself Tatus."

"Make it stop!" Tatus cried. The serpent's tongue was a dagger that stabbed into his deepest pain and twisted in the infected wound.

"Well done, good and faithful servant," the snake hissed.

"My Lord?" Tatus asked, desperate to make sense of what he was seeing and hearing. He staggered backward out of the light and fell to his knees.

"Yes, Erik," said the voice of Love, "this is your god."

"How is that possible? How is any of this possible?"

"Wyrm infected you a long time ago. The blood worms were the rage within you that gave you your strength."

"It's the shadow!" the little dragon hissed. "Don't be fooled. His words will draw your faith in him just as they drew me from your body."

"Wyrm," Love said quietly. The serpent cowered and slithered into the woods. The light swirled with rainbows. "Erik, look into my light and see the truth."

Tatus turned and saw himself in the light, crouching just outside a forest examining the ground. A shadow grew around him as a large dragon silently swooped down. The creature struck him with a snap of his tail and Tatus flew into the woods and onto a boulder. His limp body slid off the rock headfirst to the ground below. A dazzling light appeared and hovered over Tatus.

"Why are you here?" The dragon hissed into the brilliance. "He asked for me."

The light didn't move.

"Haven't you made him suffer enough?" Flames lit the serpent's mouth as he spoke. "He gave himself to me."

Suddenly, the light shrank and disappeared.

"Coward," the dragon growled.

Tatus recoiled as he watched the winged serpent encircle and infect him with blood worms.

"On that day, so long ago, you became Wyrm's slave," Love explained. "When you found that your family had died, you ran from the pain into the snake's trap. You gave yourself to wrath and ran from anguish. In time there was nothing left but rage, and the serpent entered. His black maggots did their wicked work, corrupting your senses and twisting your mind."

Tatus clenched his fists. "What do you know about my family? Who are you really?"

"They are safe," the voice of Love said. "They were always safe with me, even when they were with you." The light danced before Tatus. Swirling amber wisps of radiance wove together and parted to reveal his wife's face, and then her body clothed in light, her arms outstretched. His daughters appeared, wrapped in radiance as well, their smiling faces greeting him. Tears of joy fell from his oldest girl's eyes. Tatus's son appeared last and he waved to his daddy from within Love's illuminating presence.

"Oh, God!" Tatus wept as he reached toward his wife and children, "I did the best I could." Tatus buried his face in the dirt road and cried again, "I did the best I could!" He clawed at the ground. "I did the best I could." Time slowed, and then the sense of it flowing at all disappeared. The road and the wagon were gone. All was dark. The only thing that existed was Tatus and his lament, "I did the best I could."

"You did," Love's voice spoke into the darkness, "and they are grateful. Nobody could have done any better for them." The light of Love appeared and moved toward Tatus to soothe him. Love reached to envelop him in the penetrating peace of home, offering endless comfort, another moment filled with another eternity, but Tatus pulled away and time started to flow again.

Tatus looked at his family in the light. "I couldn't save them. They're gone," Tatus objected. "The shadow took them!"

"No, they're not gone. I was there when they got sick. Look into the light and you'll see."

Within the light of Love, Tatus saw his wife drawing water from the stream that flowed near their home in the woods. He saw his children laughing with their mother at the table by the hearth, eating and drinking in its warm glow. He watched as, one by one, the children fell ill. Then his wife became sick as well. As weak as she was, the desperate woman tended to her three children the best she could. She became so sick it was painful to move. Tatus's wife and children curled up in bed with one another and waited for death to take them.

Tears streamed down Tatus's face. "Why? Why do you torture me with this vision?"

"You must see the true fate of your family instead of your twisted memories."

Through tears, Tatus looked back at his wife and children huddled together in bed, their gaunt faces surrendered to the inevitable. Then the room filled with light. Their faces brightened. The light of Love lifted Tatus's wife out of bed and she beckoned her children to follow. Each of them joined her and they all walked together, hand in hand, into the light.

"The disease was in the water," Love explained. "It came from Wyrm's victims upstream. If you weren't away hunting, you would have died too, Erik. I saw them suffering and I came to them in their helplessness. I comforted them. I took their pain and brought them home where all things are made new. Then you walked into the room, but in your grief and the strength of your anger, all you saw was my shadow."

Tatus wiped the tears from his face. "So, that thing that came out of me was right? You are the shadow."

"You only saw the shadow of Love. Now, in your helplessness, you see the light of Love. Your family would like you to join us in the light, but you'll need to trust me."

"Why didn't you save them?"

"I did. They're right here with me."

"You took them!" Tatus struggled to his feet. "Enough of this madness!" He staggered toward the ladder on the wagon.

"No, this is a moment of sanity," Love replied. "I pulled Wyrm from you so you could see clearly enough to make the choice that is before you. I know this encounter with your brokenness has left you feeling ashamed, but there is healing on the other side of the pain if you will follow me through it."

Tatus looked for the little dragon and caught a glimpse of him peeking from behind a tree. He turned to the light and yelled, "You took everything from me!"

Love sighed. "I have shown you the truth, but your bitterness blinds you. Let me help. I have a gift for you, if you will receive it."

"I don't want anything from you," Tatus said. He grabbed a wagon wheel and pulled himself to the ladder.

"I know," Love replied, "but you could be with your family forever. I have planted a tree in the center of the labyrinth. All of my power dwells within him and he has the ability to heal you. He is my essence, my very life. Go into the labyrinth and eat the fruit from my tree and then, even though you die, you will live. It will not be an easy journey without the worms giving you strength, but you can make it with my help."

Tatus tried to climb up into the wagon, but he was too weak. The serpent slithered out of the woods and stopped in silence next to him, just under the wagon.

Love continued, "You can help free my children. Lead them out of the labyrinth and you will no longer be Erik, 'ever powerful.' Your weakness will remain, but so will I, and your name will truly be Tatus. I will comfort and guide you, as you guide them."

Tatus looked at the little dragon. "So, I serve him in strength . . . or you in weakness."

"Yes, the pain you feel now will never fully subside, but one day death will mercifully usher you into my eternal joy with your family."

"You offer me a life of pain in exchange for my murdered family?" Tatus asked. "Repulsive."

"Turn around and look down the road behind you," Love answered. Tatus turned away from the light and saw his shadow stretching down the forest road into the darkness. "If you turn away from my light," Love explained, "then you will see only my shadow. It's your choice. If my seed of light doesn't fill that hole in your broken heart, the dragon will gladly take my place and fill your emptiness with his dark, raging fire."

"He wants you as helpless as your children when he took them," the little dragon's mouth twisted Love's words. "I am the only thing standing between you and history repeating itself."

"Follow him and you'll feel strong for a time, but at what cost?"

Tatus trembled. "If I follow you, I get only weakness."

"If you turn away from the source of life, the result will always be death. I set you free to choose, even if it kills me."

Tatus turned back around. He looked at the little dragon, then up at his wife and children in the light. "I'm not falling for your tricks," he said. "My wife and children are dead, you killed them. Madeline and Roark are still here and they need their Tatus to protect them from you. I'll do everything I can to make you pay for what you've done to my family. Your life for theirs. That's my choice . . . shadow."

At that, the dragon leapt onto Tatus and curled around his neck. "Together, we can take him." The snake's forked tongue tickled his ear. "Open wide."

"Yes, Lord," Tatus said, then he stretched open his mouth. The shimmering scales of the serpent started to quiver and became the black maggots again. The dragon disintegrated into thousands of worms that swarmed all over Tatus, burrowing into his ears, nose, and eyes. They poured into his gaping mouth.

Tatus's fury and fearsome strength began to return, and he looked up into the light. His wife and children disappeared in a flash as the light of Love surged and exploded with a forceful blast. Tatus turned his face toward the ground to protect his eyes and saw the shadow of a tree burned into the road in front of him.

The lantern swinging on the wagon provided the only light left in the forest. As Tatus's eyes adjusted, he saw the lantern's light was absorbed into the void in the road. Tatus watched as the shadow slowly got up.

"I knew it!" Tatus exclaimed. "You didn't fool me."

Love reached out to Tatus. "Please . . . you don't know what you are doing."

But Tatus couldn't hear him. He scrambled to back away and bumped into his wagon. He leapt up the ladder, grabbed his spear, and turned around to acquire his target.

"Erik, don't," Love cried. His shadow stood in the middle of the road giving Tatus a clear shot.

All Tatus heard was the shadow saying his name wrapped in rumbling thunder. "I am Tatus!" The dark power of the dragon's blood surged through him and he sent the spear flying through the air. The spear hit its mark, but vanished into the shadow.

Tatus scowled. He leapt down from the wagon in a fit of wrath and rushed the shadow of Love, diving at it, but the shadow disappeared. Tatus went flying and landed in the ditch on the side of the road. He stumbled to his feet and scanned the road and trees, but the shadow was nowhere to be seen. Tatus dropped to his knees and screamed at the top of his lungs in uncontrolled rage.

28

Light in the Labyrinth

"That's better," Roark said as he held his pipe and watched the smoke rise beyond the top of the wall and into the night sky. He imagined himself rising with it, high above the labyrinth, drifting upward and disappearing in the dark.

Why couldn't he fly away like a puff of smoke, free to leave his bricks behind and become nothing? "Poof," he said looking up and longing, but it wasn't that easy. It wasn't just fear. He couldn't deny that Tatus scared him, and he couldn't risk the shadow finding him in the wilderness. If he left, he'd be hunted by both. Still, there was something else. The labyrinth itself had a strange power over him. He didn't want to walk away from everything he built. Persevering for so long left him weaker than ever, but his work mattered. It had to. Abandoning his walls would mean all of his suffering was for nothing. More than his fear, it was his determination that kept him captive. Even so, he could still escape in the smoke.

As he watched the smoke rise, Roark noticed he could see more stars than usual. "Maybe it's the weed." He snickered and took in the splendor through heavy eyes. He breathed deeply. The air smelled cleaner. Something had definitely changed. The new clarity in the sky was unmistakable, and the surprising number of stars revealed that he hadn't noticed when they disappeared in the first place. Over the years, the thick haze above the labyrinth must have slowly clouded the sky like a cataract.

He lit his pipe again, only to smoke ashes and burn his throat. Roark coughed and tapped the pipe on the heel of his hand. He rose and took another deep breath.

He climbed a ladder to the top of the wall. The night air was crisp and invigorating. A light, aromatic breeze greeted him as he stood up and looked to the starry sky sparkling above. Roark lifted his arms and gave himself to the experience, his senses swimming in smoke and beauty. For a moment, all felt right with the world, until he thought about Madeline. He looked toward the center of the labyrinth. He didn't expect to see anything except a sea of walls reaching into the darkness, but instead he saw a warm glow radiating far off in the clear night.

Roark's arms flopped to his sides. "What the . . . ?" He tried squinting, but he couldn't see the source of the light. "It looks like a star landed in the labyrinth." He realized how ridiculous that sounded. "I've done it now, I've smoked too much." He blinked, opened his eyes wider, and stared until his eyes got dry, but he couldn't make out any details at that distance. "A fire? It doesn't look like flames," he said.

While they were building the tower, Tatus told him about great oceans and the men who rode on the water in their wooden sailing ships. In darkness or bad weather they needed towers on the land with lights to guide them safely to shore. Roark imagined that the glow in the labyrinth called to him in the night like one of those lighthouses calls to a sailor long lost at sea. He thought of the good years he spent living with Madeline in the tower, and in that moment, he wanted to go home. Roark closed his eyes. He wished he could remember her face. Dark waves of yearning and regret crashed over him. She was so sad, and he knew too well that she blamed him for her sorrow. Roark once again looked toward the radiance. The lighthouse beckoned him home and, at the very same time, warned him of dangerous waters ahead. Then he heard the distant sound of Tatus's wagon approaching from behind.

A lone cloud of moonlit dust rose in the distance. Tatus was moving fast, and Roark could hear him shouting, but he couldn't make out much more than Tatus calling his name through the cacophony of camel moans, harnesses, and wagon wheels. "Just what I need," Roark said as he turned his attention back to the curious light in the labyrinth.

"Roark! Roark!" Tatus yelled as the team of camels reached the outermost wall of the labyrinth. Roark turned and looked down from on top of the wall as Tatus arrived. "Whoa! Whoa!" Tatus ordered as he pulled back on the reins. The exhausted camels stopped and the cloud of dust trailing the heavy-laden wagon engulfed it.

"What's the hurry?" Roark cried to Tatus. "I didn't expect you back until morning."

"The shadow is in the labyrinth!" Tatus yelled.

"What?" Roark turned back toward the light. "That's impossible. The labyrinth is secure. Nothing got past me."

Tatus leapt from the wagon and started to unharness the camels. "Oh, no! Nothing gets past you," he said. "Your weed has dulled your senses, boy. And now Madeline will pay the price." Tatus led the camels away from the wagon to get water and looked up at Roark as he passed. "Time for you to sober up . . . and grow up! This is it, our chance to kill the shadow! What are you doing up there?"

"I . . . was on watch," Roark said. "I spotted a strange light . . . near the tower."

"A light?" Tatus asked. "What kind of . . ." Tatus paused and rubbed his eyes. "I'm coming up there. Unlock the door." He left the camels and ran toward the entrance to the labyrinth.

Roark scrambled down the ladder and lifted the large wood beams barring the door. Tatus burst in as soon as it was open and climbed up. The old man stood on top of the wall and looked toward the center of the labyrinth. Roark grabbed a torch and joined him. He froze, taken aback by Tatus's appearance. He looked haggard and crazed.

Tatus growled. "It's the shadow."

"But . . ." Roark turned to the light.

"It's a trick."

Roark looked into Tatus's eyes. They were bloodshot, deep red. "How do you know?"

Tatus squirmed and twitched. He seemed somehow uncomfortable in his own skin. "The shadow attacked me on the road."

"What?" Roark asked in shock. "What happened?"

"He struck me down. When I was at my weakest, the demon appeared as an angel of light; light just like that one in the labyrinth."

Roark looked at the light, then back at Tatus. "You think that light is the shadow? That doesn't make any sense. And if the shadow attacked you on the road, why do you think it's in the labyrinth?"

Tatus turned, stuck his finger in Roark's chest and said, "I'm lucky to be alive. I was helpless. He held me there and forced me to listen to him. The shadow's powers of deception are . . . maddening."

"Wait, you *talked* with it?" Roark questioned. "How?"

"Don't be fooled, Roark. There is no light. That's the shadow. Our eyes are being deceived."

"Slow down. What did the shadow say?"

"He told me . . ." Tatus hunched and rubbed his mangy head. "He told me he planted a tree in the labyrinth. He wanted me to eat its fruit . . . probably poison." Tatus seemed to be trying to make sense of it all himself.

"A tree?"

Tatus grabbed Roark's shoulders and pulled him close. "I'm telling you, he planted a tree!" His breath stank like rotting meat. "I don't know how he got in to plant the damned thing, but we have to destroy it before Madeline . . ."

Roark got free of Tatus's grip and took a step back. He briefly considered pushing the crazy old man off the wall and making a run for it, but the light in the center of the labyrinth beckoned.

"We have to save her." Tatus turned toward the light and paused. "But are we strong enough? Why do I still see . . . ?" He looked at Roark and pointed. "You see that light?"

"I said I did!"

"Well . . . Madeline is in there too. Something's going on in the labyrinth and it's connected to the shadow attacking me on the road. I just know it's that damned tree. You have to believe me."

"Okay," Roark agreed. "I get that something's not right. That strange light appears in the labyrinth, and at the same time you say the shadow has shown itself after ages of hiding. It can't just be coincidence. You've obviously gone through something horrible, but do you hear yourself? The shadow is attacking us with a poison tree? Even if that were true, why would it tell you? It all sounds . . ."

"Crazy, I know." Tatus popped his neck. He grimaced. "Roark, I believe it in my bones that this is the moment we've been waiting for. Everything in me tells me it's true." He clenched his fist and shook it. "We can finally have justice and be rid of the shadow forever. Our labyrinth will work. It will trap him. We have to go in."

"Do you know how long it would take us to get to the tower? Years ago I traveled maybe a third of the way in and it took me almost a full cycle of the moon. At this point, the path winds round and round and back and forth on itself for . . . getting to the center will easily take three moons!"

"Then get moving," Tatus replied. "Unload the bricks and the rest of the materials from the wagon. Add all the food and water you have here to what's already loaded. Get the camels ready."

"They won't survive the trip," Roark objected.

"Shut up and do what I say. There's enough grass and water pooling in the labyrinth. They can eat the vines if they get desperate enough. They'll make it. We can replenish our supplies from Madeline's garden and the well. We'll leave in the morning once the camels have rested. And don't forget the axes."

29

Learning to Love

Warm waves of peace passed over Madria as she slept suspended in Ilan's twinkling canopy. All of her doubt, fear, anger, and pain were washed away. A song gently woke her from her sleep. Ilan's leaves were dimmed and darkness surrounded her little shelter in his branches. It was still night. The soft light of Love from Ilan wrapped her in the comfort of home as Duron sang above. She closed her eyes again, completely relaxed, and listened to Duron's singing.

Madria couldn't understand the words, but the emotion in Duron's voice spoke directly to her heart. It was a sad song, a lone voice in the night like a flickering little candle trying to push back the darkness. Suddenly, a chorus of voices joined Duron; light and airy voices filled with hope. She opened her eyes and Ilan's branches slowly opened above her. The night sky was filled with luminous white ravens. The Leukos had joined Duron as he circled in the sky singing in the middle of the night. Duron's lonely mourning was wrapped in the Leukos' joyful expectation. Ilan reached up to receive their song. His leaves trembled and brightened.

Madria couldn't help but stand and reach to the sky as well. Looking up at the white ravens, she realized that more and more they resembled the beings of light she saw in her visions of the past.

Duron finished his part of the song. The Leukos had overcome the darkness of his dirge. They flew away singing triumphantly. Duron descended to Madria in the fluttering of wings and perched on one of Ilan's branches.

"That was beautiful," she said. "What do the words mean?"

Duron looked down and a tear fell from his eye, landing on Madria's arm. "It's an old song of the Leukos about how Love never fails," he said.

"Duron sings to comfort me," Ilan's voice rose from below. One of his glowing leaves touched Duron's tear on her arm and it disappeared in a little flash. "It's a song to help me remember the light of Love in the darkness."

"What do you mean?" Madria asked.

"Come, let's talk." A branch reached out to her.

She sat and Ilan lowered her to the ground.

Ilan looked at her with sad eyes. "When I hand myself over to Wyrm, the light of Love will leave me."

"No," she objected. "You can't . . ."

"Madria, I can't bear for you and Ruak to pay the price for setting Wyrm free and handing the world over to him, so I will pay it for you. That's the deal we made to make things right."

"There has to be another way. Why can't we just live here together in the labyrinth?"

Ilan reached toward Madria and touched her cheek with a leaf. Its light warmed her face. "I will not settle for anything less than your complete freedom and trust. Besides, my canopy is filled with seeds for the rest of Love's children. My life will make them free too."

"I don't care about the rest of Love's children. I can't lose you." She hung her head. "You just got here."

Ilan's leaf lifted her chin. "I'm not asking you to care about all of Love's children, just one, and you have already received enough Love to care for him. Soon Ruak will arrive with Wyrm, and I will lay down my life. Love Ruak the way I show you. You'll feel the sting of self-sacrifice, but trust the light of Love within you. Choose to lay down your life for him despite the pain, and be my lone image bearer in the world. And, listen to me, even if you can't do that, enjoy my freely given Love. The water of light will flow into you until Love flows out again. When Love is lavished on the unlovely, the Love Fractal grows."

"I don't understand."

"You will, in time."

Madria turned away. "All I know is that I can't lose my home again."

"I know how you feel. I lost my home within you."

Madria sat on the ground and thought about what he could mean. She looked up at Ilan. It was still hard to believe that she used to be treeish and filled with light just like him. Then it occurred to her. "You mean the water of light? Nali filled us with the water of light."

"Yes." Ilan's canopy flashed with all the colors of the rainbow. "Remember, Love and I and Nali are one. We are the Love Fractal and we welcomed you into our life of joyous being, selfless giving, and grateful receiving. When we filled you and Ruak with the water of light, we joined with all of creation through you. We made our home in you just like you made your home in my tree house. It was a sad day when Nali could no longer flow through you, but now the source of the water of light is forever within you, and the Love Fractal will grow."

"Please don't go," Madria begged. "I'll do whatever you ask. Please stay."

Ilan bent down and touched Madria's chest with one of his long, green fingers. "The eternally repeating pattern of the Love Fractal always was and always will be."

She looked down to where Ilan touched her. Her heart beat faster and lit up inside her chest.

The voice of Love spoke from within her, gently vibrating her whole body, *Whatever happens, remember, I don't Love you for what you do, I Love you because I am Love and you are mine. I will never leave you or forsake you.*

She looked up at Ilan. He smiled and said, "Wyrm can kill treeish flesh, but death has no power over Love. I am both. I am deeply rooted in Love. When my roots are severed, Nali will pour into this world through them."

"But you said we'd go together. How can that happen if you're dead?"

"Love never fails."

She stood up and hugged Ilan's trunk. "I won't let it happen!"

Ilan embraced her, lifted her up, and looked into her eyes. "The Love Fractal must grow, just as all living things do. For that to happen, you have to see Love." He cradled her in his arms. "Love's true nature is to give up his life for his beloved—self-sacrifice solely for the good of the other with no expectation of anything in return except pain and rejection. But those words won't come alive in your heart until you see Love's passion for you. When you do, and you see the power of Love in action, you'll be able to trust Love enough to act like him."

30

Roark's Resolve

A full moon rose above Tatus and Roark as they pushed through the labyrinth. Tatus rode ahead in his wagon and Roark followed on his camel. A huge section of wall cracked and fell to the ground in front of them. It wasn't the first time. The vines were winning their slow war with the labyrinth. The animals bellowed and stopped.

Tatus dismounted. He tugged on the reins and his lead camel growled.

"The beast has more sense than you do, Tatus," Roark said from atop his mount. "He doesn't want to end up like his little brother."

"An unfortunate accident," Tatus grumbled as he pulled again. A rumble grew deep inside the camel until it let out a belch and spit all over Tatus's face. "Watch it or I'll cut you into little pieces and cook you up too!" Tatus yelled at the animal. The camel let out a series of grunts that sounded like laughter as Tatus tried to clean himself off.

"Ha!" Roark exclaimed. "You deserved that! You've been pushing them too hard. We should go back to the water we passed and stop for the night. That was a good place to camp."

"No," Tatus declared. "And quit bringing that up. We're not going back to water the camels again. They'll be fine for weeks. The labyrinth is trying to trick you. Forward. That's the way it's designed. Change direction and the labyrinth will eat you."

"I don't know, Tatus. The labyrinth isn't what it used to be." Roark surveyed the gaping hole that just opened up in the wall before them. "It's in worse shape than I had ever imagined. The vines are huge this far in. I can't believe the amount of damage that's been done."

Tatus cleared debris, lifting large sections of wall and tossing them aside. "The power of this place isn't in its walls alone . . . never has been." He stood up and wiped sweat from his face. "I've prayed over every inch of this labyrinth. It's the perfect prison." Tatus shook his head and winced. He looked like he was in pain. "Yes, Lord!" he shouted into the sky. Tatus glared at Roark. "This is God's house and he protects it."

Roark loathed Tatus's rants about God and hoped he wasn't about to launch into one.

Tatus went back to tossing aside bricks and chunks of wall. "The labyrinth is dedicated to God's glory. It's filled with a spiritual energy you've never understood. Our selfless sacrifices will buy us safe passage. Only the pure have the resolve to keep going forward. Again and again, we've done the right thing! Don't give in to doubt. You need to have faith, Roark."

I hate you, Roark thought.

Tatus went on, "God is with us, but he helps those who fear him and honor him with their hard work and determination. Now listen, you need to pray and promise God that you'll get serious about cutting back these vines and making repairs. God will bless us, you'll see."

The thought of taking on the thorny vines and toiling over the work he thought long since completed was intolerable. "That's insane," Roark objected. "It's too much for one man, with or without God's help."

"What do you suggest, Roark?" Tatus asked and stood up straight with a brick in each hand. "Do we just give up and let the labyrinth crumble? All our work over the ages would be for nothing!"

"Isn't it already?" Roark asked. He climbed down from his camel and walked toward Tatus. "If you're right about the shadow being in there with Madeline, then what good is the labyrinth? Your big plans couldn't save her, could they?"

"You ungrateful . . ." Tatus's red eyes were windows to a fire burning within. "Watch your mouth, boy," Tatus ordered as he raised one of the bricks above his head.

"What are you gonna do, smash my head in? Go ahead," he taunted. "Kill me. Take me out. I want out. What could the shadow have done to me and Madeline that's worse than what you and this labyrinth did to us? Do it! Then what will you have? The two people you've been trying to protect, dead in your crumbling fortress."

Tatus snarled and wound up. Roark turned away. Tatus screamed and Roark heard the brick smash into the wall beyond the hole that had just opened up in front of them. He looked up and Tatus sent the other brick flying through the hole after it. Tatus turned back toward him and sneered, "I will not accept defeat. We can still trap the shadow. We can still save Madeline. And don't forget, you wanted this labyrinth as much as I did!"

Roark stared. Tatus hunched to remove more of the fallen bricks. "Yeah, well I'm doubting my judgment," Roark said as he walked away and inspected the opening in the wall. "You know, we could bust the rest of this down, load the supplies from the wagon onto the camels, and they could get through here. We could save days, maybe weeks!"

Tatus grunted as he heaved a piece of wall out of the way. He wiped his brow and turned to Roark. "Tell me this, genius, are you going to go left or right? Do you hear yourself? You should know better. You're doubting the power of the labyrinth, you keep trying to go back, and now you want to go through that hole! The labyrinth is in your head, and it has revealed your lack of faith. Tell me, left or right? Make the wrong choice and you could end up back where we started, or worse, going back and forth constantly doubting your judgment until you run out of supplies and die! Just do what I tell you. Forward! Forward, forward, forward!"

Tatus pulled on his camel's reins again and this time the team got underway. "Forward!" he yelled again as he walked on.

Roark sighed and watched Tatus and his camels maneuver through debris, pulling the wagon over bricks and past the huge hole in the wall. He was so tired of following the old man, but at least he wasn't slaving away building the labyrinth.

Roark climbed the pile of bricks and pulled himself up on top of the wall. They had traveled for forty days, and it would easily be another forty days on the winding path before they reached the center of the labyrinth. He took in the vast amount of ground they'd already covered. There were so many walls; walls that took Madeline long before the shadow did. Or was she still alive? *Maybe she's in there nagging the shadow to death.* He smiled at the thought and looked toward the tower. From his vantage point, Roark could clearly see the tree's glowing canopy. "What are you?"

"Forward!" Tatus's voice echoed ahead in the labyrinth.

"And what is he getting me into?" Roark considered taking his camel and leaving Tatus and Madeline to their decaying home. If he didn't turn back, he might be following the crazy old man right into the shadow itself. The distance behind them was steadily growing, and with it, Roark's fear of what lay ahead.

A sweet-smelling breeze blew across the labyrinth. Roark turned his face into the light wind to enjoy the refreshing scented air. He saw something move out of the corner of his eye and looked down at the wall. One of the thorny vines was at his feet, and it held a cluster of giant, purple grapes.

"What's this?" Roark muttered. He bent down, picked up the fruit, and examined it. "Strange." Plucking a grape from the bunch, he squeezed too hard and it burst open. Juice squirted all over his hand and ran down his arm. He sniffed at it. The juice smelled sweet. He licked a finger. The taste reminded him of the wine Tatus carried with him when he returned with supplies. The old man tried to hide it in his wagon and keep it all to himself, but once Roark got a taste, Tatus's stash was never safe. Roark carefully popped another grape from its stem and took a little bite. It was good, and very juicy. "Hmm." He smiled. "They're filled with wine." He looked down the path to see Tatus disappear around a corner, then quickly chewed and slurped up the rest of the grape before going on to finish off the entire cluster of sweet treats.

Roark inspected the vine to see if there were any others. He pulled a few more vines from the wall, but found them all fruitless. He stood up on top of the wall and looked out over a multitude of winding paths toward the center of the labyrinth. The tree was shining brighter than ever. "How could you be the shadow?"

Roark stood motionless, enjoying the lingering flavor. He felt warmth in his face and chest. He was light and energetic and, if only for a moment, less despairing. "Some wine," he said. Roark wished Madeline were there to share the experience. He looked to the tower for any sign of her, but there was nothing. He took a deep breath of fragrant air, closed his eyes, and exhaled. He tried to remember Madeline's face, but instead recalled a song. Her singing seemed to drift to him on the breeze.

> "O northern wind, rise,
> come to me, the south!

Blow on my garden,
that spice may flow out.

My love put out his hand
to unlock my door,
I rose from my sleep,
my heart yearned the more."

He smiled and tears dripped from the corners of his eyes. The years of fighting and distance between him and Madeline faded as her long forgotten song continued in his mind.

"My hands scented with myrrh,
longing, I find the door,
but my sweet love was gone
and my heart yearned still more.

Come to your garden, love,
and eat its pleasant fruits."

Roark opened his eyes. The silhouette of a woman in the moonlight stood on the wall beyond the hole and bricks below. "Madeline?" Roark asked, surprised and hoping he was right.

She didn't move. There was no answer.

He couldn't make out any of her features, but it had to be her. Tears pooled in his eyes.

"Help me," she whispered on the wind.

Roark's face went blank. "What?" A tear fell. He quickly wiped his cheeks and hid behind the wall that provided safety from the pain of their failed relationship. "What are you doing out here? It's not safe. How did you . . . ?"

Flames appeared at her feet. They began to lick at her legs, and at the façade of his protection. She stood absolutely still.

"No!" Roark scrambled down the broken wall. He tried to reach her, but the fire spread too fast. The blaze engulfed Madeline. His heart pounded in his chest and he fell to his knees. Roark stared at the fire. "What's happening?"

"Look at what you did to me!" she shrieked.

He couldn't bear to watch and turned away as the fire consumed her. Her words echoed in his mind. The flames sizzled and popped, then, in an instant, went silent.

Roark looked back. The fire was gone, and Madeline along with it. He climbed up to where she was standing. There was no sign of her, no charred bricks, and no ashes. "But . . . how?" Roark clenched his fists until his whole body was shaking. "Madeline!" Roark cried. "I did the best I could!"

He looked at the moonlit path ahead. He scowled and turned to leave Madeline and Tatus behind. As soon as he did, he heard giggling. It was Madeline's voice again. He scanned the twisting pattern of the labyrinth. It stretched on and on into the night, empty and dark.

"We're pretty trees." Madeline's voice whispered the words in his ear.

Startled, he spun around, then looked to the glowing tree shining its light on the tower he built to protect them from the shadow. "Madeline . . . have I been deceived? Is this some kind of trick of the enemy?" His heart thumped in his chest. "That must be it." The sound of blood pumping in his head dizzied him. "It's trying to scare me and get me to turn back. Tatus is right, the demon appears as an angel of light."

Roark turned, stumbled, and slid on his heels down the rubble from the wall. He looked at all the bricks on the ground around him and remembered what Tatus said about the supernatural power of the labyrinth. *What if he's right about that too?* Roark thought. *What if this is our chance to cut down the enemy and be rid of the shadow forever?*

Roark mounted his camel. "I may not be able to help you, Madeline, but I'm not going to give up without a fight. I'll try to save you, but even if I can't, when I leave, there'll be no one to hunt me. I'm dealing with the shadow once and for all. My labyrinth will do what I built it to do, then I'll be free." He looked at the path ahead. "Forward it is," he muttered. Roark made a clicking sound and the camel started after Tatus.

31

The Seed of Love

Tatus climbed up out of the shadow of the wall on the thorny vines that covered the first ring of the labyrinth. The sun stabbed his eyes. He squinted and turned his head. Roark stood on the ground below, ax in hand, with his back to the wall by the open gate. Tatus reached the full height of the wall and froze. He had seen the top of the tree from a distance, but now the full magnitude of what they were up against stood before him. "My God, that's no tree," he whispered. "It's . . . a monster."

Branches rose like arms from knotted shoulders and reached as high as the top of the tower. The canopy grew thick and formed a living cage of branches and eerily glowing leaves. A little further down, bark gave way to smooth, green wood that looked like skin stretched across a muscular, hunched back. The torso rose and fell with the creature's breathing. Twisting roots extended from tree trunk legs, dug into the dirt and wrapped around the base of the tower. A large crack splintered out of the ground and up its wall.

"It's an abomination," the blood worms whispered in Tatus's ears, "the evil of the shadow in tree and flesh. Remember what he told you on the road, all of his power is within that tree. The fool has made himself vulnerable."

Tatus thought about his encounter with the enemy and how helpless he was without the worms. If it really was his weakness that made the shadow appear as a light in the woods, he had cause for concern. He and Roark could both see the tree creature's light and he wondered if that revealed a lack of strength in them that might lead to defeat. Tatus looked down at Roark waiting for him at the entrance. Roark wasn't filled with the Lord's power. He was blind to the forces set against each other at this decisive moment in the center of the labyrinth. Tatus considered telling him about the dragon's blood worms that strengthened him, but that would surely be met with too many questions that he couldn't answer.

The worms spoke to Tatus's unspoken concerns. "Don't doubt. The labyrinth has trapped your enemy and your victory is at hand. Tell Roark the monster has Madeline in his branches and that the evil must be cut out of the labyrinth. That will be enough."

Tatus climbed down the vines. He crept to Roark through the thorns and whispered, "Madeline is alive."

Roark looked at him wide-eyed.

"The shadow is holding her prisoner in his tree's branches."

Roark turned toward the gate, but Tatus grabbed his shoulder and yanked him back. "No matter what you see in there," Tatus said, "don't doubt for a second that we have the shadow trapped in our labyrinth . . . the shadow, Roark." Tatus smiled. "Have faith, this is the day we've worked so hard for. We're going to free Madeline from the shadow's cage, and we're not going to stop chopping at that tree until we've cut the evil out of God's house."

Roark gripped his ax tighter, his hands shaking. He looked into Tatus's eyes. "This really is the day, isn't it?"

"Yes, it is," Tatus replied. "Now, before we go in, bow your head and let's say a prayer."

Ilan stood rooted in the center of the labyrinth with Madria sleeping in his canopy. Nali filled him with the joy that he and Love shared in each other's presence. He took great comfort that her water of light still coursed through his body. Madria's dry, withered gardens surrounded him, a constant reminder of what happens when plants are cut off from their source of life. His impending end would be no different. Of course Ilan knew this hour would come, but now that it had, ripe with the fullness of time, he wondered if there might be some other way. It wasn't just the pain he knew he'd feel, it was the darkness of separation from Love that distressed him the most.

Ilan wished Madria were awake to share a few more moments with him in the light of Love. She would need the strength for what was about to happen, plus, he enjoyed her company. "Madria," Ilan said hopefully, looking up into his branches above. There was no answer. She slept for sorrow, unable to accept that he had to die.

He closed his eyes and searched the water of light. Memories of life with Love flooded his mind, but each perfect moment in time only served to remind him that life with Love was about to come to an end. He tried to find a path from eternity past that didn't lead to darkness. He strained to look beyond the present hour, but all he saw was the shadow of Love, and it wouldn't let him pass. The water of light boiled within him at the thought that it was impossible to escape being cut off from the light of Love. Was it the only future within Love's will? Great drops of sap dripped from Ilan's forehead and ran down his face.

What are you looking for? Love asked in the water of light.

Ilan groaned in anguish. "You know."

Yes, but it will make you feel a little better to say it anyway.

"Daddy," Ilan took a deep breath, "I know that nothing is impossible for you, so I thought . . ." He stared into the darkness ahead in the water of light. "I will trust you no matter what, but I was hoping there might be another way."

If there were, I would spare you in an instant.

"Then I'm already dead," Ilan said trembling.

This is the only way the Love Fractal will grow.

Ilan wept.

Remember my promised joy, Son.

The water of light cooled and calmed Ilan.

Remember the children's homecoming beyond death.

He wiped his brow. "For the joy then?"

For the joy.

Ilan opened his eyes to see Duron flying to him from the wall. In his beak, he held a piece of vine with a cluster of grapes hanging from it. Ilan wiped glowing tears from his face and reached out to the brilliant bird. Duron flapped and fluttered and, in a flash of white, dropped the grapes in Ilan's hand. Duron landed on one of Ilan's branches and said, "You looked like you might need these."

Duron's kindness managed to make Ilan smile. "Thank you, my friend." He ate some of the grapes and lifted the rest to Madria. "Madria." He gently shook the branches on which she slept. Madria stirred. "Madria, would you like some grapes?"

Ilan heard something drop behind him and turned to see Roark standing stunned with an ax at his feet. "Ruak," Ilan whispered.

Roark stared and said, "The creature speaks."

"Ruak?" Madria asked. "He's here?"

Ilan looked up and said, "Madria. It's time."

"No, it's too soon." Ilan felt Madria wrap herself around one of his branches.

"Please trust me." Ilan lifted the branch she was holding and turned it over to hold her in his leaves. "I'm so sorry for the pain this will cause you, but just imagine the joy we will share when this is all over and you can once again soak your roots in Nali. That joy ahead will help you get through this."

"Don't leave me!" she yelled, beating on Ilan.

"Madeline?" Roark shouted. "Tatus, I can't see her!"

"Tatus?" Madria whimpered.

"Are you all right? Tatus and I are here to save you."

"Madria," Ilan said, "listen to me. Don't forget in the dark what I taught you in the light."

As Ilan spoke those words, he was hit from behind. There was a loud *whack* and sharp pain shot through his body. Madria yelped above. Ilan's trunk buckled backward and shook. He dropped the cluster of grapes, and the light in his leaves flickered. Ilan twisted to see the one who called himself Tatus behind him. The old hunter lifted his ax for another cut.

Duron jumped from branch to branch and then flew away.

Thwack! Ilan cried out in agony as he was hit in the back of his trunk again. His leaves stopped shining, then began to crackle and glow once more.

Ilan turned away to see Roark coming at him with his ax lifted high. He swung at Ilan's legs and hit him hard. His canopy went dark.

Roark watched black blood pour from the wedges they took out of the tree creature's trunk. Shadows rose like steam from the blood and swirled around the winding roots in a dense cloud. Tatus swung at the darkness with his ax.

Madeline peered at him through the thick leaves above. "No, no!" she screamed.

"Don't worry, we'll get you out of there!" Roark yelled.

The ground began to shake. A deep rumble grew in the creature's roots and traveled up its trunk. It turned, glared at Tatus and said, "Wyrm, get out!"

Tatus was in mid swing when it looked like something struck him in the stomach. He buckled over and his ax went flying. Tatus clawed at his chest and fell to the ground.

Roark stood staring in silence at the sight.

Suddenly, Tatus choked. He couldn't breathe and stiffened in pain. His mouth opened wider and wider and he vomited. Writhing worms poured from his mouth and Tatus went limp in a broken heap.

"Tatus!" Roark gagged at the sight of the black maggots. He fell backward and dropped his ax. He looked up at Madeline watching from above, trapped by the tree monster. "What's happening?" Nothing made sense anymore. The world itself had gone mad.

Tatus could barely lift his head. He stared at the black cloud from the trunk then back at Roark. "Don't be deceived," he croaked. "Only the weak see the light. It's the shadow."

Roark ran to Tatus and shook as he tried to pull him away from the tree creature. "We have to get out of here."

"Attack. I can't . . ." Tatus began to cry. "It's going to kill her."

Madria struggled to part Ilan's branches. The only light she could see came from beyond his faded leaves. She looked down from Ilan's darkened canopy and saw the water of light shining all over his bark-covered legs. Tatus and Roark stared wide-eyed toward Ilan's trunk. The light of Love hovered in the air and drifted toward them. Wisps of color begged them to enter the light. It was beautiful, but they looked horrified.

"Mother," Ilan said, "we'll see each other again soon. I . . . Love . . . you . . . forever."

"No!" Madria cried.

Ilan called out, his voice booming, "Wyrm, nobody takes my life from me. I give it freely. I grant you my life for theirs. Take me now and set the children free!"

The worms from Tatus gave off a shrill buzz and a deafening shriek replied in the sky above the labyrinth.

Ilan opened his branches, picked up Madria, and set her on the ground by the well. Roark fell backward. Madria turned around to see light pouring from three large wounds in Ilan's trunk.

"Ruak," Ilan said tenderly, "this is Madria. Take good care of each other."

"Madeline," Roark quaked. "Get away from that thing!"

Ilan looked down at his trunk and watched the light of Love flowing from him. "Light rolls away before the darkness," he whispered, "and the darkness from before the light." Ilan moaned. "Into Love's hands . . ." His branches trembled and his leaves quivered. "I commit my spirit." He winced and squinted as he turned his head away from the light. "The shadow!" he quaked. "The shadow of Love has come for me." Ilan started crying. "Why? Why are you abandoning me?" he wailed. "Father, please." Ilan reached toward the light, his head turned in the opposite direction. "Don't go."

A screech came from above. Madria saw Wyrm shooting toward Roark and Tatus. Without thinking, she ran to Roark, grabbed him under the arms and tried to pull him away from the diving dragon.

Roark looked up and kicked himself backward with Madria's help. They scurried out of the way and looked back at Tatus.

"It is finished," Ilan cried. There was a blinding flash and a powerful gust of wind. The light was gone.

Tatus started laughing and coughing. He had a twisted look of satisfaction on his face as he stared at Ilan. He pointed and yelled, "My shot hit its mark!" Madria looked at Ilan's trunk where the light shone moments before. A spear was stuck in his side. "I knew it!" Tatus hacked. "You were the shadow. My shot on the road hit its mark!"

Roark grabbed Madria's arm and pulled her toward the gate to the labyrinth. "We did it. The shadow is dead. Let's get out of here!"

"Let me go!" she screamed.

Tatus turned and crawled to the mass of blood worms on the ground. They buzzed and swarmed, rising in the air away from him. "No! Please give me my strength back," Tatus begged.

Wyrm pulled out of his dive and hovered above, his giant black wings beating the air creating a cloud of dust. His shredded tail swished back and forth on the ground. The serpent let out an ear-splitting cry. The blood worms flew toward Wyrm and met him in the air, then disappeared under his scales.

"Run, Tatus!" Madria yelled, Roark still dragging her away.

Tatus reached up to Wyrm. "Help me and I'll cut this abomination out of the labyrinth."

Wyrm landed and slithered toward the helpless old man. "Your work here is done," said the snake. In an instant, Wyrm coiled around Tatus and he wheezed. He groaned and his bones cracked as Wyrm squeezed the life out of him.

"Well done, good and faithful servant," Wyrm hissed. "I grant you the darkness of death as your reward." The dragon released his grip and Tatus's crushed body flopped to the ground.

"Tatus!" Madria held on to the gate with one arm while Roark tugged on the other.

Wyrm turned to Ilan.

"We have to stop Wyrm!" she cried.

"What are you talking about? We have to get out of here!"

She couldn't hold on much longer. Kicking at Roark she yelled, "Let go of me!" She yanked her arm away from him and he fell backward to the ground. "All you have to do is take him by the tail!"

Flames erupted from Wyrm's mouth and set Ilan on fire. A wall of heat hit Madria and Roark. "You want me to grab that thing by the tail? Have you lost your mind?" The flames burned up Ilan's trunk and set his branches and leaves ablaze.

"Oh no!" she cried with a sudden realization. "The seeds!"

The dragon flew to Ilan's flaming body and wrapped around him, blowing fire in all directions. The serpent flapped his wings and fanned the blaze. "Burn," Wyrm growled.

"Get up!" she yelled at Roark. "You have to eat one of Ilan's seeds if you want to live."

Roark scrambled to his feet. "Madeline, please. Let's go, the camels aren't far."

"My name is Madria."

"Stop! Just stop it! This is crazy. You're not staying in here with that . . . that snake. Did you see what it did to Tatus?" He pointed at his dead body on the ground.

"I'm not going anywhere," she said as she reached out to Roark. "Ilan is our only hope."

Roark looked at Wyrm attacking Ilan, and then at her. "I don't know what the shadow did to you in that tree, but you're . . ." He rubbed his face and pulled his hair back. "She's lost her mind," he said to himself. Roark's eyes filled with tears. "I can't . . . I'm sorry." He turned away, and then turned back. "I can't make you, but please, follow me." Roark left her and disappeared into the shadow of the labyrinth's wall.

Madria wept as flames swallowed up Ilan's canopy.

"Damn vines!" Roark yelled as he struggled on the other side of the wall. "And you'll be damned too if you stay here, Madeline!"

Madria ran to Ilan, but the heat pushed her back. "Ilan!" she yelled. Tears flowed down her face as she watched the fire consuming him. "The seeds, the seeds! They're gone. What am I supposed to do now? Don't leave me all by myself again. Ilan!"

A pillar of fire rose from the center of the labyrinth and within it, Wyrm tried to pull Ilan out of the ground.

"Why?! Why are you doing this?" she screamed.

Madria couldn't watch any longer and turned away. Smoke surrounded and choked her, engulfing her in grief. She buried her face in her hands and wailed. All hope disappeared. The crackles and pops of burning wood filled the air. Madria dropped to the ground and curled up into a ball, sobbing. Despite all that had happened and everything Love showed her, she was once again utterly alone. "He gave me back my name," she lamented.

Suddenly, there was a snap, then another and another. Snap. Snap. Madria looked up to see that with each snap from Ilan's canopy, white, fuzzy little floating seeds burst from their burning pods and rose above the center of the labyrinth. Soon, a cloud of sparkling seeds surrounded Ilan. The wind from Wyrm's wings sent them spiraling into the sky, over her dead gardens and beyond the wall.

Madria stood up and stared wide-eyed as tears ran down her cheeks.

The dragon tried to burn the seeds with his breath, but he just blew them further away. In a frenzy, Wyrm slithered from Ilan's trunk and gnawed on his roots. Wyrm ripped and shredded Ilan with his fangs like a mad dog. When he was done tearing at the roots, the dragon set them on fire too.

Looking to the sky, the seeds were all out of reach, billowing away with the smoke rising from Ilan. How would she get one for Roark? Even if she could, how would she get him to eat it? It was an impossible task. She fell to her knees and stared at the seeds while they disappeared into the sky.

Wyrm was relentless. He kept attacking Ilan as the sun slowly made its way toward the horizon. The dragon's fiery breath kept Ilan's green wood burning and thick smoke filled the air above. As the day wore on, Madria wouldn't leave Ilan. She just sat there on her knees. The seeds were gone and she wasn't able to help Roark. If Wyrm came for her next, she was doomed.

Then something flashed bright white in the sky. She squinted and tried to make out what it was through the smoke and tears. It was Duron!

32

The Freeing Flood

Wyrm flew toward the wall. The winged serpent slithered on top of the first ring of the labyrinth, coiled and launched himself at Ilan with a mighty roar. The impact knocked Ilan sideways and ripped some of his roots from the dirt.

With all his leaves and most of his branches burned off, Ilan looked so frail and small compared to the dragon. He was completely black from his roots to the tips of his two largest limbs that were raised to the sky in a "V." Deep holes pocked the base of his trunk where the serpent had tried to shred Ilan's roots; roots that were still wrapped around the foot of the tower.

Wyrm shrieked. He set the newly exposed roots on fire and growled, "Get out of my house!" He threw himself at Ilan again, pulling up more roots and cracking his trunk.

Duron flew toward Madria. She stood and the faint sound of fluttering wings blew in on a breeze that cut through the serpent's smoke. For a moment, she could breathe easier. He glided down and landed in front of her.

She noticed something shining in Duron's beak. He released it and it floated toward her. Madria reached out and it drifted into her hand.

"A seed!"

She cupped it in her hands and held it close to her chest. It glowed and looked like a miniature tree. The seed itself was tiny and brown, but it had a slender, almost transparent shoot topped with a fuzzy white canopy that allowed it to float on the wind. "Oh, thank you . . ." her voice shook as she held the gift that could fill Roark with light. She smiled. All hope was not lost. "Thank you so much!"

Duron started to sing. It was the song she heard that night the Leukos flocked above her in Ilan's canopy; the song they sang to help Ilan remember the light of Love in the darkness.

Wyrm took to the air, then wrapped around Ilan. He choked his charred trunk and flapped his wings wildly. Wood snapped and popped. Dirt and rocks flew through the air. Wyrm screeched with dark delight.

"Duron, what do we do?"

He kept singing and wouldn't move.

"Duron!"

Wyrm pulled and pulled until a deafening crack made Madria cover her ears. Wyrm tumbled backward, his body twisted around his prey. He had pulled Ilan from the ground. The dragon slithered to get on top of Ilan and his head snaked into the air. He spread his wings and blew a column of fire into the sky in victory.

Madria wept at the sight.

Wyrm torched Ilan one last time and then lit up the ground around him with flames.

Duron stopped singing. "Madria," he said, "no matter what happens, remember Love never fails."

Wyrm turned to Madria and hissed at her, exposing his teeth. Madria screamed and scrambled backward as the dragon slowly slinked toward her.

Duron stood his ground and stared at the snake. Wyrm looked right past him and said, "Madeline, get back into your tower and stew in fear. Killing Ilan has made me hungry for your despair."

Madria scurried away, but a loud shaking brought her and Wyrm to an abrupt halt. The earth quaked. She fell and Wyrm writhed as he tried to grip the ground. She looked past the well, behind the dragon, and saw what he couldn't—a gaping hole in the base of the tower. Ripping Ilan's roots from around the tower left it unsupported and the shifting ground was causing it to collapse. Wyrm managed to steady himself, but by the time he turned around, there was no escape. The dragon flapped his wings, but the huge structure came down, crushing Wyrm and burying him in a pile of rubble. Madria covered her head with her arms as a cloud of dirt and debris billowed toward her.

The earthquake subsided, and in the quiet, Madria rolled over and opened her eyes. Dust settled around Duron still perched in the same place. He looked regal, illuminated from within. She wiped the tears from her face. Beyond, one of Wyrm's wings stuck out from under the tower's bricks, motionless.

Ilan's dead body burned in her garden.

Duron leapt into the air and once again started singing the old song of the Leukos that comforted Ilan. He flapped and hovered over the hole that Ilan had left in the ground.

Madria walked toward Duron, stunned. From a distance, she could see the shredded ends of Ilan's roots that wouldn't let go of the ground.

Duron flew higher and circled above, singing.

"Love never fails?" she asked in reply. She looked down into the pit. Splintered wood twisted in the darkness and dirt. Tears kept coming. Then something caught her eye in the hole: radiant water dripped from one of the severed roots, and then from another, and another. Hundreds, then thousands of droplets, shone like candles flicking away the darkness. The dripping turned into trickles and soon water of light poured from Ilan's roots and filled the hole. Minutes later, the water overflowed into the center of the labyrinth and Madria stood in a shining puddle.

"Love never fails!" Duron cried out to her.

"I am deeply rooted in Love," she said, recalling Ilan's words. "When my roots are severed, Nali will pour into this world through them."

Duron kept singing as he took off again and headed for Ilan. Madria followed, splashing as she ran. The water bubbled up right out of the ground all around her and rose faster and faster. "Love never fails," she said. The water of light reached Ilan's burning trunk and put out the flames.

Madria gripped Ilan's seed tightly with one hand and cupped the other. She drew the water and drank. It tasted like sweet liquid sunshine; like the seed Love gave her once she had swallowed it.

A gleaming geyser burst from the hole and high into the air. Madria fell backward into the water of light, suddenly soaked with memories of Love and her former home. "Nali!"

She got up and her own reflection caught her eye. "The source of the water of light is forever within you," she said to her wavy image in the water. "Wyrm can kill treeish flesh, but death has no power over Love." Joy bubbled up within her and she began to laugh. Drops of happy tears fell from the sky, fed by the fountain of light. "The water of light will flow from you, filling the world with life and Love!" She spun around crying tears of joy and sadness mingled together. "You did it, Ilan! Love is flowing from your roots!"

The water poured through the gate and into the labyrinth, gushing from the hole Ilan left. It flooded the inner circle of the labyrinth and Ilan's lifeless body started to float. Duron landed on one of Ilan's blackened branches. Madria swam for him and pulled herself up onto his charred trunk. They rose with the water of light as it pushed them along, out of the center of the labyrinth. The vines parted for them and they rode the River of Love running between the walls of Madria's prison.

The water of light kept rising until it filled the center of the labyrinth, overflowing its walls to form the beginning of a luminous lake.

Roark drove his camel hard. The violence in the center of the labyrinth echoed behind him. "Run! Run!" he cried as he whipped the beast, the riding crop smacking. "Faster!" Splashing replaced the sound of the camel's feet on the path. Roark looked at the ground. The camel slowed to a trot through shallow, black muck. Water was coming up through the dirt. "Run if you don't want that flying snake to roast you!" He whipped the camel again and again, then noticed a roar behind him. He looked back. The roaring grew louder and a dark wall of water surged toward him on the path like a wave from a tsunami. Murky water poured over the walls and took out large sections of brick that had been weakened by vines. Thorny jumbles twisted in the wave like tumbleweeds.

Roark directed his camel toward the wall and prepared to jump. When he got close enough, he leapt onto a section covered in vines, barely holding on against the impact and the thorns piercing his hands and arms. He climbed up the wall and jumped onto the soaked path on the other side. He splashed across, then scaled the next wall. His camel on the path behind wouldn't make it, along with the other camels and the wagon. The supplies were lost, but it didn't matter. Looking back, black water poured over the wall and bubbled up from the ground. Even if the bricks across from him held, it wouldn't take long for the water to wash him away too.

Roark stood on top of the wall and tried to figure out what was going on. In the distance, a dark fountain was shooting into the air. The column of water gushed where the tower once stood and reached even greater heights. A growing black lake poured into ring after ring of the labyrinth sending out rivers into its winding pattern.

Roark noticed his side was strangely warm. His hand smeared with blood as he swiped it. He had landed on one of the larger thorns. Roark pulled his bloody shirt away from his body to see how bad it was. The thorn went deep.

The wall across the path from Roark gave way and water poured toward him. For a moment, he thought he saw Madria in the distance bobbing among the debris in the churning water, then she was gone. A large white bird appeared in the sky. Below, Madria emerged from behind a clump of floating vines. She rode the rising water on a large, charred tree. At one end, she held on to its broken roots. At the other end, two large branches parted from the trunk and kept the tree from spinning in the water. She rushed toward him and shouted, "Ruak! Jump on!"

Roark barely had time to think. He ran on top of the wall toward Madria and leapt again, splashing into the water a few feet from the black trunk. The smell of the water made him gag and it stung his wounds from the thorns. He swam with the current and managed to grasp one of the tree's longer roots. Madria climbed down to Roark and reached for him, grabbing his arm as he clutched hers.

"Gotcha!" Madria exclaimed. They both climbed up the wall of roots and clung to each other.

"Thanks," he said, panting. "You're full of surprises today." He looked at the woman he left so long ago. "How is any of this happening?"

Madria wiped her long black hair out of her face.

He stared and asked, "Am I dreaming?"

"I know exactly how you feel." She smiled. "It's kinda exciting once you get used to it."

Roark held his breath. A foul wave splashed across the log and soaked him. He gasped for air and vomited from the stench. The inky water kept rising and rolling, fed by the growing geyser behind them and bursting forth from the ground all around them. The couple held on to the roots as the water lifted them above the walls of the labyrinth. It churned like a boiling cauldron and spilled into the once arid plain beyond. Roark watched in disbelief as the water rose ever higher until a great, bubbling, black lake stretched out in all directions. Eventually, the water got deep enough for the surface to calm. The white bird circled above as the sun set.

Madria noticed Roark's torn and bloody shirt. "You're hurt," she said.

"The thorns."

"Let me see." Madria grimaced and lifted his shirt with her thumb and index finger. Her face relaxed. "There's nothing."

"What?"

He pulled his shirt up higher and stared wide-eyed. There wasn't even a scar.

"It must be the water," Madria said.

"The water?'

"I think it healed you."

He looked down into the deep darkness. "But . . . it's so disgusting."

"What? It's . . ." Madria stopped. "Of course. You can't see the water of light." She looked at her closed hand and extended it to him. "You need to eat this."

Roark backed up. "Look, Madeline."

"Madria."

He remembered what the tree creature called her. "Right. Look, I don't blame you for losing it."

"What?"

"I can't imagine what it was like for you to be trapped alone in there with the shadow for so long. I can understand you got a little . . ." He held his tongue and looked at her reaching toward him. How long had it been since he'd seen her? She looked younger somehow, and nowhere near as crazy as she sounded. Her face was soft and radiant. He had forgotten how beautiful she was.

Madria's arm dropped to her side. "I can explain," she said.

"You can explain?" He laughed. Everything he saw seemed beyond explanation. "Okay, start with the shadow's tree monster. Can you explain that?"

"He wasn't a monster, his name was Ilan." She bent down and put her hand on the blackened log that saved them from the flood. "He came to set us free."

"Wait, we're riding on it?" He looked down at the charred wood. "What happened?"

"Wyrm killed him."

"Wyrm?"

"The dragon."

Roark stared blankly.

"The flying snake," Madria replied to his silence. "He burned Ilan and ripped him from the ground, but the tower collapsed and crushed him."

"The tower? How . . ." Roark tried to make sense of it all. "Tatus said that if we chopped down that tree we'd kill the shadow," he thought out loud. "I doubted it at first, but I saw the darkness bleed out from where our axes hit and the shadow disappeared into the wind. If that snake took down the tree, it just finished what we started. My labyrinth worked. We don't need it to protect us anymore."

"No, we never needed the labyrinth."

"Nobody hated the walls more than I did," he replied, "but they did their job. The labyrinth's power trapped the shadow long enough for us to kill it."

Madria looked down into the water. "The labyrinth's only power came from our fear. Wyrm had *us* trapped."

He thought of all his years of hard labor. "Well, we're free now. We can start over."

Madria smiled.

He looked into her bright eyes and suddenly felt ashamed. She could have died. He ran away, leaving her with that snake, but she rescued him. It made him sick to his stomach. "I'm sorry I left you . . . I . . ."

She hugged him.

He froze and stared at her, puzzled. "I did try. Why wouldn't you come with me?"

"I know. I would have run too, but I couldn't leave Ilan." She held him closer. "I missed you."

He gave himself to her embrace and wrapped his arms around her. "I missed you too." He wondered if she could feel his heart thumping. He pulled away and held her arms. "Look, if we're going to make it off this log alive, we're going to have to work together, but we need to think straight."

Madria dropped her head and shook it. Then she kissed him softly on the lips. His heart beat even faster. Madria looked him in the eyes. "You're right. We do need to think straight. That's why you're going to sit there and listen."

He looked at the water surrounding them. "Do I have a choice?"

"Yes. Yes you do, Ruak." Madria held up something fuzzy and white. She took his hand and placed it in his palm, closing his fingers around it.

33

The Sea of Love

Nali changed the entire landscape in one afternoon while her water of light freed Madria and Roark from the labyrinth. That night, they floated away as a full moon emerged from the horizon. The couple talked while the lake of light lifted them ever higher, growing into a sparkling sea that covered the land as far as the eye could see.

Roark sat while Madria told him everything that happened to her since she decided to leap from the tower. She told him about the light of Love and the shadow of Love, about Duron and the seed. She recounted the visions of the past Love gave her, describing the Tree of Love and explaining that they had once been treeish like Ilan. She told him about Wyrm and the Tree of Trust. Roark listened intently with the light of the moon beaming on his face. She described waking up and the miraculous grapes in the labyrinth that helped her remember his name. She spoke Ilan's words with tears in her eyes and told Roark he could have a new name and a new life like her if he would simply trust Love and eat Ilan's seed.

When she was done telling him all she experienced, Roark
sat and thought while examining Ilan's glowing seed. After a long
silence he said, "That's some story." He put the seed in his leather
pipe bag he had hanging at his waist. "You know, I ate some of
those grapes you talked about."

"Really?"

"Yeah, on our journey through the labyrinth."

She hoped Roark's experience would help him believe her.
"What happened?"

"I found a cluster of grapes on one of the vines."

"Yeah, but what happened when you ate them? Did they help
you remember anything?"

"Now that I think of it, they did. I remembered a song you
used to sing." He paused. "I also saw you burn. I couldn't save you."

"That could have been a memory of what happened at the Tree
of Trust," Madria thought out loud.

"I doubt it," Roark replied, "I think I was fooled by the enemy.
Have you ever considered that? Maybe everything you saw was a
trick of the shadow."

"Of course, but what about all you saw? You saw the dragon's
blood worms come out of Tatus. You saw what Wyrm did to him.
Who's really the one doing the deceiving, Ruak?"

"Will you please stop calling me that?"

"No, it's your true name."

Roark looked up at the moon. "I need to get some sleep." He
sat still and thought some more. "Do you remember that song you
used to sing for me?"

Madria smiled. "I do."

He turned toward her. "Would you?"

It delighted Madria to think that he remembered her song,
and it delighted her even more to hear him ask her to sing it for
him. "I'd be happy to sing for you."

Roark leaned back against the tangled roots and closed his eyes.

Madria sang until Roark fell asleep.

Duron soared high above in the cloudless sky. The warmth of the sun was welcome after a cool night on the water, but by afternoon they were enduring the heat in silence. Through the hottest hours of the day, Roark lay quietly on his back with his eyes closed. Madria cooled herself in the water of light and reflected on all that had happened. She sat wringing out her hair when Roark started thinking out loud. "Tatus said the shadow was a demon that appears as an angel of light." Roark just lay still as he spoke. "What if it was so evil it didn't even know it was lying? Maybe that's why you trusted it."

Madria scooted closer to him. "Why would you believe anything Tatus said? Ilan told me he was a slave to Wyrm from the day we met him."

Roark scowled. "I hated him . . . but Tatus was like a father to us." He opened his eyes and turned toward her.

She reached to him and touched the scar on his face. "That's a lie. Love is our father."

Roark pulled away and sat up. "It doesn't matter now. I'm so thirsty. We need to figure out how to get to land and find some drinkable water."

She turned to watch the shining water lap against Ilan's dead trunk. "We're surrounded by the most amazing water you've ever tasted."

"Let's not do this again," Roark said. "You saw that I can't get any down. It makes me throw up. With all the fluids I've lost, I'm worse off because of your vile water."

"The water isn't the problem. If you'd just eat the seed, you'd see. The water is sweet. The seed changes you." She got down on her belly, cupped the water of light in her hands, and slurped it up.

She hoped he would give in and eat the seed when he got thirsty enough.

Roark gagged. "That is so nasty." He gagged again. "I can't believe you're drinking that stuff."

"Suit yourself."

Roark pulled his shirt over his head and shifted to get comfortable. She sat up and dangled her feet in the brilliant water while looking out into the distance. "We could get in and kick," she suggested.

"Yeah? Kick in which direction? We haven't seen land since the labyrinth flooded yesterday. Besides, I'm not getting in that water."

She scanned the horizon. "This is the Sea of Love," she said. "Nali, the sea that came from the tree!" She laughed at her silly rhyme.

A school of fish broke the surface and flew on their fins just inches over the water of light. They passed right in front of Madria and glided toward the horizon. "Did you see that?" she shouted.

Roark pulled his shirt down. "What?"

"Fish. They flew! There must have been a hundred of them. They were a brilliant blue with fins like . . . dragonfly wings."

"Did they give you any magic seeds to eat?" Roark replied.

"You're as impossible as ever." She smiled. "It's so good to be together again."

Roark pulled his shirt back up over his head. "Try to catch one next time. We're going to need something to eat out here."

Roark looked out over the water. "Two days without a drop to drink and no land in sight." He gripped his forehead. "I wish the sun would set already." He rubbed his temples. "I'm starting to worry I'm not going to make it. My head is killing me."

Madria stared at him. His lips were cracked and bags had formed under his eyes. There was no way she would let him die of thirst while surrounded by drinkable water. She reached down and splashed Roark with the water of light.

Roark grunted and squirmed. "Stop it!" He held his nose and wiped himself off. He stood up and looked overhead. "Where's your bird?"

"His name is Duron."

Roark grinned. "His name will be Dinner if I can get my hands on him."

"I can't believe you."

Roark shrugged and turned his attention back to the sky. "Is it just me or does the sky look hazier?"

She looked up. "Yeah, I suppose it does."

"Good. At least I'm not seeing things yet." Roark's foot slipped into the water and he clung to Ilan's roots to keep from falling.

"You're not looking good," she said. "You better sit down before you fall down."

"I'll sit when I feel like it." Roark looked off in the distance and snuck a look back at her. Then he sat down. "How are you doing?" he asked.

"I'm okay now. The hunger comes and goes."

Roark leaned against Ilan's roots and went back to staring at the horizon. "There's something familiar about that sky."

She grew impatient. "Please. Eat the seed. Drink the water."

Roark scoffed.

Madria stood up and slipped out of her clothes. She tossed them onto Ilan's roots and jumped into the water of light, splashing Roark. She rose to the surface and floated on her back, bathing in the comfort of home. She turned her head to drink, then spit water in the air.

"Get out of there. That's so gross."

"You're missing out."

"Aren't you the least bit concerned about how we're going to get off this log?" Roark croaked. "You may have the stomach for that water, but you'll still need to eat."

"I know it's hard to believe, but I'm not worried," she replied. "Look at us. We're free from the labyrinth and it's because I trusted Ilan. He knew what he was doing by doing nothing. He didn't fall for any of Wyrm's tricks. He trusted Love; he wouldn't move. Even something as awful as his death made the way for Nali to flow again and carry us out of our prison. It's strange—it's like I can feel Ilan with me here, and I'm really not sad or afraid. I trust Love for what's next. Even if we die out here, the Love Fractal will grow . . . somehow." Madria swam next to Roark, grinning. "But we're not going to die, are we?"

Roark opened up his leather sack. He poked around and pulled out Ilan's seed. "So how is it supposed to work?" Roark asked.

Madria hung onto one of Ilan's roots. "You just eat it and it fills you with light. Then things start changing."

She watched Roark looking at the seed. "If you're not going to eat it, why keep it?" she asked.

Roark examined the seed. "The shadow flowed from the tree creature. Why would you trust it?" He blew on the fuzzy white top. "Honestly? I've kept the seed because I wish I could believe what you're saying," Roark answered. "You look . . . happy, but what if you've been deceived? Who knows what the seed is doing to your mind? The things you told me sound so crazy."

"Love showed me that if you keep trying to understand and never let go and trust, you really will go mad. Ilan said that belief is just a choice to act on what you hope to be true and then evidence follows. If you really want to trust Ilan, all you need to do is choose it. Eat his seed and see for yourself."

"I don't know," Roark said. He put the seed back in his pouch and tied it shut.

"You don't know what?" she asked.

Roark snickered. "I just don't think it's wise to believe everything strange voices and lights and trees tell you." Then, all of a sudden, he looked very serious. "Besides, if everything you say were true . . . I'd be a complete failure." Roark turned away. "Is that what you want me to believe?"

She pulled herself up and reached to Roark, turning his head back toward her. "We've both failed, but Love hasn't. Ilan said that Love's true nature is only revealed in response to the unlovely. I want you to believe that. I want you to believe it's because of Love that we're here together."

Roark grinned.

"I've missed that smile," she said. She watched Roark look down and then back at her face.

"I've missed . . . yours too," Roark said haltingly.

"And now Ilan has given us the chance to start over again," she said, "free of the labyrinth."

"I am glad to be done with that exhausting prison, but . . ."

"But what?"

Roark took a deep breath. "Nothing. A fresh start sounds good."

Madria remembered how much hope she'd placed in the labyrinth, how she'd traded Roark for safety behind walls, and how she ended up with neither. "I'm so sorry . . . for everything."

Roark pulled her closer and gave her a kiss on the cheek. She returned the kiss, wet on his dry lips.

Suddenly, they heard Duron's singing. They looked up. He flapped his wings and glided toward them. "Where have you been?" Madria shouted. Duron circled overhead and then flew away. They watched him until he disappeared in the haze on the horizon. Roark squinted. "Whatever's in the air is really thick over there."

Madria shielded her eyes from the glare off the water. She looked for Duron but couldn't see him. "What a strange cloud," she said.

"Wait . . . that's not a cloud." Roark looked down at her, his eyes sparkled. "That's land!"

34

Life by Death

Madria woke up in Roark's embrace, her head cradled between his chest and arm. She thought about getting up to see if they had drifted any closer to the land during the night. Roark was still sleeping, but his heart beat fast. He was so weak and she didn't want to disturb him. Besides, she hadn't eaten for three days and she needed a little more rest too. She closed her eyes.

The sun warmed her skin. Ilan's dead wood bobbed up and down in the water and a cool breeze blew across their bodies. She listened to the lapping water until she noticed another sound far off, the splashing of waves. She had to investigate.

Roark's arm was draped over her. She slowly moved it to his side. She stood and looked beyond the roots against which Roark rested. The sun hung above treetops in the hazy sky. Nali did it! She brought them within sight of the shore. It was so exciting, Madria couldn't wait to share her discovery.

"Ruak," she said softly. "Wake up. Look."

Roark stirred, "What, more flying fish?"

"No, better." He opened his eyes and she pointed. "See, I told you we could trust Love. He's brought us safely to land."

Roark slowly got up, bracing himself against the roots. He looked dizzy. His skin was sunburned and his eyes were sunk in dark circles. He stared at the trees. "Land." He rubbed his head and groaned. "But the way I'm feeling, it may be too late."

"Don't talk like that," she replied. "Let's go ashore. We'll find water you can drink, a stream or something. You've survived so much, there's no way I'm going to let you die of thirst."

Wind and Nali's rolling water continued to carry Ilan toward the land. When they floated close enough, Madria jumped into the water and kicked, pushing Ilan toward the trees while Roark clung to the roots above.

Before they reached the shore, Ilan's roots ran aground. His trunk rolled back and forth with the push and pull of the sea. Roark was too fatigued to hold on and slipped into the water. He went under, then emerged gagging and coughing. She let go of Ilan and swam to Roark as his head sunk below the surface again. She heaved him up and kept kicking on her back, pulling Roark toward the shore. He was heavy. She was so weak and they still had a long way to go. "Kick," she urged, "kick!" He tried, but wasn't much help. She barely managed to drag Roark until they could touch the ground.

Waves of light splashed against trees, illuminating their exposed roots reaching into the dirt. The Sea of Love had stopped advancing at the edge of a forest. Madria helped Roark stand. The waves pushed them forward and they tripped on the roots. Stumbling into trees, with Roark in a half-crawl, they finally made it to dry ground and collapsed, gasping for air.

Madria looked back to the great glowing sea behind them. She sat up to see Ilan through the trees, rocking in the surf.

Roark lifted his head and coughed. "We're lucky we made it alive," his voice cracked.

"Luck?" she asked. "Love saved us. Nali and Ilan carried us here."

He groaned, held his stomach and doubled over in pain. "Cramping . . . getting to land took a lot out of me."

"We need to find you water." She took one last look at Ilan. Tears pooled in her eyes as she watched the waves wash over his dead body. "It doesn't seem right to just leave him there. He was so beautiful."

He struggled to sit up. "There's no use," Roark said softly. He lay back down. "I don't think I can go with you."

"What?" Madria wiped her eyes and stood. "Don't quit on me." She bent down at the water's edge, cupped her hands, and held the water of light out to him. "Don't be a fool. It's no trick of the shadow. Look at me. I'm fine. All the water you can drink is right here. Is it so hard for you to eat a simple seed? You're dying, Ruak."

"Please stop," Roark asked.

"No. I'm never giving up on you."

Roark fumbled around and opened his leather bag. He dug through it and pulled out Ilan's seed. "Go find yourself something to eat." He held the seed up and then flicked it into the water.

"No!" Madria shouted. She splashed in after it. "Why did you do that?" She searched, frantically looking all around her, but she couldn't find the seed that would save Roark.

Roark scowled. "We were talking about a fresh start . . ." he grimaced, holding his stomach with one hand, the other clenched in a fist on his chest, ". . . with no labyrinth."

She got down on her hands and knees with her head near the water, scanning the surface for any sign of the seed.

"I hated those walls, but they were mine."

Madria stopped and looked at him.

Roark gritted his teeth. "You said we never needed the labyrinth to protect us from the shadow."

"So what?" She stood in the water. "That was our only seed! Why would you throw it away?"

"The labyrinth was all I had." His lip quivered. "Eating that seed would mean I believe your story . . . that I was a coward . . . that I let you burn. I can't accept that. You have no idea how much I suffered to keep us safe. My work . . . my life . . . I won't believe it was all wasted." Roark's sunken eyes rolled back and his head dropped to the ground.

"No." She went to him and knelt, taking his face in her hands. She slapped him.

He came back to consciousness and looked intently into her eyes. "Go, find food. You're safe. The labyrinth worked. We trapped the shadow. We killed it." He nodded slowly, his eyes closing. "Now it's time for me to rest."

"Listen to me, I know you just want to slip into the darkness. I did too, but I can't lose you again. Don't do this." She hung her head feeling the tears welling up again. "Just choose to live, that's all. Just choose it. I'll go find you water."

"I . . ."

"Yes?" She held up his drooping head.

"I've made my choice," he said, "You're free from the shadow now. Let me die knowing my life mattered." Then he slumped into the dirt.

Roark opened his eyes and looked up. The tower was nearly finished. He had decided to take a break in the shade it provided and he must have dozed off. He was so thirsty.

He watched Tatus and Madeline scatter seeds in rows of tilled earth. Tatus drew bucket after bucket from the well as Madeline watered their new garden. When they finished, Tatus took her hand and walked to Roark. He stood to meet them.

"It's just a matter of time now," Tatus said. "Soon you'll have more than enough." He looked back at their work. "Gardening always reminds me of that old poem from Ai. Remember?"

Roark didn't, but Madeline nodded.

"'Earth's Tribute,'" Tatus said.

> "First the grain, and then the blade—
> The one destroyed, the other made;
> Then stalk and blossom, and again
> The gold of newly minted grain.
>
> So Life, by Death the reaper cast
> To earth, again shall rise at last;
> For 'tis the service of the sod
> To render God the things of God."[1]

"That's so beautiful," Madeline said.

"What does it mean?" Roark asked.

Tatus thought. "It says life comes from death, from sacrifice. It's about our duty to God to give so others may live. Like what I'm doing to help you two." Tatus put his hand on Roark's shoulder. "I'm sacrificing for your safety. The poem is about hard work and selflessness so that, in the end, God is pleased with the fruits of our labor."

Suddenly, Madeline was gone and Roark and Tatus stood by the tower surrounded by a black void. Tatus held both of Roark's shoulders and said, "I did the best I could. You know that, right?"

Roark heard something move behind Tatus in the outer darkness.

Tatus let go and looked over his shoulder. "I have to get back to the bricks." Hissing came from the void. "God is calling, but before

---

[1] John Banister Tabb, "Earth's Tribute," *Poems,* ed. John Lane (Boston: London Copeland and Day, 1894).

I go to my reward, I have to warn you. Don't be weak, ask the Lord to fill you with his strength. Never give up on your labyrinth and he will accept your sacrifice. Render to God the things of God, and you will live with him in the safety of your walls for all eternity."

"The labyrinth is gone," Roark answered.

"Rebuild."

"Please," Roark begged. "I'm so tired . . . so thirsty. I just want to sleep."

"You've been working hard," Tatus said, "that's good. Here, drink." Roark looked down and Tatus held a bucket. Roark grabbed it and as he peered at the water inside, instead of his own reflection, he saw Tatus's face. He stopped.

"Drink," Tatus demanded. The old man turned and walked into the darkness.

Roark was so thirsty. He lifted the bucket to his mouth, but the water began to boil with black maggots. Disgusted, he threw it away, but the blood worms had already crawled up his arms. They covered his face and poured into his mouth. He gagged but couldn't stop them or catch his breath.

"Ruak. Ruak, wake up. I found you some water."

Roark opened his eyes. Madria held him, pouring water from his leather bag into his mouth. "I found a nice stream not far from here."

Roark sat up and coughed.

"There's not much here, but I'll go get more."

He looked inside the bag, blinking, then guided it to his mouth and drank.

"Careful, sip it. Look, I also found some blackberry bushes." Madria held up a frayed piece of fabric full of berries. "Eat these while I go get some more water."

Roark drank the rest of the water, then asked, "Where's Tatus?"

"What?"

"Tatus, I just saw him," he said as he looked among the trees surrounding them.

"That's impossible," Madria answered. "Don't you remember? Wyrm killed him. You're delirious. Rest here and eat what you can. I'll be right back." She stood with his bag, flashed a smile, and ran off.

Roark scooted to sit with his back against a tree and looked down at his hand still closed in a tight fist. He devoured the berries with the other hand and licked his lips. He closed his eyes and savored the flavor. Madria had saved him again. She was so different than he remembered, sure of herself and fearless. He smiled, took deep breaths, and waited for her to return.

After resting awhile, he felt a little better. The cramping stopped and his head seemed clearer. He looked around for Madria then stared beyond the trees at the edge of the forest. To his surprise, the sea was gone. It was as if the tide went out. The dead tree was gone too. Only a flowing, black river remained, winding through the land.

He heard footsteps behind him and turned to see Madria running with his leather sack in both hands out in front of her. It was nearly full with only a little water dripping from its soaked skin. "You're awake. Good." She knelt at his side and held the bag to his lips.

He drank it all, being careful not to spill any.

"How are you feeling?"

"I think I'll be okay, thanks to you." He smiled.

She touched the back of her hand to his forehead, then his cheek. "I'll get more." She got up to go.

"Alright. Thank you. Oh, wait!"

She looked down at him.

"Did you notice . . . the water?" He pointed. "The tree is gone."

"What?" She turned to look, and as soon as she did, the winged serpent swooped down and slithered around where the tree used to rest.

"Oh, no," Madria whispered, "Wyrm." She whipped around to Roark.

Roark got up, but he was soon too dizzy to stay up. He held onto the tree and slid back to the ground.

The snake lifted his head. His tongue darted out of his mouth. "Roark," he called. "I can taste your fear."

The dragon's body was covered in sores and blood worms. It looked like he had been boiled in oil. A large gash stretched across the serpent's head and his wings were torn. He licked the air and abruptly looked to the trees where Madria and Roark hid. Wyrm snaked toward them.

"Run," Roark said.

As the dragon approached, Madria tried to pull Roark up, but only helped him stumble a few feet. Wyrm would soon be upon them.

He sat and waved her away. "Leave me," he snapped at her. "I'm still too weak."

Madria stared at Wyrm. "The Love Fractal must grow . . . we can't be stopped." She looked into Roark's eyes.

"Go! I'll just slow you down."

Madria grabbed Roark's face. "Look at me," she said. "You're going to live." She started to cry. "I don't care how you feel. Get up and run straight into the woods. You can't miss the stream."

She stood and faced the dragon, but Roark grabbed her arm. "What are you doing?"

Madria bent down and kissed him. "I'm going to Love you," she said with tears running down her cheeks. "I'm going to show you Love, just like Ilan showed me. You and I will be together again soon." She tore her arm free of his weak grip and ran toward the dragon.

"Madeline!" Roark yelled, clutching for her.

He watched with horror as she stepped into the open, waving her arms. The dragon saw her and she yelled, "Come and get me, Wyrm." She took off running and the snake followed.

"No!" Roark struggled to his feet and lurched after her, steadying himself against trees.

Wyrm opened his wings, launched into the air, and struck. He snatched Madria off the ground, piercing her body with his fangs. Wyrm angled skyward and flew higher and higher with Madria hanging limp in his mouth. He beat the air and hovered.

"No," Roark whispered, too stunned to move.

Wyrm opened his mouth and shook his head to whip her free from his teeth.

Roark watched helplessly as Madria's body hurtled to the ground and landed with a heart-shattering thud. He started toward her, but Wyrm spotted him from the air and shot at him in a rage.

Roark stumbled into the woods. The soaring serpent scorched the trees behind him. Wyrm shook the earth as he landed, then slithered after him. Roark weaved, bouncing off trees and tripping over roots. His head pounded and he couldn't catch his breath. A large tree with arching roots stood before him as the crashing and snapping behind him grew louder. His strength evaporated, he couldn't run any longer. He dove headfirst toward the tall roots and crawled into a hole under their twisting wood. He collapsed onto the dirt in the dark.

For a moment he couldn't hear anything except his breathing and a dripping near his head. Then the snake hissed behind him. Roark kicked and pulled to inch deeper into the darkness of his hiding place beneath the tree.

"You always were a coward," Wyrm growled.

He could feel the heat of the dragon's breath as he talked.

"My worms will heal you of your fear."

Roark looked back and saw the dragon's mouth at the entrance to the hole. Black venom dripped from his fangs. The drops singed the ground, pooled, and bubbled.

"I will give you strength, and you will give me eternal rest."

The puddles of inky ooze beneath the dragon's mouth smoked and churned. The snake extended his tongue and licked at Roark's legs. Trembling, he pulled away as far as he could.

"But first, together we will free the world from the torture of existence. Then you will take my tail and rule a kingdom of death."

Black maggots, like the ones he'd seen come out of Tatus, rose from the boiling venom. Roark covered his head in his arms.

"Madeline is dead, and so is Love. Now that he is, you are mine."

Roark braced himself, waiting to feel the wriggling worms or the dragon's flames on his skin.

35

Becoming Ruak

The ground shook with a thud. Roark heard a crunch followed by wheezing. The smell of sulfur surrounded him and thumping rocked the ground beneath him.

He waited for Wyrm's fire, but the flames didn't come. No maggots crawled across his flesh. The thumping continued. Roark stayed curled up, too scared to move.

"Ruak, don't be afraid," a voice said from beyond the arching roots that sheltered him.

He peeked from behind his arms and stared out of his hole into the black eyes of Wyrm. The dragon's head was pinned under a network of roots and surrounded by his blood worms.

"I have the snake under control. You can come out."

Suddenly, the roots above Roark creaked and shook, then rose into the air. He tried to look up, but falling dirt and clumps of grass made him cover his eyes. He scrambled out of what was left of his hiding place and away from the trapped dragon, then got lightheaded and fell to the forest floor. The ground shook again.

Looking back at Wyrm's crushed head beneath the roots, he saw the trunk above. Next to it stood another trunk above the roots where he had hid. The two trunks formed hulking, bark-covered legs. Roark looked higher still to see smooth, green wood and a beard of leaves on a smiling face with bright jade eyes. It was Madria's tree.

"Ilan?" Roark quaked.

"I am," Ilan replied. His canopy lit up with the light that called to Roark in the labyrinth.

"But, you burned. We thought you were dead."

"I was," Ilan said. "You can kill treeish flesh, but death has no power over Love. I am both."

"Madeline . . ." Roark got up and backed away, putting some distance between him and the giant creatures. "You're too late." Wyrm's flailing tail struck the forest floor, shaking the ground around him. Roark scurried away and fell again. He looked back at Ilan. "This snake killed her."

"Madria chose to save you. She gave her life for yours."

Roark looked down at his clenched fist. "Why?" He punched the dirt. "Why did she do that?" He hit the ground again. "You should have stopped her!"

"She wanted you to see Love and give you another chance to trust."

Roark remembered what she told him, that Love's true nature is only revealed to the unlovely. "Love?" Roark's voice cracked. "No, not for me." He started shaking. "Not for me! Bring her back! You're here; you can bring her back!"

"Yes, Madria will rise. She has joined the repeating pattern of Love in the Love Fractal."

Roark looked up at Ilan, desperate to understand. "What is that supposed to mean?"

"You'll see. Eat my seed and even though you die, you will live. You can be with her again."

Wyrm growled and struggled but he couldn't get his head from under Ilan's roots.

"Take this serpent by the tail," Ilan implored. "All that Madria told you is true. Stop doubting and believe. Take the staff of power. Choose to become who you were created to be . . . Ruak . . . king."

Roark looked at the dragon's thrashing tail and thought about Madria's story. He thought about the Tree of Trust and looked at Ilan crushing Wyrm's head under his roots. "I already made my choice," Roark objected. "And if everything she said was true, it wasn't the first time."

"Yes, you've made many choices," Ilan replied tenderly. "Like the choice to pretend that you threw away my seed."

"What? I didn't . . ." Roark stammered.

Ilan pointed down at him and asked, "What's that you've been holding so tightly in your hand?"

Roark sat up, stared at his fist, and slowly opened it. There, glowing in the palm of his hand, was Madria's gift to him . . . the seed of Ilan. "How did you know?"

"I know you better than you know yourself." Ilan smiled. "So, why do you think you tricked Madria like that?"

Roark looked up at Ilan. "I didn't want to believe her story. I didn't want to hear it anymore."

"Hmm." Ilan scratched his leafy beard. "You know what I think? I think maybe you were holding onto a little bit of hope."

Roark glanced at the seed. "Maybe."

Ilan's eyes lit up. "You still have today. Choose to take what I've already given. You can decide your destiny right now and grow into your true self, Ruak. Choose to be free like you were before the Tree of Trust. Eat the seed. Take your scepter. Use it to free Love's children from their labyrinths and lead our brothers and sisters home to the Love Fractal."

Roark plucked the fuzzy seed out of his hand and it shone brighter. After being chased by the dragon and seeing Ilan save him, Roark couldn't help but believe everything Madria told him. He looked at the dragon's tail and thought of all the years he spent running from the shadow and toiling away at the bricks. He felt the full weight of his failure and it threatened to snuff out his little spark of hope, but the enemy he helped to kill was now standing in front of him offering another chance, fanning his spark into a flame. Roark knew he didn't deserve the seed, but the desire to make things right and be with Madria was stronger than his self-contempt. "Can I really see her again?"

"Yes, trust me and you will live forever with her in Love."

The kiss before Madria saved him from Wyrm couldn't be their last. He had to hold her in his arms. He had to tell her that Love didn't exist for him until she gave her life for his; only then could he see. If there were the slightest chance he could be with her again, he had to take it, even if it meant letting go of the hope he put in his labyrinth. He had to thank her and tell her that the light of Love touched him through her sacrifice.

"For her then," Roark said.

"For her, and you and me and the whole world," Ilan replied. "Let me fill you with the light of Love."

Roark lifted the seed and dropped it in his mouth. It was bitter and difficult to get down. He coughed and winced, then forced himself to swallow it. It tickled his throat. "Can I get something to wash this down with?"

"Yes." Ilan laughed. "You're a delight."

"I'm serious. I'm thirsty."

"I know. I'll take you to drink from Nali." Ilan kept laughing and his leaves glowed brighter. His blossoming branches swayed back and forth creating an aromatic breeze. "Receive the breath of life," he said as the sweet-smelling wind swirled around them. "You are no longer Roark. The rock has become the wind and you will breathe new life into the world as Ruak, the father of the free."

Ruak inhaled the fragrant air from Ilan's flowers. He exhaled and noticed that the bitterness from the seed disappeared leaving a sweet aftertaste. Despite drinking the water Madria brought him, his mouth was still painfully dry, but the seed quenched a different kind of thirst. A peculiar peace refreshed him, washing over his heavy heart and soothing his troubled mind. Ruak took another deep breath and smiled.

"Oh, Ruak, you've worked so hard, but now your younger self has died and you can rest. Soon the light of Love will begin to illuminate your memories. Drinking from Nali will help."

Smoke started to billow out of Wyrm's nostrils. His body writhed and he flapped his wings. "Be still, Wyrm," Ilan ordered and pressed harder on the dragon's head. The dragon groaned and twitched.

"Before we go, let's deal with this snake. Go ahead, take your scepter."

Ruak stepped back and looked at Wyrm. The dragon was now motionless on his belly, crushed by Ilan. Within the cage of Ilan's roots, Wyrm's big black eyes seemed to beg Ruak to put him out of his misery. Courage rose up within Ruak and he looked to Wyrm's tail. "Just grab it?" he asked.

"Just grab it."

With Ilan at his side, Ruak felt safe enough to approach the dragon. He walked the length of the serpent. He looked at the shredded tail, then turned to see Ilan grinning at him. Ruak smiled and said, "What the hell?" He reached out and took Wyrm by the tail. In an instant the snake shrunk into a rod of polished ebony. Ruak threw it on the ground in shock.

Ilan bent down and looked Ruak in the eyes. "Now, that wasn't so hard, was it?" Ilan started laughing again, stirring the air with his branches. He picked up the staff and held it out to Ruak. "Here, you're going to need this," he said.

Ruak looked at it. He marveled that the rod was actually the dragon and not the work of a master craftsman. A detailed serpent's head adorned one end. Smooth scales covered its length and it flared at the other end to resemble Wyrm's shredded tail. The staff was as tall as Ruak and straight as an arrow. Ruak remembered running from Wyrm and how afraid he had been of the dragon. He thought about how much pain his seed of doubt caused. The scepter belonged in Ilan's hands, not his. He hung his head and said, "I don't deserve it."

"Love doesn't require you to. All he asks is that you receive the gifts he gives with the trust of a child."

Ruak nodded solemnly.

"When Love is lavished on the unlovely, the Love Fractal grows. Come, let's get you that drink," Ilan extended the ebony rod toward him again, "son of Love."

He looked up and Ilan's eyes sparkled. A memory flashed in Ruak's mind. He sat on shimmering leaves. Stars filled the sky and a laughing river flowed far below. Light, like the light in Ilan's eyes spoke to him, "Guardian of the garden. Only a true son of Love can take Wyrm by the tail."

"Son of Love?" Ruak asked. "Me?"

"You," Ilan reassured him. "You are a son of Love just as much as I am. Love's life is within you now."

Ruak took the staff and felt its heft. "Could this all be a dream?"

Ilan smiled. "No, you've just woken up."

Ruak wrapped his hand around the staff, planted the tail on the ground, and said, "This will make a good walking stick." He leaned hard on it and almost fell over. Looking up at Ilan, he smiled too. "I guess I'm still pretty weak."

Ilan reached out to Ruak. "I will carry you." Ruak rested against Ilan's hand and slowly rose into the air.

Ilan stepped out of the woods. He carried Ruak toward a brilliant stream that flowed where he once saw a ribbon of black cutting through the land. "So that's what Madria was talking about."

"What's that?" Ilan asked.

"The water of light. I couldn't see it until now."

"Yes, that's Nali. Her joyful water will be your strength." Ilan walked up to the stream and lowered Ruak to the ground.

Ruak heard singing and looked up. Duron circled over a bed of white flowers in the distance, light seemed to radiate from him.

"Here, drink," Ilan said.

He turned to see Ilan kneeling and holding out the water of light cupped in his hands. Ruak lowered his head and drank, slurping and gulping. Cool sweetness filled his mouth and soothed his throat. He gasped for air, then drank some more.

When he was done, he looked up into Ilan's eyes. Radiant tears dripped down his cheeks and into the leaves of his beard. "You're crying," Ruak observed out loud.

"I have longed for this day, but it is so bittersweet," Ilan said as he lifted his head. "And so is Duron's song. Listen."

Ruak leaned on his staff and watched Duron gliding above, singing words he couldn't understand. "It's beautiful . . . and sad. What do the words mean?"

"He sings, 'The giver is the gift, and they have inherited all things.' The lyrics are about you and Madria; about how you have grown into your names . . . and what that cost."

Duron finished his song with a mournful cry and landed far off among the white flowers.

Ilan stood and offered his hand. "Come, let's join him at Madria's side."

Ruak stared into the distance. "That's where she . . . ?"

"Yes." Ilan gently lifted Ruak and held him close, then carried him to Madria.

She came to rest in a bed of lilies next to the flowing water of light. Her body was twisted and pierced. Blood speckled the white flowers standing tall among strands of her long black hair.

Ilan knelt and set Ruak on the ground next to her.

Ruak dropped his staff and shook as he cradled Madria's head in his arms. "We wasted so much time," his voice quivered. "We gave our hearts to the labyrinth instead of each other."

Big, glowing tears dripped down Ilan's cheek. "Not one bit of it will be wasted, I promise," Ilan assured him. "And you will spend an eternity together outside the constraints of time in the Love Fractal."

"Take me there now," Ruak begged as he held Madria.

"You are already part of the Love Fractal. You have received Love."

"What do you mean?" Ruak asked. "What exactly is the Love Fractal?"

"Me, Nali, Madria, you . . . our daddy. We are the repeating pattern of Love in the world—a tree of life—life freely received and freely given."

Ruak cried and laid Madria's head to rest on the ground.

Ilan gently picked Madria up.

"Where are you taking her?" Ruak asked.

"I am going to plant her by Nali. There she will spread out her roots to the water of light and grow into a beautiful tree. In her new home, there will be no more pain or death. She will trust Love forever and have nothing to fear."

"Plant me too. I want to grow with her."

"You will. Bathe in Nali, let her flow over you and wash away your sorrow with the comfort and warmth of home. Then you can begin your journey."

"Journey?"

"Ruak, as a son of Love, you are free to go where you will and do as you please. No matter where you go or what you do, I will guide you back to Madria's side. However, there are many people in many labyrinths who need your help. Actually, the labyrinth of Ai is just beyond this forest. The people who live there are forced to build its walls, generation after generation. The king and queen are infected with blood worms. Their cloud of despair hangs over this whole land. You now have a unique understanding of the people's plight. Choose to be the image of Love to them, the way I revealed him to Madria, the way she revealed Love to you, and the children of Love will follow you home. You will free many from the worms that have warped their minds."

Ruak looked down at his staff on the ground next to him. He picked it up and said, "I thought this was the end of the dragon and his worms."

"It is. Wyrm is slain, but his influence over this broken world remains. You can use the staff's power to redeem evil for good. Cast out the worms wherever you find them and they will be made harmless."

"If I go, will you come with me?" Ruak asked.

"The light of Love is now forever within you and, if you will go, I promise to help along the way. My seeds are everywhere, floating free . . . a consequence of burning me Wyrm did not foresee. Duron will soar on the wind from my canopy and guide you through many storms. Follow him to those who see my seeds floating on the wind and water. Show them Love and invite them to eat."

Ruak thought back to his doubt and how hard it was to let go of his labyrinth. He looked to the wilderness and considered leaving the people of Ai to their walls. "Whether I go or not, I'm not in for an easy journey, am I?"

"No," Ilan replied. "The way of freedom is often painful, but it is also filled with great joy. I'm sad to say that if you choose my way there will be times when bearing the image of Love is unbearable. In fact it will send you running in the other direction. When you go your own way, just trust my presence within you and enjoy my freely given Love. I will overflow from you again and again. We die a million little deaths for one another, but the Love Fractal must grow."

Ruak looked at Madria's limp body cradled in Ilan's arms and considered the price of freely given Love. He wasn't sure that he had the courage to pay it.

36

Home

Madria lay perfectly still as she gazed into the water of light flowing into her. There was no darkness in the past or the future; both were filled with Love's eternally repeating pattern of joyous being, selfless giving, and grateful receiving. All at once, everything was caught up in the ever-expanding mystery of the Love Fractal. She watched Love, Ilan, and Nali overflow with joy and laugh the world to life. She saw herself entombed in bricks receiving Love's gift. She witnessed the birth of Ilan, his death, and Nali's freeing flood of Love. She saw herself give her life for Love and Ruak. She delighted to see Ilan rise and watched Ruak eat his seed and take Wyrm by the tail. She also watched Ruak turn away as Ilan buried her body in the ground like a seed planted by the River of Love.

Ruak waded into the water of light, dropped to his knees, and cried. He cupped his hands and splashed water on his face, then drank. She could feel his grief through Nali. *Don't be sad*, she thought, *I'm right here.*

Ruak lifted his head. "Madria?" he asked. "Is that you?"

Ruak could sense her presence in the water of light too! Nali welled up inside Madria with happy tears. Ruak's song filled her heart and mind. *Come to your garden, love, and eat its pleasant fruits.*

Ruak heard her singing and smiled. She sensed his hope rise in the water of light and it drew her to him. She felt herself growing. She pushed away the dirt that surrounded her and stretched her arms to the sky. Tears dripped down her cheeks. "Oh, Ruak," her voice trembled. "Come home. Come home to me."

The water of light bubbled within Ruak and washed away his grief with the joyful comfort of home. Hearing her, his hope blossomed into anticipation. He believed that he would see her again. He spun like a child with his hands skimming the water, then fell backward and splashed into Nali. Surrounded by her water of light, he looked to the sky and whispered, "Thank you, Madria. Thank you for showing me Love." Madria felt a strength rise up within Ruak. It was unlike anything she had felt before. It was a power born of desire, a fiery passion for her and Love.

She got the chills and heard leaves rustling in the wind. Her joy danced with the joy Love and Ilan shared in Nali. Ruak's emotion mingled with theirs and mysteriously added to her experience of Love. In that moment she knew—with a knowledge that permeated her entire being—that Love gave Ruak to her, just as he gave her to Ruak, so they would know Love in a way that would be impossible without each other.

Duron soared in the sky above Ruak and called out to him.

Then something floating in the River of Love caught her eye. It tumbled on the water toward Ruak and bumped into his leg. He looked down and picked it up. It was the little wooden karimba the old man gave her so long ago. The flood had washed it out of their prison.

Ruak turned it over to see the design on its back. He traced the lines of the labyrinth with his finger. Madria could feel his relief and deep gratitude. He set the karimba afloat again and teared up as it drifted away on the water of light.

Madria watched as Ruak took another drink and waded out of Nali. He picked up his ebony staff and leaned on it as he watched the white raven circling above. Duron caught a gust of wind and soared toward the forest and a labyrinth beyond. "I'll be home soon, Madria," Ruak said with quiet confidence, and then he started walking.

A fragrant breeze blew across Madria's body. She inhaled and opened her eyes to see a familiar face smiling at her. Ilan's jade eyes twinkled with the light of Love. "Ilan!" she exclaimed.

He reached to her and held her hands as they stood in a grassy field by Nali's stream, bathed in a warm glow.

She looked down; her skin was a radiant light green. She had branchy fingers and glowing leaves grew from her arms. "We're alive with the light of Love!"

Ilan laughed and his canopy lit up. White flowers blossomed in his leafy beard and on the lush vines growing from his head. "Yes, we are. Treeish flesh can die, but death has no power over Love. We are both."

Madria stared wide-eyed at her bare belly, down to the supple bark around her waist and her long, slender legs below. She stood as tall as Ilan. "I'm, I'm . . ." she stammered. "I'm just like you!"

"Isn't it exciting?"

She looked up. "Where are we?"

"We are where we have always been," Ilan answered, "with each other, here in the eternal now."

The water of light babbled and splashed next to them, then flowed off to a forest in the distance. "Is this where you buried me?" she asked.

"Yes"

"Where's Ruak?"

"He'll be along with the rest of Love's children in no time."
Ilan winked. "Ruak is alive with the light of Love too! Come with
me, I have a surprise for you."

Madria's leaves brightened. She tried to move toward Ilan, but
she was stuck in the ground.

Ilan let go of her hands and slapped his knee. "Ha! You were
walking around on stumps so long, you don't remember what it's
like to have roots."

"Roots?" she asked as she looked down at her treeish legs in the
grass. She pulled one leg up out of the dirt and then the other. She
stood up on her roots and fell forward into Ilan's arms, laughing.
"I have roots!"

"Isn't it wonderful?" Ilan helped her stand. "It gets even better.
Just wait until you see what I have to show you. Now, close your
eyes and look into the water of light within you."

Madria closed her eyes. "Okay . . ."

"And don't open them until I tell you to."

"Alright."

"Ready?"

She smiled. "Probably not." She held Ilan tighter.

"What do you see?"

Suddenly, a verdant, misty garden stretched out below her in
the water of light as if she were flying above it. She took in the
beauty and tried to catch her breath. Mountains rose in the distance. Flowering fields, rolling hills, a variety of fruit trees, and
meandering streams of light passed beneath her. "It's Love's garden!" she exclaimed.

"Remember what Love said, 'All I am and have is yours.'"

A resplendent orchard labyrinth appeared on the horizon. It
filled an expansive plain. Trees full of apples wrapped back and
forth as far as the eye could see. The sparkling River of Love flowed
between the arching rows of the orchard, feeding it with living
color and then running on into the garden beyond. In the center

of the labyrinth, the water of light rose in a glistening fountain of light and filled a luminous pool that fed the river. "Nali . . . oh, she's beautiful."

"The joy we share with Love now overflows into all of creation. I will give of the fountain of the water of light freely to anyone who thirsts."

In an instant, she felt water soaking her roots and a fine mist kissing her leafy body. The sound of water splashing and pattering filled her ears.

"Okay, open your eyes." Ilan's voice burst with delight.

She looked and found herself standing with Ilan knee-deep in the orchard's pool staring at Nali's fountain. Misty rainbows surrounded them and the light of Love in Nali took her breath away. Her legs gave out and she almost collapsed into the water, but Ilan held her up.

Ilan laughed and held her hands as she stood on her own. "Traveling like that is going to take some getting used to."

She nodded her head. "How . . . ?"

"Remember, I've never been bound by space and time. The here and now is all there really is—the eternal present wrapped in the light of Love. I've always lived free in the now. Now you do too."

The water of light flowed into Madria, bubbling and fizzing with overwhelming joy at the endless possibilities of her new freedom.

Ilan let go of her hands. She watched him turn and gaze into the orchard labyrinth. The water of light flowed from the pool and filled the familiar pattern. He looked back at her, grinned, and said, "Just imagine how happy Ruak will be that all of his hard work didn't go to waste."

"What? What do you mean?"

"He gave so much of himself to this labyrinth. I started planting the seeds of the trees in the wall the day the first bricks were laid. Once the vines and the water of light broke it up, the wall created the perfect soil for an orchard. Madria, this is what has become of your prison." Ilan giggled. "Ruak is going to be so surprised."

Madria stood in awe, staring at the rows of giant apple trees populating the labyrinth. Red, yellow, and green dotted the design. "How could something so ugly be transformed into something so beautiful?"

Ilan lifted his limbs high. "With Love, all things are possible."

She splashed toward Ilan and hugged him. "Thank you. Thank you, thank you, thank you."

"You are welcome," Ilan said as he held Madria in a warm embrace.

She relaxed into his arms. His luminous branches wrapped her with the light of Love and gave her a deep, still, familiar calm. The sensation of home reminded her of life with Love in the tree house from her visions. Suddenly curious, she pulled away from Ilan.

"What is it?" he asked.

Madria looked to the horizon. "Everything's perfect," she said, "except . . ." She circled the fountain in the center of the labyrinth looking to the sky beyond.

"Except what?" Ilan called out over Nali's splashing.

She came back around to Ilan and asked, "Where is our home in the tree?"

Ilan stretched his limbs above his head and his canopy grew even more lush. "I am your home. . . . I am now the Tree of Trust too."

"I don't understand," Madria said. Then she paused and grinned. "But I don't need to. I trust you."

"And that is the key to life in union with Love. Now you have a home *and* trust, forever as one in me. You are one with all of Love's children in the Love Fractal—filled with the light of Love—just as Love and I and Nali are one. I in you and you in me: perfect in one."

"I . . . I'm speechless."

Ilan smiled. The light of Love twinkled in his eyes and he started to sway. He skipped toward her, twirled around, and reached out his hands. "Come, dance with me."

Ilan delighted her with his childlikeness. Madria laughed and the urge to join him made her leaves quiver. Before she realized what she was doing, she was gliding on her roots with Ilan as he led her in a flowing dance of leaves and light. Ilan sang as they spun and splashed in circles around Nali's fountain.

> "Rise up, my Love, my fair one,
> you are home with me.
> The drought is over and gone,
> Love has set you free."

Ilan sang in the same language she'd heard sung by Duron, but now, she understood the words. She let go completely, free of self-consciousness. They twirled away, spinning and jumping through the rainbows in Nali's mist with their shining leaves creating trails of light in the air. Tears of joy welled up in her eyes as Ilan sang on.

> "The time of singing has come,
> Love shines on your face.
> Water, light, and earth now one,
> let me hear your voice."

Madria opened her mouth and, to her surprise, she sang in Ilan's exotic tongue. The song sprang up, sweet and effortless.

> "I am my beloved's
> and he is freely mine.
> Love's fountain never fails,
> beyond the end of time."

Ilan held her close as they glided on their roots singing. She was home. She closed her eyes and gave herself to the sensation. Suddenly, Ilan lifted her off the ground. She opened her eyes and found herself high above the orchard labyrinth surrounded by Ilan's branches and shimmering leaves as they swirled in Nali's fountain of light. Ilan's limbs grew larger and larger and wrapped around her. She swam in the sweet smell of Ilan's canopy. The wood wound and wove together surrounding her and spiraling ever higher until all grew still and Ilan's branches lowered her onto a bed of leaves.

She found herself reclining in a large, comfortable room, complete with arching openings that overlooked the orchard labyrinth and all of Love's garden beyond. An ornate door opened onto a big, branching hallway.

Madria grinned, got up, and glided to the door on her roots. She peeked out into the hallway and flowers blossomed from its living walls. Lush vines arched over a multitude of doors, bursting with grapes. Madria walked down the hall looking into the other rooms and marveling at the organic architecture and decoration. She came to a winding wooden staircase and followed it down. The stairs ended in a sweeping leafy room with grand arches and more hallways beyond. In the center of the room a larger spiral staircase with a thick banister invited her to keep exploring. She wound down the stairs and they led her into a majestic, circular banquet hall with soaring, elegant arches of twisting wood. Nali's fountain flowed and splashed in a sparkling pool in the center of the vast space.

A grand, wooden table encircled the pool. Above, in ever larger circles, tables extended from the walls creating an immense bowl. Stairs rose from level to level and spiraled up to table after table as high as the eye could see. All along the tables, fruit trees grew right out of them. Oranges and mangos and apples and lemons and limes and peaches and cherries and grapefruit hung on the trees' branches, hovering over large platters and bowls filled with a wide variety of food. Vines bearing Ilan's miraculous grapes adorned the tables and grew on the walls, plump and begging to give up the wine within.

Nali flowed from the pool that surrounded her fountain and poured out of a magnificent entryway. Paths on each side of the flowing water led out to Love's garden beyond. And there, hovering in the entrance, shone the light of Love. The sweet comfort and safety of home radiated from him. His brilliant beams reflected off the water of light and color danced on the walls and the tables that grew from them.

The water of light bubbled within Madria and happy tears welled up in her eyes. "Daddy," she whispered longingly. A gentle breeze blew through soaring entrance and filled the great hall.

"Welcome home, my child." Love's light burst into the room and wrapped her in bliss. "Madria."

"Daddy, oh Daddy. It's so good to be home."

"My little girl, I Love you."

"I Love you too, Daddy."

In a flash, Madria stood outside of the Tree of Love. She stepped backward in awe at the sight of the shining canopy, massive and filled with the Leukos darting back and forth. She gasped. "Ilan!" She turned to see they were in the center of the orchard. The River of Love flowed out of the Tree of Love and encircled them over and over again in the repeating pattern of the labyrinth.

The Leukos began to sing. "Love never fails!"

Love laughed and Ilan swayed with delight. "Madria, look!" he exclaimed.

She lowered her gaze and saw Duron riding on the wind swirling from Ilan's branches above. Shouts and cheers erupted behind him and the ground began to shake. The Lord of the Leukos soared toward her and flew right over her head into Ilan's canopy.

A multitude of treeish people appeared among the labyrinth's apple trees. They were a great forest of illuminated children of Love running toward her on their roots and splashing through Nali. A kingly son of Love led them, a treeish Ruak with his staff of power held high above his head.

"Well done, my child," Love whispered to her on the wind. "You have become who you always were, Madria, the mother of all the living." The light of Love surged with peaceful power. "Death has passed away, and now you and Ruak will fill the whole world with my image. There is no more sorrow, no more pain. You have inherited all things, for you are truly my children."

Madria smiled and began to run to Ruak.

"Madria, wait!" Love called out.

She stopped and looked back at the light of Love shining bright in the entrance to her home in Ilan.

"Madria, do you remember why I Love you?"

"Yes, Daddy," she replied. "You Love me because I'm yours."

Living color swirled within the light of Love and he reached out to embrace all of his children with the warmth of home. "That's right. I Love you because you are mine."

There Is No End

Acknowledgments

Paisley, Hannah, Madeline, and Ezra, thank you for continually showing me that Love is alive. (And thank you for your patience during the years of my obsession with this book.)

Many thanks to George Abihider, Steve Brown, Robin Demurga, and my editors, Mick Silva, Travis Gasper, and Gretchen Logterman. You helped me to hear Love tell this story and to get it written in a way people may be interested in reading. I am deeply grateful for the crucial role each of you played in making this book a reality.

To the president of Key Life, George Bingham, my agent, D.J. Snell, and Barbara Juliani at New Growth Press, thank you for your guidance and support in getting this book published.

Jenni Young, thank you for crying when you first read the seed of this story. You helped me believe I could write, and your encouragement kept me going when I wanted to quit.

Also, there were many who read this story (or listened to me drone on about it) at various stages in its creation and provided valuable feedback and encouragement. Mom and Dad, Jeff Adams, Clay Bailey, Nino Capozzoli, Lori Fox, Douglas Gresham, Sharon Hersh, Lottie Hillard, Sharon Kidd, Dan Linden, Jason and Sam Little, Mark Marsden, Carly Mason, Dave and Rachel McDaniel, Andy Meisenheimer, Jordan Munroe, Mike Morrell, Aaron Nee, Matthew Porter, Brian Shriner, Scott Smith, Shari Silva, Sharon and Tim Tedder, Zach Van Dyke, Mark Warner, Aaron and Keri

Wiederspahn, Chad and Nancy West, Cody Whitaker, Holly Wilson, and Cathy Wyatt . . . thank you.

Thank you to my professors, Dr. Chuck DeGroat, Dr. Mike Glodo, Dr. Reggie Kidd, and Dr. Scott Swain. Your teaching inspired many of my theological musings written here. However, if any heresy is found in this book, I want to go on record and say that these fine scholars are not responsible for how I twisted the material in their classes. I take full responsibility.

Finally, Brad Young, thank you for your compassionate counseling. Our time together was one of the most intimate, profound, and transformative experiences of my life. What you helped me to see about myself is woven throughout this book.

Can anything **good** come from addiction?

You did it again. You drank. You got high. You slept with him/her. You surfed porn on the Internet. What gift could you possibly find in so much failure? But when your helplessness drives you to turn to God and admit your need, you will experience the greatest gift of all—his presence, his kindness, his forgiveness, and his peace.

Author Erik Guzman wrote *The Seed* as a metaphor for his spiritual journey, including his struggle with addiction. In this minibook, he explains how coming to the end of what we can do is the beginning of faith. That is the gift of addiction.

New Growth Press
www.newgrowthpress.com

KEY LIFE
God's not mad at you

Are you tired of
"do more, try harder" religion?

Key Life has only one message, to communicate the radical grace of God to sinners and sufferers. Because of what Jesus has done, God's not mad at you.

On radio, in print, on CDs and online, we're proclaiming the scandalous reality of Jesus' good news of radical grace...leading to radical freedom, infectious joy and surprising faithfulness to Christ.

For all things grace, visit us at **KeyLife.org**